My Dream Man

Copyright © 2018 Nae T. Bloss

Chapter One

Renea

I'm sitting courtside at the Playoff game with my best friend Shanice enjoying the game that is now going in to the fourth quarter, and our team is up by ten points. I watch excitedly as the man of my dreams runs from half court, up to the basket, and leaps into the air dunking the shot. Dejuan Washington is 6'2, dark mocha skin, chestnut brown eyes, and a body that was sculpted by god. The man is breathtaking and watching his tight ass flex in those shorts with every twist and turn sent a tingle between my thighs. But he's also smart, talented, athletic, and everything that I've dreamed of. He is perfection. The kind of man that would surely complement me and my beautiful curvaceous frame, butterscotch toned complexion, hazel eyes, and long shoulder length curls.

Now don't get me wrong I'm more than just a pretty face. I'm also well known as Renea Dubley the queen of R&B and Pop, 18- time Grammy award winner, and actress, with two Oscar, wins under my belt and all by the age 25. I'm living out my dreams but failing at one thing, love. I was ready for love, a husband, and eventually a family. I'd dated a few guys from the industry and a few that weren't, but none of them had that husband/ family man potential. I mean in a world with so many women throwing themselves at you left and right there's really no need to settle down or play house with only one woman. This lifestyle is way too enticing and addictive for these types of men. But there was something about Dejuan, he seemed different from the way he interacted with women, he was always a gentleman.

I've run into him at several times mostly during mutual friend's gatherings and occasionally out on the town, enjoying the nightlife with his boys and a couple of females that looked more like groupies. He keeps a clean image no pictures with random girls, leaks of nudes, and he's never been linked to anyone that I know of.

"Renea', hello, do you hear me talking to you?" Shanice said snapping her fingers.

"What?" I say sitting up straight in my seat "Sorry, I'm a little out of it."

"Mm-hmm... More like you over there daydreaming with your pussy lips again," She joked giggling as she took a sip of her drink.

I turn and pout my lips at her. "Shut up! I'm watching the game," I say rolling my eyes and adjust myself in my seat once more.

"Yeah, I bet you are," she replied as she stood up in front of her seat fixing her clothes. "I'll be right back, I have to go to the restroom."

"Ok, hurry up. The games almost over."

"Yeah, yeah." She replies, waving me off. "Oh, wait. Watch out for sugar daddy over there he's been eyeing us all night. He just might try and come steal my seat now that it's empty." She laughs then turns and waves over to him before continuing up the steps.

I turn slowly and look to my right and I see the old man looking my way with a big smile on his face. He looked to be in his late 60's or early 70's. He was staring so hard that he was practically drooling on himself with this creepy looking smile on his face. I returned the smile and quickly turned away focusing back on the game. I'm lonely, not desperate and besides any man that's old enough to be my father and is trying to get me in the sack is beyond disgusting. I'm not looking to be anyone's trophy wife that is not my style.

The buzzer sounds startling me, and I turn just in time to see the winning shot being made. Without hesitation, I leap out of my seat screaming and cheering with the rest of the crowd. Our home team had scored the winning shot and were the new champions. I was so freaked and excited that I couldn't contain myself I turned to my right staring down at an empty seat, I was so caught up in the moment that I'd forgotten Shanice left to go to the restroom. She must've gotten stuck in line because she'd been gone for a while.

She'd better hurry up I didn't want to be late to another after party and the traffic that comes with a home win is massive.

As I take my seat Shanice plops down in her seat pulling me down with her fanning herself as she tries to catch her breath.

"What the hell Shanice?"

"I'm sorry," She begins "You'll never guess who I ran into coming from the restroom."

"Damn Nesse. Who was it, Obama?" I say in a sarcastic tone.

"NO," she said "Jonathan DeClair," she shouts bouncing around in her seat.

"The billionaire?" I ask my eyebrow raised. "And you just casually ran into him, in the hall, coming from the public restroom. Girl stop playing and come on, so we can beat this traffic." I start to get up from my seat, but she pulls me back down.

"I'm serious Renea'," She said, with a hint of annoyance in her voice and I look at her like she'd lost her mind.

"Ok…I'll play along. So, what he approached you because you were the finest women standing in line for the restroom and sparked up a conversation. Oh wait, and I bet he ask you if you'd like to accompany him to the after party. Am I right?" I say squinting my eyes at her.

"Ha-ha. Very funny." She smirks at me as she grabs her Gucci handbag from the seat. "Actually, he did stop me and yes we had a spark and a conversation."

"And," I said, sarcastically.

"And… He also asked me if I would like to accompany him and his friend Dejuan to the team's celebration party." She places her hands on her hips, as her lips part into that wicked smile of hers.

"Don't play with me Shanice Asceno," I said in a calm voice trying to hide the excitement that was building inside me.

"Mm-hmm... but I told him I had to check in with my BFF first then I'd give him an answer."

I give her a side eye then turn to pick up my handbag from the seat beside me when I hear a husky voice call out to Shanice. I sit up straight and turn just in time to catch a glimpse of a tall handsome guy waving over to us. My mouth dropped as I stood frozen in place watching as Jonathan DeClair comes walking over towards us.

"Hello again," he leans in and kisses her on the cheek "Is this your friend?" He asks as he stood towering over her with a huge smile on his face.

"Yes, it is. Renea' Dubley meet Jonathan DeClair." She said, looking over at him then back to me.

I could hear the "Ha, what!" dancing around on her tongue as she spoke, but it was ok, I'd let her have this one "I told you so" victory. I extend my hand out to him but instead, he walked over and gently kisses me on the cheek and gives me a quick a side hug.

"Pleasure to meet you Miss Dubley. I'm a huge fan of your music."

"Pleasures all mine, Mr. DeClair," I reply, as I shot a piercing glance at Shanice out the corner of my eyes.

I tried not to look to intrigued, but damn he looked even better up close, and he has the kind of smile that can make a woman come out her panties instantly. And as for looks, he was about 6'1, butterscotch skin tone, gray eyes, hair low-cut, and the way his shirt hugged his body you could clearly see that he was cut underneath those clothes.

Now my girl Shanice is bad as well. 5'9, dark chocolate skin, deep brown chestnut eyes, and a body that was curvy but fit. Her ab game was impressive, I don't even think Janet Jackson could compete with those abs, but she also didn't really seem like his type either. I'd mainly seen him out and about with woman let's just say not of color, so I'm shocked, to say the least. Then again what do I know maybe he entertains whatever flavor he's in the mood for and well when you're a billionaire I'm sure it's fair play.

As we turn and head toward the exit but stop when we hear a deep voice call out to Jonathan and he turns back and throws up his hand.

"Hey bro, you ready?" a voice calls out to him.

I look over and see Dejuan walking across the court heading over to us. My heart began to pound hard into my chest. He walks up to us with a huge grin on his face stopping beside Jonathan and resting his hand on his shoulder.

"What's up bro you ready to party?" Dejuan beamed before turning his attention towards me and Shanice.

"Of course," Jonathan responded bumping fists with him. "but first let me introduce these lovely ladies that are going to accompany us tonight. Meet Shanice Asceno and—" he begins.

"Renea Dubley, nice to meet you." He said cutting Jonathan off before he could finish his eyes locked on mine as he held out his hand for me to take.

"Pleasures all mine," I say reaching out and taking his hand smiling with both sets of lips.

I was lost in his gaze and confused by my body's immediate reaction to his presence. I've performed at sold-out arenas, award shows, and I've even given speeches to millions without breaking a sweat but somehow this man had me nervous as hell.

Shanice clears her throat to get our attention and we break eye contact turning our attention back to our friends. They were both standing there grinning at us and for a second there was an awkward silence.

"So, ladies shall we go?" Jonathan asks, looking from Shanice to me and then to Dejuan.

"Sure, after you," Dejuan replies motioning towards the door.

We head toward the exit once again. A woman walks over as we approach the VIP Parking she's standing by the gates calling out to Dejuan and he turns in her direction and waves to her. Shanice and I turn and look at one another then at Jonathan, but he just gives us a shoulder shrug and continues to walk to the Lincoln SUV parked a few feet away from us. I glance over my shoulder once more at the two of them before continuing to catch up with them.

I could feel the lump in my throat and the knot tightening in my stomach. I reached the SUV and climbed inside, and Shanice looked over giving me a half smile, I guess she could see that sad look in my eyes. She mouthed the word "I'm sorry," before turning her attention back to Jonathan.

I sat quietly as we made our way to the party staring out the window wondering who the woman was that called out to Dejuan. My heart sank into the pit of my stomach as an uneasy feeling washed over me, of course, he's in a relationship most of the good men are I don't know why I got my hopes up.

"Hey," Jonathan calls over to me. "don't read too much into alright it's not what you think," he winks at me.

It was like he could read my mind or maybe just the shift in my mood. I hadn't said much the whole ride and I could sense that my mood was throwing Shanice's off, so I perked up and put a smile on my face because I didn't want to ruin the night. Besides we were headed to a party where there was going to be plenty of sexy bachelors and I'm sure that I can find someone suitable to be my Mr. Right now. I haven't had sex in over 8 months and my lady soul was craving a good pounding and hopefully, that happens tonight.

We pull up to the front door and I could see the lights flashing as the paparazzi captured shots of the celebs as they entered the building.

Waiting to catch a million-dollar shot or a juicy story to put in the headlines tomorrow morning. I take out my mirror from my purse and check my makeup and hair that's still neatly tucked in place, I don't need the paparazzi catching me slipping. The driver opens the door and Shanice and Jonathan step out first and then I follow behind them.

Out the corner of my eye I see Dejuan walking over to us he nods to Jonathan who looks back at me and smiles before heading inside.

"Hey Beautiful," he said, walking up and putting his arm around my waist and kissing me on the cheek.

I smile up at him and shake my head before wrapping my arm around him and continue towards the door.

"Hey, Dejuan and Renea overhear." Shouts someone from the crowd of flashing cameras.

They snap a couple of shots before we make our way inside the building. He wraps my arm around his and leads me up the steps and into the party. The music was loud, and the dance floor was packed. He stopped to dap it up with a few of his teammates who looked surprised to see me on his arm.

Once we reached the V.I.P area were the team was seated we took our seats by Shanice and Jonathan on the couch. Drinks were flowing, and the dance floor was heating up as we danced the night away grinding on each other vibing to the music. I wished for the night to never end but I knew it would for me as soon as the clock struck 1 am.

***

The party was lit, and the memories of Dejuan's body pressed up against mine grinding slow left me hot and dripping wet. But as much as I wanted to invite him back to my place tonight, I didn't. As for Shanice, she left with Jonathan and at this very moment is probably getting her back blown out.

I go into the bathroom and turn on the water filling the tub and adding a few drops of my scented oil into the water before turning on the jets. Looks like the only orgasm I'm getting tonight is the one that I have the pleasure of giving myself. I strip down and ease into the water laying my head back on the cushioned pillow and closing my eyes. Letting my mind drift off and memories of tonight replay over in my mind, as I let my hand slide into the water and over my sex. I began to massage my clit when the sound of my phone startles me as it chirps letting me know that I have a text message. I dry my hand on the rag hanging on the side of the tub and grab my phone, opening the message from Shanice.

Shanice: Details in the AM!!

I read the message over again, but I was still confused. What details? She was the only one with tea to spill in the morning and I'm sure she'll be giving me every juicy detail. I turn to set my phone down and it chirps again, and I glance down at the new message.

Shanice: Please don't be mad at me you need this. I love you!

Me: Oh no, what did you do Nesse?

I sit up straight in the tub with my knees pressed against my chest. What is she up to now, it's obviously something that's going to have me biting her head off because she never replied. A loud buzz came from the monitor in my room, I reach over and grab my towel, get out of the tub, and dry off quickly. I rush over to the monitor and pressed the button.

"Yes Nick," I say into the speaker.

"Good evening Miss Dubley. I have a Mr. Dejuan Washington here to see you."

I press the mute button on the speaker and lean up against the wall. It felt as though the room was closing in on me as my breathing became shaky and then grew rapidly. "Ugh, I'm going to kill her. She's going to get every ounce of crazy in the morning," I say to myself. I turn back to press the button just as Nick began speaking again.

"Ma'am?"

"I'm sorry Nick, it's fine you can let him up."

"Yes, ma'am. Right away."

I remember that I'm standing in my towel and freak, "Oh shit," I shout then run into my closet and grab a pair of shorts and a tank top to throw on.

"Hello," I hear him call out from the foyer.

"One second," I answer poking my head out the closet.

I slip on a pair of fluffy socks then run out of the closet and down the hall coming to a sudden stop right before I enter the living room. I take a deep breath then walk slowly and calmly into the room. He was standing by the entrance with his hands in his pockets and my eyes immediately dropped to the bulge in his sweatpants. He cleared his throat and my eyes jumped back up to him and he licks his full lips before turning them up into a smile.

"What's up Beautiful. Is it ok if I come in?"

"Omg, I'm sorry. Yes, please, come in." I say motioning him inside.

Why is this man so damn fine?

The scent of his cologne sent chills through my body and I had to remember to keep control. He walks over and takes a seat on the sofa stretching out with his arm resting on the back and I walk over to the chair beside the sofa and take a seat. I was trying to keep a little distance between us because my hormones were already out of control and one-touch would send me spiraling, ripping his clothes off, and sexing him right here on the sofa.

"So, I'm guessing you didn't know I was going to be popping up on your doorstep?" He asks with a smile as his eyes study my expression. "You know you can come closer, I won't bite."

"But I might!" I think to myself.

I stand and walk over to the sofa and He scoots over to the middle and I pause mid-step and look at him with my lips pressed together in a playful way. He smirks at me, and I shake my finger at him before waving him back over to his side of the sofa.

"To answer your question, no, I didn't know that you were coming," I say, pulling my legs onto the sofa and tucking them under me.

"Oh, so I should probably go, huh? Yeah Imma go," he says as he begins to get up from his seat

"Wait—I mean you don't have to leave." I blurt out placing my hand on his arm.

He sits back down and pulls me closer to him and my heart skips a beat. He leans in to kiss me, but I lean away, and he sits up straight removing his arm from around me and laying back on the sofa.

"I'm sorry. I don't mean to make you feel uncomfortable."

"I'm not."

"You seem tense," he looks at me with a raised eyebrow. "Did I read too much into this?" he asks.

"Umm...depends. What exactly is it that you were expecting?" I question.

"I guess—I thought that I was here to you know," he lowers his eyes to his waist and then back up to me.

I laugh. "Well I'm sure that's what Shanice would love to happen, but that's not the reason I let you up to join me."

"I see, well this is definitely a first."

"Why is that? Because I wasn't ripping your clothes off as soon as you walked in the door and fucking your brains out."

He shrugs his shoulders at me nodding his head with a huge smile.

"Sorry handsome but it takes a lot more than that to get inside these panties," I say, winking at him.

Our conversation from that point was so easy and laid back and I learned that we actually have a lot in common basketball being one of those things. His phone rings, and he pulls it from his pocket and glances at the screen quickly.

"I'm sorry I have to take this," he gets up from the sofa and walks towards the foyer.

His voice was low, but I could still hear the anger as he spoke in a hard tone to the person on the other end of the phone. As I waited for him to return my mind flashed back to the woman from earlier tonight, I needed to bring it up once he returned. Several minutes later he walked back over to the sofa and reclaimed his seat.

"Sorry for that. Now where were we," he said calmly as if he'd flipped a switch and his anger was immediately turned off.

"Everything ok?" I ask a bit curious seeing the way he played it off like he wasn't just upset.

He takes a deep breath. "Yes, now back to you." He reaches over and pulls my legs onto his lap, but I slide them off and pull them to my chest.

"Question. Who was the lady that you left with earlier?"

He sits up straight on the sofa and leans forward placing his elbows on his knees, rubbing his hands down his face, as I watch his movements which let me know immediately that I wasn't going to like the answer. He continues sitting quietly for a second before turning to face me.

"I'm just going to be all the way honest," He mumbled, "That was Jaylyn, my wife."

The voice in my head was screaming "WHAT THE FUCK!" but on the outside, I was trying to remain calm but that didn't work out to well.

"What?" I snapped "you have a wife?" I say scooting towards the edge of the sofa.

"Let me explain," he said, placing his hand on my leg, but I reach over and push it away.

I think carefully about what I'm going to say next, should I let him explain or should I kick his cheating ass out of my place. Every ounce of me was screaming "kick this no-good motherfucker out on his ass and move on," but I went against my better judgment and decided to let him explain. I close my eyes and take a deep breath before slowly exhaling to calm myself.

"You should talk fast before I change mind," I demand.

"Look I'll start by saying I'm sorry I didn't mention earlier tonight. But like I said before I thought this was going to be a one-night thing, so I didn't bother mentioning it." He pleaded.

"Ok, no, you know what it's time for you—" I begin getting up from my seat, but he places his arm in front of me.

"Wait. Please let me finish." He begged.

I cross my arms and take my seat. "Ok, go ahead."

"Jaylyn and I are in the middle of a divorce, but we've been separated for a year now. She called me a couple of weeks ago and ask if we could meet after the game to talk about the divorce. In the beginning, she didn't want to go through with it because she thought that we could work it out, but I was done. I've been done for a long time now I promise you."

"So, what it's final now and she's letting you go?"

"Yes, she handed over the signed documents tonight we took them and drop them off at my lawyer's place together."

I took another deep breath and relaxed into the sofa. I can't even lie a small part of me was happy to hear the word divorce fall from his lips, but I was still a little skeptical about the whole situation. But I'd decided to give him the benefit of the doubt.

"Ok, I believe you. But I want to see those papers as soon as it's final."

"Promise, as soon as I receive them." He said, with a smile.

I glance over at him giving him a side eye with my arms still crossed in front of my chest. I was still upset but also still horny and he was looking so damn edible. I wanted to rip off his clothes climb on top of him and ride his dick until my pussy couldn't take anymore.

"So, what now Beautiful?" He asks, tearing me from my thoughts.

"I don't know. How about a movie or—"

"Or we can go back to your room and you can do all those nasty things that are clearly running through your mind right now." He cuts me off staring at me with lust filled eyes and biting his bottom lip.

My breath hitched as I watched him stand to his feet and reach down to lift me up from the sofa and into his arms.

"Which way is the bedroom?" He asks his voice a low growl.

I use my foot to point out the way and he heads towards the hall and down to my room. Gently he lays me on the bed and pulls his shirt off letting it drop to the floor. His body was perfectly chiseled, and his abs were rock solid. My body trembled as he slid his hands under my shirt and pulled it off then removing my shorts and tossing them to the floor. He looked down at my fluffy socks and then back up at me with a grin on his face.

"Cute," He winks, "I think we'll leave those on."

He licks his bottom lip and spreads my legs as he climbs in between them. He presses his lips to mine kissing me gently letting his tongue slip between my lips opening them so that he could deepen the kiss. He trailed little kisses from my neck and over the top of my breast as he cupped it gently in his hand bringing it to his mouth. He softly begins tugging on my nipples with his teeth sending a shock wave through my body. He continues down my stomach stopping and circling my belly button with his tongue before going lower between my thighs.

He parts my lips with his tongue and begins making small circles around my clit teasing it before taking it into his mouth and gently sucking it. I let out a soft moan as I raise my hips and he slides his arms under my legs gripping my thighs pulling me in closer placing his face deeper between my thighs. I could feel the pressure building inside me with every flick of his tongue.

"Talk to me Beautiful, tell me what you like," he whispers looking up at me meeting my gaze.

"It feels—omg it feels so good. Yes… right there."

"Mm… you like that? You like it when I do my tongue like that beautiful."

"Yes, aw…yes Dejuan…" I say, panting as he worked my clit with his thumb.

He eases his finger inside of me, and my pussy was so wet I could feel my juices soaking his fingers. He returned to teasing my clit with his tongue as he moved his fingers in and out of me moving a little faster each time. I rock my hips matching his rhythm as the feeling of pleasure builds and becomes even more intense.

"That's right beautiful cum for me," he whispers, and my hips began to rock faster.

"Omg," I scream out arching my back as I climax squirting my juices all over him.

He pulls back and stands to his feet and licks his lips then grabs his shirt and wipes off his face. My body was still shaking and trembling with pleasure as I watched him pull off his sweatpants freeing his erection. It was amazing, long, thick, and far bigger than what I was used to which made me take in a nervous breath then exhale slowly. He reached out to take my hand, so I placed my hand in his and he pulled me up from the bed.

"Are you ok?" he asks pulling me into his arms.

"Yes," I replied still breathy.

"Good, come with me."

I followed him into the master bathroom and over to the shower. He presses the button and the overhead shower turns on and we step into the shower, he pushes my back up against the wall before lifting me up allowing me to wrap my legs around his waist.

"Tell me what you want me to do Beautiful."

"I want to feel you inside of me," I answered him while gazing into his eyes.

I place my hand between us and take his dick into my hand and rub the tip over my opening before putting them tip inside. He smiles back at me and then eases me down on to it. I wince at the pain as he enters me, and I buried my face in his chest as he pushes deeper inside me.

"Damn baby you are really tight," he says, as he slowly pulls out of me.

"I'm sorry," I say softly feeling embarrassed.

"Don't be," he said in a low and seductive voice. "I like it, but I'm going to need you to relax beautiful."

He leans in and kisses me letting the water run over us and I melt into his arms and relax. After a few moments, he eases inside of me again gently pushing inside of me and holding still allowing me to adjust. Sensitive to the touch I respond to him instantly as he starts to move in and out of me so painfully slow, my body was craving him, and I wanted him deeper inside of me, moving faster, pounding me harder.

"Faster—please, Dejuan baby please go faster," I begged breathlessly.

He does as I ask and begins moving faster slamming into me hard, I could fill him getting harder as he got closer to climaxing. I lean back pressing my back against the wall as he gripped my waist thrusting deeper inside me until he exploded reaching his climax. I feel him as his dick spasms inside of me spilling his seeds and I tighten around him milking him as he sends me over the edge. He reaches up and pulls me back into his arms, turning around and pressing his back against the tile as he tries to catch his breath.

He pulls out of me and his body trembles from the sensation and places me on my feet in front of him. I lean against his chest and we stand there for a minute. I step out of the shower and grab a couple washcloths so that we can wash up. We dry off and then head back to my room to gather our clothes and get dressed.

He looks at me and smiles as he takes my hand and leads me out of the bedroom and down the hall to the living room. We stop in the foyer and he turned to face me pulling me into his arms. I reach up and wrap my arms around his neck standing on my tippy toes.

"So beautiful when do I get to take you out?"

I laugh. "So that's how you do it, huh. Sex me and then ask me out on a date?" I ask my eyebrow raised.

"I mean when your girl told me to come over I thought maybe you were just needing a quick orgasm then tossing me back into the streets."

"And now?"

"And now that I know it's not like that I want a chance to do it right." He says, biting his bottom lip.

"Mm… I guess I can give you that chance." I wink at him and his lips part into a smile and he leaned in pressing his lips to mine.

I pull back and catch my breath, I've never had someone kiss me the way he does it sends a shiver down my spine and a tingle in between my thighs. I release him and take a step back watching him walk over to the elevator and press the button disappearing inside once the doors opened. I wave to him one last time as the doors close and as soon as they shut I throw my hands in the hair and do a little dance before running down the hall and back into my room.

I cannot believe I just made love to Dejuan Washington, I was screaming on the inside

Chapter Two

Dejuan

I hadn't gotten much sleep last night. I'd left Renea's at 4 am came straight home and climbed into bed but I couldn't sleep my mind was still reeling. I can't believe that I had the one and only Renea Dubley sweating in the sheets. I let out a chuckle that filled the silence in my room. If someone would've told me before last night that I'd win the championship and get with the hottest chick in the music game, all in the same night I wouldn't have believed them.

My eye's shoot open when I hear my cell ringing. Damn when did I fall asleep, I look over at the clock and it read 9:03 am. I grab my phone and answer without checking the caller ID.

"Yo," I shout into the phone.

"What's up Bro?" Jonathan said in a cheery voice.

"Yo, what up man." I reply "It's a little early for you, isn't it? You must not have gotten lucky last night huh bro." I said, rolling over on to my back rubbing the sleep out of my eyes."

"Real funny. So, how did it go last night did you have her clawing at the sheets?" He chuckles.

"You know it." I sang.

"Damn, well at least one of us got some action."

"No way the friend didn't give up? Bro, you must be slipping on your pimping man." I laugh, sitting up on the bed and resting against the headboard.

He took a deep breath then replied. "Tell me about it. I woke up this morning with the worst case of blue balls that I've ever had in my life. These females right here are different breed I'm going to have to work to get her panties wet."

I let out a gut-busting laugh at the sound of desperation in his voice. Getting females in the sheets was never an issue for my brother but these two women were unique. They knew what they wanted and knew exactly what they were going to make us do to get it. You know I love me a confident woman it's a major turn on for me, and I love the chase. But as for my big bro he has no chill he must have it on the regular, so he's not really into chasing the ladies. He's more of a hit it and move on to the next kind of guy.

"Well, I guess you've got your work cut out for you."

"I suppose I do. Yo, you know you and the gorgeous Renea Dubley are a hot topic on every social media plate form this morning."

"Say what?" I ask.

"Yeah man, everywhere I click your face is there with the words 'new couple' alert in bold letters."

"Damn, it's pictures from the celebration party isn't it?"

"Yes, sir." He beamed.

My line beeps and I look at the caller ID and see my lawyers name flashing on the screen.

"Aye, man, let me hit you back I have another call."

"Alright, later."

I click over and answer the call hoping that he was calling to give me some good news. This divorce had gone on long enough and I was ready for it to be over so that I could move on with my life and put the whole nightmare behind me.

"Hey, Harlan. Give me good news my man." I say, anxiously.

"Good morning Dejuan. Man, I thought I told you to stay out of the headlines until your divorce is final. And here I am this morning scrolling through my news feed and up pops a picture of you and Renea` Dubley."

I take in a deep breath, hold it for a second, then close my eyes and exhale. "Yeah man, I know. The paparazzi were all over the celebration party after our win, so they got a couple of shots of the two of us together that night."

"All I'm saying is be cautious and don't rush into anything."

"I hear you, man. So, you got something for me?"

"As a matter of a fact I do. The judge phoned me this morning and your divorce will be final in 30 days. Congratulations!"

I pump my fist out in front of me. "Great. Thanks, man!"

"No problem. Enjoy the rest of your day."

I hang up the phone and fall back on to my pillow rubbing my hands over my face and letting out a deep sigh of relief. It was over. She was finally out of my life and I was finally free to move on hopefully with Renea`.

I pick my phone back up off the bed and scroll through a few of the social media sites until I find the pictures of Renea` and I from the party. I take a snapshot of it and send it to her with a message that read.

Me: We're making headlines already Beautiful. #Newcouple

I press send and lay my phone back on the bed smiling to myself. A few seconds later my phone rings and I reach over and grab it unlocking it and reading her reply.

Renea: Wow, they practically have us married. Lol

I send her back a picture of myself looking panicked and she replies with a picture blowing me a kiss and a message that read.

Renea`: You should come to the studio and keep me company. That is if you're not busy?

Me: Never too busy for you Beautiful. Shoot me the address.

Renea: Great! I'll be there at 1 pm. I'll send you the address and the pass code you'll need to get in.

Me: I'll see you soon.

I look at the time on my phone and it was almost 10 am so I set an alarm for 11:45. That was enough time for me to get dressed and head over to the studio. I send Maverick a message letting him know to have the SUV out front at 12 pm and instructions to where I was headed. I placed my phone on the charger then laid back on to my pillow closing my eyes.

***

We pull up in front of the building and I check the address making sure that we were at the right place. Maverick hops out and opens my door, I step out of the SUV on to the street and nod to Maverick before I head inside the building. I walk over and join the guy standing by the other people that were waiting for the elevator. I take out my phone and take another look at the security code that she sent to me making sure I remembered it.

"Hey, man is you Dejuan Washington?" A male's voice said coming from behind me.

I turn my attention to the older gentlemen who was now standing beside me. He adjusts his glasses as he continues to stare at me.

"I'm sorry, what were you saying?" I ask.

"You're Dejuan Washington, right?"

"Yeah man, that's me. Nice to meet you." I say as I extend my hand to him.

"Pleasure's all mine brother. Congratulations on your championship win, I'm a huge fan." He says a bit overzealous as he grips my hand giving me a firm handshake.

"Thanks, man, I appreciate it. Um, what did you say your name was again?"

"Names Darron—Darron Tristan." He speaks up quickly.

The elevator doors open and we all walk inside of the elevator. We were each calling out our floor numbers as the lady pressed them in. I caught a glance of the overzealous fans eyes on me and I noticed that he never called out his floor, he just stood in the corner grinning. Once the elevator reached my floor it was only me and the strange fan left.

"You have a good day Dejuan." He said as he nods to me.

"Uh—yeah, thanks, you too," I reply politely.

I approach the very attractive redhead sitting at the entrance speaking into the phone. She holds up her finger to me as she finishes up the call.

"Hello, sir, what can I do for you?" She asks, with a very thick accent.

"I'm here to see Renea` Dubley."

"And you are?"

"Dejuan Washington," I reply, thinking to myself she must not watch basketball very much.

She punches in a few things on her keypad then turns her attention back to me.

"Yes, sir she's expecting you. If you don't mind just type in your security code, there on the keypad for me please." She points to a small black keypad in front of the computer and I enter the code. She punches the keys on her keyboard a few more times before standing up from her seat and smoothing out her pencil skirt that hugged her hips nice and tight.

"Right this way Mr. Washington." She says, turning and leading the way.

Shorty has a nice little frame on her and I tried not to look too hard or too long but the sway in her hips was mesmerizing. I focus and began looking straight ahead once we reached the glass doors at the end of the hall. She opens it and motions for me to continue straight ahead to the 2nd hallway where the studio would be to my right.

I thanked her then set off down the hall alone. I reached the second hall and continued to the room off to the side at the end as she instructed. I opened the door slowly and walk inside, I spot the two men sitting at the switchboard and Renea inside the booth. I wave to her and she winks at me as she continues to belt out her vocals. One of the fellas turns and looks over at me and nods, but the other guy at the computer he hadn't even noticed that I walked in. I take a seat on the couch and listen to her sing and her vocal range was crazy. The music was a different sound then what I was used to hearing from her.

Once the music ends she rushes out of the booth and over to me wrapping her arms around me. I hug her back tighten my arms around her waist lifting her off the ground.

"'Thanks for coming." She said, taking my hand and leading me over to the sofa.

"Of course, Beautiful."

"So, what did you think?"

"About what the song?"

"Yes!" she says in a high pitch voice.

"Oh, the song was hot. A little different, but it was dope."

She smiles at me excited. "Yeah, I figured I'd give my fans something new. You know more of me, more of the kind of music I want to make rather than the type of sound others think I should have.

"I feel you on that Beautiful."

I could tell that she was really in love with her craft and the music that she was giving her fans. I could feel her light beaming off her by just being there with her and watching her work. She was confident and relaxed, you could see the light in her eyes as she sang the lyrics to each song, this was her reason for being it was exactly what she was meant for. She has me hooked I'm drawn to her beauty that lies both inside and out and I can't believe this amazing woman is feeling me.

After a few hours, her crew left out to grab lunch and take a break for a while. Finally, we were alone again just the two of us, we sat and talked for a while. I love how the conversation flows so easy with us. She's so wise and level-headed with set goals and so far, she's crushed half the list.

When her crew returned I got out of their way, so they could get back to work. Giving her one last hug and kiss I head out of the studio and out to elevators. Maverick hurries out of the car once he sees me walking towards him and opens the door and I climb inside.

"Where to sir?" he asks, looking in the rear-view mirror.

"Head over to Jonathan's office please," I answer, and he nods then pulls into traffic.

I take out my phone and send Jonathan a quick text letting him know that I was on my way. I was hoping that he wasn't busy so that we could grab a bite to eat because I hadn't really eaten much before meeting up with Renea. We pull up to the building and Maverick lets me out in front before heading to the garage to park the Escalade.

I head inside and step inside the elevator pressing the button for the 16th floor and watching as the doors close. I step out into Jonathan's office and I spot his assistant at her desk tapping away at her keyboard.

"Hello lovely lady," her eyes shoot up from her keyboard and a smile replaces the seriousness that was on her face.

"Good Afternoon sweetie. How are you?" She asks, shuffling a few papers in her hand.

"I'm great. Is he busy?" I nod towards the doors.

"No sir he is not. You can go right on in hun."

"Thanks, lovely." I wink at her then walk over to the door and head into his office.

He was sitting at his desk on a phone call. I nodded to him then took a seat on the couch in the corner of his office grabbing a magazine from the table to flip through while I waited.

My homeboy had done well for himself he had turned a once small business into a billion-dollar company and was known worldwide. He would always talk about buying companies and flipping them for a profit and I'll admit I never knew what the hell he was talking about. But I could tell he knew what he was doing and that one day he would be great and of course rich, but I honestly never imagined a billionaire.

He was the reason I pushed so hard towards my dream and attended college. He was always on me about the type of crowd I was hanging around and I'll never forget what he said to me the night I told him I wanted to give up.

"You're going to get pushed out of your comfort zone and you're going to want to give up, but I won't let you. I'll never let you throw away the talent that God has blessed you with. Because right now you only have two options you can either live to die or live to thrive. The streets will only bring you heartache and pain. Is that what you want?"

I thought hard and long that night and I decided that I wasn't going to live to die. I wanted more, I wanted to make my mother, my stepfather, and my grandmother proud and become the man they raised me to be.

"What's up Bro?" he said, as he hung up the phone.

"Aye man what's up," I reply, getting up from my seat and walking over to the chair in front of his desk bumping his fist before taking my seat.

"Where are you coming from?"

"I just left the studio."

"Studio?" he looks at me with a raised eyebrow. "What are you trying to start a rap career or something." He chuckles, fixing his tie and leaning back in his chair.

"Nah," I laugh "I was there with Renea."

"Oh, so you're hanging out in studios now, huh. You run into anything interesting?"

"There's a nice little red headed receptionist with a nice little frame."

"Oh really?" he sits up in his seat leaning forward onto his desk.

I shake my head at him. "Yo, come on man aren't you trying to get at her friend? Don't be tryna start no trouble." I laugh.

He leans back in his seat once again letting out a sigh. "Yeah, you right."

"You're crazy man. I dropped by to see if you wanted to go grab something to eat?"

"Yes, I'm starving, and I need a break." He gets up from his seat and walks over to the door grabbing his jacket. "Let's go."

We head out the door and he let his receptionist know that he's stepping out for a while and to forward his calls. We decided to take his car, so I call up Maverick and tell him it's ok to take the rest of the night off.

MY DREAM MAN

Chapter Three

Renea

I stare into the vanity mirror replaying my night with Dejuan in the back of my mind as my make-up is being applied. My body ached to remind me that he'd been there, and my lady soul tingled at the thought of his mouth on me.

"Are you ok?" ask my makeup artist staring at me.

"Hmm… Oh, yes I'm good." I reply, raising my cup to my mouth and taking a sip of my tea.

"Mm-hmm…" she said eyeing me as she leans up against the make-up table "So are you going to sit there blushing letting on that tea boil over or are you going to spill it?"

"What?"

"Now come on you know I spotted that glow when you walked through that door this morning. So, go ahead and give up the details!" She demanded.

"I have no idea what you're talking about. I'm just in a really good mood this morning." I say with a straight face trying to convince her, but I knew I was caught.

"Ha! Lies!" she picks up the brush and brushes me over the nose "I know you got some last night from that sexy ass Dejuan Washington. So, go ahead and spill the tea on his stroke game boo." she says moving her hips back and forth with her tongue out.

I bust out laughing almost spitting my tea everywhere. She continues swaying her hips and I put my hands over my eyes.

"OMGOSH… Stop, stop!" I call out to her waving my hands in front of her.

"Okay, okay. Now go ahead talk." She insists as she walks back over to me out of breath.

"All I'm a say is… He got a big ego, such a huge ego." I sing to her as I grind my hips into the chair.

She laughs as she joins me dancing in place as we both laugh.

"They're ready for you Miss Dubley." I hear a voice say from the door.

We straighten up and she gets back to finishing up my make-up then I slip into my heels and head for the door. My assistant Kiani comes over and joins me to go over a few last-minute things as we head down to the set.

My interview with Steve was great, he's great and I always have an awesome time whenever I visit his show. I change and head out to the car where Francisco was awaiting my arrival. He opens the door and I climb inside and take my seat pulling my phone out of my purse and unlocking it. I have several missed calls from Shanice and a couple of text messages. So, I press the icon opening my messages.

Shanice: Seriously! I know you're not ignoring me. Call me back ASAP!

I roll my eyes then press the call button putting the phone up to my ear as I let out a loud breath. The phone starts to ring, and she picks up after the third ring.

"Hello"

"Hello ex-BFF of mine," I smile looking out the window and hoping that my tone makes her feel like shit.

"Oh, so you're breaking up with me, just like that, after 20 years and all that I've done for you." her voice cracks and she makes sniffling noises for dramatic effect.

I pull the phone away from my ear and cover my mouth. The line goes silent for a moment then we both burst into laughter.

"Come on love, you know I was just trying to help you out." She says speaking in a gibberish way.

"Mm-hmm... sure you were." I roll my eyes and suck in my teeth. "I guess I can forgive you only because it was the best sex I've ever had in my life," I scream into the phone.

She gasps. "You didn't!"

"Oh, I did, and it was so fucking good." A flash of that night creep into my mind and my lady soul awakened.

I could hear her clapping her hands on the other end of the line. "Way to go. It's about time that you threw caution to the wind and let someone fuck your brains out."

I shake my head with a bright smile on my face as I listened to her go on and on. We talked until I reached my next interview and then we made plans to get together for dinner at her place later tonight before saying goodbye.

***

I change into something a little more comfortable before heading over to Shanice's house for dinner. I stop for a moment to think whether I should pack an overnight bag because I'm more than likely going to end up passed out on her couch after a couple of bottles of wine.

I pull up to Shanice's Bel-air mansion and hop out of my Range Rover grabbing my bag and heading for the door. I love coming to this area it's so beautiful and the houses are so immaculate.

Shanice had done well for herself and made partner at her father's law firm and she's also very successful in her field might I add. She'd always dreamed of having a house in Bel-air and she accomplished it. After she graduated, she worked her ass off and proved all the naysayers wrong especially those men who see themselves as the alpha males that work for her father.

I walk up to the door and reach out to ring the doorbell, but the door swings open before I'd even gotten my finger anywhere near it.

"Hello Renea, come on in. Shanice is in the kitchen waiting for you," Jonathan says, leaning in and kissing me on the cheek then turning to close the door once I got inside.

I look at him puzzled, she hadn't mentioned that it would be the three of us having dinner tonight. I drop my bag on the stairs and began to walk towards the kitchen when the doorbell rings and Jonathan swings open the door and in walks Dejuan. Ok, correction she left out the part where the four of us would be having dinner this evening.

He looks at me with a sexy grin on his face, but it quickly faded into a confused expression once he noticed the look on my face. He turns and looks towards Jonathan, and he throws his hands up as if he was surrendering looking back and forth from Dejuan and me.

"It wasn't my idea," he adds before he closes the door and turns walking ahead of us.

Dejuan walks over and stops in front of me and I continue staring at him with a blank expression on my face and his lips part into a small smile.

"So, she set us up again, huh?"

I sigh heavily. "Yeah—she seems to be really good at being sneaky. I guess it's a lawyer thing." I wink at him then take his hand and pull him towards the kitchen.

We walk through the living room towards the hall that leads to the kitchen, and once we reach the hall he pulls his hand back pulling me into him and pinning me against the wall.

"What are you doing?" I gasp feeling his semi-hard erection pressing against me.

He places his hand under my chin lifting it and pressing his lips to mine kissing me hungrily. I couldn't move, I was powerless to his touch as my body trembled beneath him.

Shanice clears her throat and we release each other both reeling and out of breath.

"There are six rooms in this house perhaps you two should find one." She said, waving us off.

"Damn bro you couldn't wait for dessert?" Jonathan teased walking up beside her and putting his arm around Shanice.

"I prefer to be the main course," I reply, winking at Jonathan.

"Oh, I like that." He says with his eyebrow raised and a smirk on his face.

Shanice turns and elbows him in the side and he lets go of her grabbing his side with a pained look on his face and we all laugh.

"Come on you guys dinners ready."

We all head into the dining room and take our seats at the table. Honey lemon chicken and asparagus, it was delicious. After our meal, we headed out to the patio to unwind and have a glass of wine with our dessert, a slice of Dulce de Leche chocolate cake.

"So, it must be kind of bittersweet having the season end?" Jonathan asks.

Dejuan shrugged his shoulder and took a sip of his corona that he and Jonathan had opted for over the glass of wine that was offered to them. "Yeah, I guess you could say that. I'm going to miss my team and being on the court. But I'm happy that the time has come, we need this break we worked hard this season and it paid off."

"You damn right it did. To your championship win." Jonathan said holding up his bottle.

We all raise our glasses in the air then take a drink. It was actually nice being able to double date with my best friend and what made it twice as great was that our men were best friends as well. Dejuan and I hadn't made it official yet, but I was sure that we were headed in that direction I could feel the chemistry between us and I'm sure he could feel it too.

Or so I hoped!

Chapter Four

Dejuan

I had a great time with Renea at Shanice's place for dinner last night. Although I was a little thrown off when she didn't invite me back to her place and rejected my offer to spend the night at my place. Maybe she wasn't feeling me as much as I thought she was, or maybe she was upset that her friend had set us up again, or perhaps maybe I came on too strong when I cornered her in the hall before dinner.

I think back to her body shivering beneath me as our tongues danced around each other and the look in her eyes when I pinned her body to the wall. She was into it the way her body squirmed underneath mine as our bodies pressed against one another and she moaned into my mouth while pulling me deeper into the kiss.

"Dejuan, my man nice to see you." My agent said as he walked into the office pulling me away from my thoughts.

"Hey man," I said, standing and shaking his hand.

He leans on the desk just a couple of inches from my chair with his arms crossed and a huge million-dollar smile on his face.

"Guess who just got you the biggest deal you'll ever get in your entire lifetime?"

"No shit?" I ask, holding back my excitement until after we discussed numbers. Although I knew that it was going to be a nice deal regardless of the price tag.

"We just finished negotiating your endorsement deal and they've agreed to our terms. It's a multi-million dollar deal my man."

"Oh, hell yeah," I reply clasping my hands together. "See that's why I love you man you always come through."

"That's what I'm here for. Congratulations!" He rises from his seat and reaches over the desk to shake my hand.

"Thanks, man I really appreciate you," I say getting up from my seat and shaking his hand.

"We'll talk soon. Enjoy your day." He calls to me as I walk out the door.

I was so amped up as I walked out of the office and out to the car. Once I was seated in the SUV I pulled out my phone swiping to unlock the screen then pressed on Renea. The phone begins to ring, and her soft voice came over the line.

"HI," she said with excitement in her tone and it made me smile.

"Hello, Beautiful. Are you busy?"

"No, I actually just finished a photo shoot."

"Ok, I see you hustling."

"You know it."

"I didn't really want anything. I just got some good news from my agent and you were the first person that came to mind once I left his office."

"Awe, really." She said gushing, "Well spill it what's the good news?"

"Well, um, I just got signed two multi-million-dollar endorsements."

"Omg, are you serious." She says excitedly. "That's awesome Dejuan congratulations babe. I'm happy for you that's huge."

"Thanks! You know, I was just thinking I should do a little celebrating. Do you know of a beautiful lady that might want to join me tonight?"

"Hmm… I don't know. I mean I'm pretty sure there are a few Becky's lingering around waiting for a hot, talented, rich guy such as yourself."

I lean my head back on the seat and let out a loud laugh and she joins in.

"Ok, ok. You got me. But no in all seriousness would you like to come hang out with me tonight."

"Mm—well I'm not sure you know how busy us artist can be." She said before the line goes silent for a second and it feels like my heart stops. "No, I'm just kidding I'd love to." She laughs.

I blow out a long breath. "Ok, you got jokes," I reply "I like it. So, I'll send Maverick by to pick you up at 8 PM and we can have dinner at my place."

"Sounds great. I'll see you soon."

We hang up and I sink deeper into my seat closing my eyes and picturing Renea` bouncing on my dick, as I cup her full breast and twist her nipples between my fingers. I feel my manhood twitch at the thought, so I push it out of my mind and start the SUV backing out of the parking spot and driving away.

I call my mother and then my grandmother sharing the good news with them as I head over to Jonathan's office.

I park the SUV then head into the building. I walk over to the elevator when I get inside and press the button.

"Dejuan."

I hear a familiar voice call out to me, so I turn looking from my left to my right searching for the voice. Finally, I spot Jaylyn waving her hand at me from the seating area and I hold up my hand waving back at her. I take a deep breath and head over. I would have rather gone on about my day and not have run into her but what the hell I was in a good mood and I figured a quick hello wouldn't hurt.

"Hey baby, how are you?" She says, and I really wish she'd stop calling me that. She walks towards me with her arms extended and a smile on her face.

"I'm good, how are you?" I replied giving her a quick embrace.

"I'm doing fabulous."

"What are you doing here? If you don't mind me asking." I say.

"Oh, I'm waiting for my boyfriend. He works for the company."

"Your boyfriends employed by Jonathan?" I chuckle with an amused smile on my face.

"Yes, is something wrong with that?"

I clear my throat and then continue. "No, of course not. I'm just—" I pause for a second. "Nevermind. So, um, what does he do here?" I ask.

She began to answer just as a voice calls out to her from behind us. "Oh, there he is," She said waving him over. "You're going to love him. He's a huge fan of yours and he loves basketball." She said grinning from ear to ear.

I turn just as she falls into his embrace and he squeezed her tight around her waist with one arm and the other resting on her ass. When he finally turns to face me I immediately notice the older gentleman from the other day at the elevator, the overzealous fan.

"Hey, baby I want you to meet my ex-husband Dejuan. Dejuan this is my fiancé Darron Reed." She said, with a glow beaming through her smile.

His face dropped, and he had a puzzled look on his face as he extended his hand to me, and I smirk at him taking his hand and giving it a firm shake.

"Hey, I remember you from a few days ago. We meet on the elevator, nice to see you again man."

"Yeah you too," He said, "Um-Jaylyn, sweetheart, you didn't tell me that you were married to Dejuan Washington." He starred back and forth from the two of us in disbelief probably wondering why in the hell I let such a beautiful young woman such a Jaylyn go free. But she hadn't changed, so I was sure he would soon find out.

"You never ask," she responded and then changed the subject. "Darron works as a part of Jonathan's security team." She said gushing over her new man.

"Oh ok. That's what's up man. Well Jaylyn it's always a pleasure and Darron it was nice seeing you again, but I have to get going you two enjoy your evening."

I turn and walk away with a grin as I replay the look of her fiancés face over again in my mind. I walk back over to the elevators and press the button and the doors open instantly, and I step inside.

That woman never fails to amaze me. She's clearly only looking for someone to take care of her now that her money boat has set sell. I may have been crazy in love, but I wasn't stupid. I'd made her sign a prenup before we'd gotten married so she's leaving this marriage with what I found to be fair $2.5 million.

I'd met Jaylyn when I first got to college and she seemed like a really cool chic and after dipping into the pussy I was in love or no I was sprung. She had me so pussy wiped that I was going crazy over her ass and my friends they tried to warn me about her, but my dumb ass wouldn't listen. She cheated on me our junior year of college and I kicked her to the curb and tried to move on. And I'll admit she sweet talked me into to taking her back our senior year and we ended up married right after graduation.

My mother and the rest of my family didn't like her and told me to leave her alone because she was no good for me, but I was blinded by what I thought was love. That is until I caught her cheating on me again with some rich old man. I wasted four and a half years of my life with that woman and now it was finally over the papers were signed and I could move on with my life.

I walk into the office and nod to Jonathan's receptionist Vanessa and she waves her hand for me to go on in as she continues with her phone call.

I walk inside, and Jonathan's head pops up from whatever paperwork he was focusing on.

"Bro," he said, getting up from his desk.

"Aye, your boy just signed two deals," I say, extending my arms out to my side as I walk over to his desk.

"Hell, yeah bro. Congratulations!" he says walking over and giving me a quick manly embrace. "Hey, we have to celebrate I can call up a few of the guys and we can—"

"Not tonight man I got a little something planned with Renea," I say rubbing my hands together.

"Awe come man are you skimping out on me like that."

"Nah man it's just you know—"

"Yeah, I feel you. But we're going to celebrate this weekend. We're going to get all the fellas together."

"Bet."

I kick it with Jonathan for about an hour and a half before heading out. I stop and grab some groceries for dinner tonight and then I text and ask her if there's anything specific that she would like for dinner, but she just replies with 'Surprise me'. I walked to the line and placed my items on the belt and waited for the cashier to ring me up. She took her time running the items through as she eye fucked me the whole time that I was standing there. Once she was finished ringing up my items and the young man was finished bagging and placing them in the cart, I headed out to the car and placed my bags in the trunk and headed straight home to get started.

Chapter Five

Renea

I pull up in front of my mother's house, step out of the car, and walk up the sidewalk. I'd been so busy that I hadn't spoken to her or my father much this past week, so I decided to stop by for a surprise visit and they love it when I get a chance to come by because they miss their baby girl. The door swung open and out came my mother in her signature yoga pants and athletic jacket.

"Hello, Darling! What a pleasant surprise." She says, rushing over and pulling me into a tight hug.

"Hey, mom!" I say, the best I can as she squeezes me tighter.

She releases me and looks into my eyes with a bright smile on her face. She places her hands on each of my shoulders and plants kisses on both of my cheeks.

"I'm sorry sweetheart did I hurt you. I'm just so happy to see you."

"I'm fine. I missed you too mom" I place my arm around her. "Come on let's go inside."

"Ok, sweetheart, is everything ok?" She asks.

"Yes," I say, pulling her in closer as we walk into the house.

Visiting my mom always put a smile on my face, it was nice to come home. All of the smells and the surroundings made me relax and brought back memories of my childhood. I was an only child, so I had both my parent's undivided attention. And of course, Shanice my best friend was always around, so it was kind of like having a sister and almost everyone pretty much thought so since she was at our house more than she was at home.

"I'm going to get a pitcher of lemonade sweetie. I'll be right back." My mother said, patting me on my knee then getting up from the couch.

"Ok, and how about a slice of peach cobbler, please," I call out to her and she turns back.

"Of course, sweetie."

I slip off my shoes and stretch out on the couch and let out a long sigh, it's been such a long day. My cell rings and I fish it out of my purse sliding my finger across the screen answering the call.

"Hello."

"Hey, Beautiful." Dejuan's deep voice comes over the line.

"Hey, you. What are you up to?" I ask, smiling into the phone.

"I just grabbed a few things for our dinner tonight and I'm headed home now. What about you, what are you up to?"

"I'm visiting my mom. I haven't seen her in a couple of weeks, but I can't wait to see you tonight."

"Sounds like you're counting down the hours." He jokes.

"That I am," I say in a cute little voice. "I've been thinking about you all day."

"Is that right."

"And... I've been thinking about all of the nasty and dirty things that were done to me the last time I was—" I start to say but my mother clears her throat startling me.

I sit up straight on the sofa once I notice my mother standing beside the couch with the pitcher of lemonade and two slices of cobbler on a tray. I could feel my cheeks getting red, so I quickly turned away from my mother's gaze.

"Um—I'm sorry Dejuan but I have to go. I'll see you tonight."

"Ok beautiful see you soon."

I hang up the phone and peek out the corner of my eyes over at my mom who was standing there grinning down at me like a crazy person.

"Ugh... how much of that did you hear?" I ask, with a nervous laugh hoping that she says none of it.

"Oh, I walked in somewhere around nasty and dirty things." She replied, with a raised brow.

"Omgosh…" I said, putting my hands over my head and falling back into the cushion.

She giggles. "Oh, cut it out. You're a grown woman it's nothing to be embarrassed about."

"Yeah, that is unless you're caught talking dirty in front of your mother."

She laughs again and louder this time as she sits down on the sofa placing the tray on the coffee table and turning to me.

"So, tell me who's the lucky guy?"

"His name is Dejuan," I mumble before sinking deeper into the couch.

"Washington?" she asks, in a high pitch voice.

"Yes," I reply a small smile dancing on my lips as I look down into my lap.

"Oh my, your father will love having him as a son-in-law."

"Whoa, mom." I say holding up my hands "we're just getting to know each other."

"So is that what you all are calling it now."

I look at my mom with my mouth wide open. "Mom!" I shout.

"Renea, we are two grown women and we both know what getting to know each other means." She winks at me.

"Oh gosh mom, no, correction you're my mother. We do not talk about things like this at all." I reply placing a pillow over my face.

I pull the pillow away glancing over at her giving her a side eye and she smirks at me shrugging her shoulder. She pours us a glass of lemonade and sits mine in front of me and takes a sip from hers. I pick up my glass and take a few sips before placing it on the coaster and picking up the plate of cobbler and a fork.

"Well, I hope you all are being careful."

"Mom, please, can we not talk about this."

"I'm just saying make sure you're protecting yourself. There's a lot of things going around and I'm certain that you're not ready for a baby."

"Omgosh mom," I say, laying my fork on the plate and sitting it back on the tray.

Kiani comes walking into the livingroom stopping in her tracks after noticing the looks on our faces. I couldn't have been happier to see her gosh was her timing perfect.

"Is this a bad time." She hesitates, looking from me to my mother searching our face for an answer.

"No, come on in sweetheart. My daughter was just telling me about her recent romp in the sheets with that sexy basketball player boyfriend of hers." My mother says, and I slowly crawl back into my shell.

"Boyfriend?" Kiani, says looking at me with her eye's wide and her mouth open.

"I think we need to upgrade to a bottle of wine."

"No, mom."

"Yes. Mama Lillian wine sounds fantastic."

I pick up the pillow and put it over my face as I fall back onto the couch. My mom returns a couple of minutes later with a bottle of red wine and 3 glasses filling them to the brim and handing one to each of us. After about 20 minutes of my mom invading my privacy, we finally switched to a less embarrassing conversation.

My phone chirps and I look down and see a message from Shanice. I pick up the phone and unlock the screen, so I could see the full message.

Shanice: A few of my co-workers are going out for drinks. Do you want to join?

Me: Thanks, but not tonight. Having dinner with Dejuan later.

Shanice: Aw… Ok, have fun and do all the things that I would do.

I shake my head and lock my phone slipping it into my purse.

"I'm going to get going, mom. I need to get home and get ready for my date tonight with Dejuan."

"Ok, sweetie. I'll walk you all out."

I gather my things and my mother walks us to the SUV after kissing her goodbye we climb inside and wave at her one last time before driving away.

***

I step out of the shower and dry off wrapping my towel around me. I stand in the center of my closet contemplating on what I should wear tonight, I'm not sure of how dressy or casual I should be. It is a celebration so maybe I should dress up, but we are going to be dining in so maybe I should dress comfortably. I should call make small talk and then slide the question in during the conversation. Ugh… no, I can't do that it's a dinner date so I'm going to go with something sleek and sexy.

MY DREAM MAN

I grab the off the shoulder, thigh high, red dress and a pair of red bottoms. No bra or panties are required and if it turns out that I'm going to be dessert, well let's just say easy access.

I grab my purse and step into the elevator and head down to the lobby. I walk over to were Maverick was parked and waiting for me "Good evening Miss Dubley," He said opening the door for me. I slide inside and take my seat. I watch as he climbs into the driver's seat, starts the car, and eases out into the evening traffic which was unusually light. I ask for him turn on the air instead of letting down the windows and risking my hair blowing out of place.

We pull up to Dejuan's building and he shuts off the engine then comes around and opens my door. I take a deep breath and exhale then take his hand and step out of the car. I take out my phone and send him a message letting him know that I had arrived as I headed into the building. I step into the elevator and punch in the code that he'd given to me earlier and watch the elevator doors close.

As the elevator starts to move my palm gets sweaty and my heart begins to race. I swallow hard and step out into the foyer and walk down the small hallway where rose petals are spread out on the floor and candles lighting the way through the deem lite hall. I stop at the entrance to the dining room where the rose petals end.

Dejuan was lighting a few more candles and placing them on the table when he looks up at me and his lips turned up into a smile. He was dressed in a red button-down shirt with the top two buttons left undone and a pair of black pants looking absolutely edible.

Chapter Six

Dejuan

She looked stunning and the way her dress hugged her body in all the right places and the way her perfect round tits peeked out the top made my dick jump to attention.

"You look gorgeous," I say as I walk over and wrap my arms around her kissing her softly on her cheek.

"Thank you. You don't look bad yourself." She replies, running her finger down the front of my shirt. Sending a tingling sensation straight to my manhood.

I catch her hand before it falls and kiss it before placing it in mine and leading her over to her seat. I pull her chair out for her then go over to claim mine. Everything was perfect and so was she was sitting across from me staring at me with lust filled eyes. I wanted to clear the table and peel that tight dress off of her and fuck her on my dining room table and watch her ass bounce and jiggle as I take her from behind.

"Are you ok?" She asks, pulling me back to the present.

"uh—Yeah," I clear my throat. "You took my breath away—I'm a little speechless," I reply smiling over at her and she returns the smiles placing her napkin on her lap.

"So, what are we having?"

"Well on tonight's menu we have Steak Au Poivre with sautéed potatoes and mushrooms."

"Mm… sounds delicious."

She picks up her fork and starts with the potatoes and then the steak. She closes her eyes and lets out a low satisfied groan before opening her eye's. This woman was jaw dropping and I wanted her bad, I couldn't wait to make her mine and what better time than tonight it was a perfect time to make it official.

I'd had my chef bring me over a Lemon Spice cake since I knew It was her favorite. And after we finished our dinner I went into the kitchen and cut her slice then returned to the table sitting the plate in front of her.

"Omg is that," She looks up at me. "How did you know?"

"I have my ways." I beam.

She finished her dessert and then we retreated to the living room to just chill out and have a glass of wine and talk. She told me about her childhood and growing up in a predominately white neighborhood and I told her about mine and how hard it was to live in the projects. While she'd grown up in a suburban area with a two-parent household. I, on the other hand, grew up in the projects with my single mother that is until she met my stepfather.

"So, you had it pretty rough, huh?" she asks, and I could hear the sadness in her voice.

"Yeah, it was hard my father died when I was 5. He had a heart attack and my mother took it hard I mean I could understand why though she was left a single mother of two boys who were now going to grow up without a father."

"I'm sorry," she says, placing her hand on my leg and gently rubbing it.

"I kind of fell into a life of—" I pause. "Let's just say I made a few bad choices and fell in with the wrong crowd." I swallow hard and look away from her.

I didn't want to lie to her, but I couldn't tell her about the drug business that I had going on in Long Beach or about Montez and the fellas. I didn't want to scare her away before we'd had a chance to see where this could go.

"It's ok, we all make mistakes. My past is not all squeaky clean either you know."

"Oh yeah, what did you do get caught boosting Chanel purses from the mall or something."

She cut her eyes at me and sucked in her teeth as she reached over and shoved my arm. "Whatever!" she begins. "I was a little mischievous when I was in my teens and I did some things I'm not proud of."

"Mm-hmm…" I tease. "But seriously my step pops helped me out a lot and he's been really good to my mom. He was in business with Jonathan's father and that's when we met, and we clicked immediately we've been best friends ever since."

"That's awesome. It's amazing that there are men like that out there that will take in a child and love them like their own."

"Yeah, I appreciate my stepfather he helped me become the man I am and my brother as well. And my grandmother she was and still is the backbone of our family, she keeps us together. Maybe you'll meet them one day."

"I hope so." She said with a wide smile.

We keep the wine flowing and the conversation as well. Everything was so easy with her she made me feel relaxed and open like I could tell her anything, so understanding and compassionate. We get on the topic of food after I ask her what she thought about dinner and from there the conversation switched to talk about our future.

"So, what do you see in your future Renea`?" I ask.

"That's a really good question. Let's see!" She said, pausing and going into deep thought. "You know I haven't really thought much of the future honestly or I should say not so much so about my personal life. But as for my career, I'm always thinking ahead when It comes to that, but I can say that I would love to have children and get married someday, not just yet but someday. What about You?" She asks, smiling a beautiful soft smile.

"Well I haven't thought much about my personal life either I've been so focused on the divorce that I never really took the time to. But I can see myself married again with a family. And I would love to open my own restaurant several if possible."

"Really? So, you have a passion for cooking?" she replies, taking a sip of her wine.

"Yes, I've loved cooking and creating dishes ever since I was a young. I think it stems from watching my grandmother and helping her out in the kitchen it was my first love basketball came second." I say with a grin.

"Well, I think that's awesome."

"I think you are awesome and sexy and beautiful."

A shy smile appears on her face as she looks down into her glass I reach over and place my hand under her chin and raise her chin so that her eyes meet mine. I gaze at her with hunger in my eyes, but I don't want to move to fast I want the mood to stay just like this, so I take her hand into mine.

"Come dance with me beautiful."

She takes my hand and I help her up off the sofa. I pick up the remote from the table and turn on the stereo system and press start on my playlist and the music begins.

I pull her in close and we began to move slowly to the sound of New Editions 'Can you stand the rain'. She places her hands around my neck and stares into my eyes and I get lost in her gaze.

"I love this song." She whispers, closing her eyes.

I lean in and kiss her slow taking time to savor every moment. She put her hands on the back of my head and pulls me deeper into the kiss. The music ends, and I release her taking her hand and leading

Nae T. Bloss

her to my bedroom. As we stand in front of the king size bed I undress her unzipping the back of her dress and letting it fall to the floor. She wasn't wear anything underneath and she turns back to face me revealing her breast, they sat perfectly, and her nipples were staring me in the face.

She reaches up and begins unbuttoning my shirt and pulling it off before loosening my belt and then my pants letting them drop to the floor.

"Lay down," she tells me, and I do as I'm told. "This is your night remember."

She takes my semi-hard dick into her hand and leans over top of me then licks the tip of my dick with her tongue and I let out a groan. She begins swirling it around the top before gently closing her mouth around me and sucking it making the kind of sounds you make when you pull a lollipop out of your mouth. The sounds ringing in my ears combined with the feeling of her hot wet tongue on my dick made me stiff and hard as a rock.

She smiled up at me as she closed her mouth over me taking in as much of my dick as she could, and I let out a low growl deep in my throat. She began moving her mouth up and down my shaft flicking her tongue on the tip before taking me all in again. I'd never had anyone fit my whole nine-inch dick in their mouth, but her pretty little mouth devoured him, and she did it like a pro.

I watched as her head bobbed and weave up and down on my dick and every time I hit the back of her throat it brought me closer and closer to the edge. She wrapped her hands around my dick after she deep throated me one last time and began to suck my dick as she twisted her hands around me like she was churning butter and I begin to flex my hips. It felt so fucking good a grunt escaped my lips and my muscles tensed as my body jerked and I shot all of my seeds into her mouth.

She slurped, licked, and sucked until she'd milked me dry. I relaxed back on the bed and after a couple of minutes, I begin feeling myself coming down from the high that she put me on. She stood straight up and licked her lips then climbed on top of me.

"Are you ok baby?" she joked.

I give a weak smile and nodded my head at her when she laughs and leans in and kisses me. I lay still on the bed for a few more minutes and she rested her head on my chest with my arms wrapped around her.

"I think you're trying to make me fall in love with you," I say, in a playful voice.

She smiles into my chest then replies, "Maybe so."

I kiss the top of her head as I stroke her back with a huge smile on my face.

***

I open my eyes and the sun stings them, so I quickly close them and roll over stretching my arm out for her, but the bed was empty. I sit up straight on the bed and look around the room.

"Renea`," I call out but there was no reply.

I get up from the bed and grab my boxers off the floor and slide them on. I walk into the bathroom and then out into the living room, but she wasn't there, I guess she'd taken off early this morning. I was kind of disappointed because I'd wanted to wake up to her beautiful smile. I head back into the room and take a seat on the side of the bed and I reach for my cell so that I could send her a message, but I find a note that she'd left for me on the nightstand.

Morning handsome!

Sorry I couldn't stay but I have

two magazine cover shoots this morning.

I'll call you later. XOXO

I placed the note back on the nightstand and smile then get up and head to the bathroom to take a shower. I turn it on and make it as hot as I could stand it then step inside and let it run over the top of my head and down the rest of my body relaxing every muscle.

I close my eyes and let my mind wander back to the night that Renea` let me fuck her in the shower. I start to stroke my dick, but the sound of my phone disrupted me. I cut off the shower and dry off then wrap the towel around me before rushing into the room to grab my phone from the dresser. I was too late the call had gone to voicemail so I look at the screen to check the caller id but there was nothing there that's when I realized it was my burner phone.

I take the phone out of the draw and unlock it. I see Montez's number beside the words missed call, so I redialed the number calling him back and he answers after the first ring.

"Yo, motherfucker, where your ass at? I've been tryna get at you for three fucking days now." He yells into the phone.

"Aye first off you better calm down and watch how the fuck you talking to me," I reply in a stern voice.

"You need to get here asap. We got a fucking problem." Tez replied.

"What kind of problem?"

"The kind of problems that'll get us all locked up."

"Fuck. Alright man, I'll be there soon just sit tight."

"Bet."

Montez, Lavon, and Jerome were my boys from back in the day. Montez was a D-Boy and he put us on and everything was kosher up until we meet this fool named Maylan and he dimed us out to the feds. I knew he was a snitch when I meet him, but the rest of the crew couldn't see it they put way too much trust in that fool and he almost got us all put on lockdown.

I grab a few things and stuff them in my duffle bag and head down to the garage. I decided to take the Mercedes instead of one of the sports cars this wasn't the time to try and stand out I needed to keep it low key. I sent a quick text to Lavon and Jerome telling them to meet me at the spot in a half hour before pulling out of the garage and heading towards Long Beach.

I pull into the driveway and park the car and grab my bag from the back. I unlock the door, go inside and close the door behind me. Being in this house always brings back memories of my childhood. My mother bought this house when my brother and I were younger after my father passed away she wanted to get us out of the hood, so we'd have a chance to better ourselves and have more opportunities.

I set my bags on the bed then walk back into the living room and stretch out on the sofa. I take out my phone to check for any missed calls when I hear a knock at the door, I go over and open the door for my boys Jerome and Lavon.

"Well look who decided to grace us with his presents Mr. Pro-baller himself. What's up bruh?" Jerome said as he walked in giving me a manly embrace.

"I see now that you got a little fame you done forgot about us small folks down here." Lavon jokes dapping it up.

I close the door behind them and walk back over to the sofa and take a seat getting comfortable once again.

"Whatever man. You fools could be making some clean money as well if you'd trade in your street hustle for a more legit kind of business."

"Oh, ok big time so now you want to try and fix my life?" he said, with a chuckle. "You were doing the same shit as us before you up and went bougie on us," Jerome says, in a sarcastic tone.

"I got out and so can you."

"Well, then my brother what are you doing here now? I know it's not because you missed us and wanted to break bread." Lavon asks.

"I'm here because one of you fools are slipping and Montez called me fucking bugging out," I say sitting up on the sofa. "What the fuck happened to the shipment Rome?"

He looks back and forth from me and Lavon with a confused look on his face as if he didn't understand the question.

"What the fuck you mean dog? I'm not the one handling the shipments." He says leaning forward in his chair. "Oh—wait a min I see your boy didn't tell you that he put that oh mark ass fool on, did he?"

"Who?" I ask, confused.

"Tez recruited our old friend Maylan," Lavon replies.

"Say what?" I lean forward in my seat again staring at the both of them as my blood begins to boil.

I hand my business over to this fool and the first thing he does is go and put that fucking snitch Maylan on. Oh yeah, he really trying to make me fuck him up, he must've been high at the time. Just as I take my seat again trying to calm down in strolls Montez.

"What's up my good people?" he says coming through the door with a huge smile on his face.

"Yo, family what's good?" Jerome said.

"That's what I want to know my dude," he says, taking a seat on the sofa and kicking his feet up on the ottoman. "Where the fuck is my shit?" he asks.

"Come on man get your shoes off my fucking furniture man," I said, getting annoyed.

"Fuck dis furniture bruh." He replies, and I shot him a death stare.

"Tez now you know damn well Maylan handles that shit man," Jerome said, and he sits up straight in the chair and looks over at me with a look of fear in his eyes.

"So, you put that fucking snitch on without consulting me first?" I ask.

"Man, chill he said he wanted to work and he's still in contact with some good connects." He responds holding my gaze.

"You know we can't fucking trust him. Look what happened the last time." I said, in a stern voice.

"So now you're doubting me?" he said. "Speak up man. What you tryna say partner? Are you saying this shits on me—what you tryna say I'm not handling business, huh motherfucker?" He snaps his voice elevating.

"Yo, Tez, slow your road," Lavon said.

"Nah man let the boss man speak," Tez replies, scooting towards the edge of his chair staring me directly in the eye.

I sit back on the couch and rest my hands in my lap staring him down with just as much aggression in my gaze.

"I know you not trying to post up on me. You better sit the fuck back and calm down before you catch this heat, and you know I'm not playing, keep coming at me sideways."

"Yo man chill," Rome says holding his hand up in Tez's direction.

He huffs then sits back in his seat. "Alright, so how you would you like to handle this boss man?" Tez asks.

We hash out a plan and then I have Tez hit up Maylan and set up a meeting at the port. We strap up then head out to Tez's Escalade and head over to the port.

When we pull up Maylan is standing outside of his car leaning on the hood. He tosses his cigarette and begins walking over to the SUV as we pull up. He pauses mid-step when he sees me exit the SUV his eyes jump from each of us before locking in on Montez I could see the fear in his eyes.

"Dejuan," He said as he got closer. "Yo man what are you doing here?"

"Let's see perhaps because you can't keep shit straight," I said, stepping closer to him so that we were eye to eye.

"What the fuck happened to the shipment man," Jerome yells out.

"Tez, man I told you I would handle it." He said stepping to the side. "You didn't have to call him out here."

I snap my fingers in front of him directing his attention back to me. "Yo, talk to me man, not him," I said, speaking in a hard tone.

"Alright look our people were stopped when they were coming through customs. But I'm handling it man just like I said I would, you have to trust me." He pleaded.

I burst out into laughter. "Trust you," I turn back looking at the fellas still laughing historically. "You want me to trust you. You, the same motherfucker that almost got us killed 7 years ago. Or the you that almost got us life in prison because you decided that you were going to go snitch to the feds about our connection. No, you a bitch and I don't trust your ass."

He walks up on me like he's going to do something so Tez runs up beside me and pulls his 9mm and points it straight at him. Maylan backs away a little but doesn't break eye contact with me instead he continues to stare me down.

"That's right homeboy. Don't fuck around and get your top blown back," Tez said

"So where are the crates Maylan?" I ask.

"They're still being held," He said taking another step back. "I won't know their decision until tomorrow morning." He replies.

I turn and look over at Lavon and say, "You know what to do handle that shit bruh."

He nods then steps away pulling out his phone and makes a call. I turn my attention back to Maylan and wave my hand for Tez to lower his gun now that he got the point.

"I'm a deal with you later don't go nowhere," I say to Maylan then turn and walk back over to the SUV.

The rest of the fellas follow suit and we all climb back into the SUV. We watch as Maylan walks over to his car and gets inside and speeds away from the port. I look at Tez and he looks back at me with a smile on his face. I could tell he already knew what I was going to say so I just shook my head and turned away.

"Just drive," I said, reaching for my seat belt.

"Yo man we good. That customs agent we put on payroll last year is handling that situation as we speak." Lavon said.

"Good looking my man," I reply.

We arrive back at the house and Tez pulls into the driveway. We dap it up before the three of us step out of the Escalade, I head inside, and the fellas hope in their cars and disappear. Just as I get in the door my phone rings and I take it out of my pocket and glance at the caller ID before sliding my finger across the screen.

"Hey Beautiful," I said, smiling into the phone.

"Hi," she answers sounding exhausted.

"You sound tired. How was your day?"

"I am and let's just say it's been a long one." She replies.

I chuckle. "You miss me?"

"Yes! You should come over and help me relax." She said, in a soft and seductive voice.

My smile gets wider. "I wish I could beautiful. I'm in Long Beach right now though helping out a friend. But I can come through tomorrow."

She lets out a disappointed sigh.

"I'm sorry beautiful."

"It's ok, I'm going to go and take a hot bath."

"Alright, I'll talk to you tomorrow."

We say our goodbyes and I hang up the phone placing it on the table. I get up and go into the kitchen in search of something to put in my stomach it was growling at me I was so hungry. I open the fridge and it was empty only a few bottles of water and a half bottle of Dr. Pepper, so I go back into the living room and pull up my pizza app and place an order.

After about 35 minutes the driver arrives with my food. When I open the door to pay him his eyes go wide, and he gasps for air.

"Oh wow," he struggles to say. "Dejuan fucking Washington. What's up man oh the guys aren't going to believe this."

"How are you doing man? How much I owe you?" I say smiling back at him.

"$21.60," he says holding out his hand.

"You can keep the change," I said, handing him $50.

"Awe man thanks. Aye—uh can I get a picture or something really quick."

I take a deep breath. "Yeah man come on."

He takes out his smartphone and takes a quick selfie and then I sign the back of one of the napkins for him.

"Thanks, so much man." He marveled turning and walking back to his car holding up the napkin kissing it.

I shake my head and close the door, I still get amazed by all the attention I receive and how excited people get once they realize who I am. I take a seat on the sofa and sit down the box of pizza and the 2-liter of soda on the table in front of me before grabbing a slice. I grab the remote and turn on ESPN and relax.

Chapter Seven

Renea

After capturing a shot of my last pose the photographer yells out "that's a wrap people," as he turns and hands the camera to his assistant. He walks over to me wrapping his arms around me in a gentle embrace as he kisses both of my cheeks.

"Excellent job darling. You are absolutely stunning my dear, it's always a pleasure."

"Thank you, love. You know our chemistry is what makes each session a success." I say, returning a hug and kiss on his cheek.

"Indeed, it is darling."

I thank him and head to my dressing room to change with Kerry right beside me. Kiani hands me my latte as she joins us, once we reach the dressing room we go inside. I sit my cup down and walk behind the folding screen to strip down, I couldn't wait to get out of this expensive dress and into my jeans and t-shirt.

"We have to be at the show taping in 2 hours and after that, you have a meeting with the editor of Rock out magazine about your cover shoot," Kiani says, flipping through the agenda on her tablet.

"Also, Elan is asking for an appearance on her upcoming season of the show," Kerry adds in.

"Of course, set it up," I reply.

I slip on my shoes and pick up my cup taking a long drink before grabbing my purse. I take out my phone and check my messages and I see that I have two texts from my mom and Shanice but nothing from Dejuan. I hadn't heard from him since the other night when he was supposed to come over once he'd gotten back from Long Beach, but he never showed up. I send a quick reply to Shanice then open my mother's message.

Mom: Hello Sweetheart! I just wanted to invite you and that handsome boyfriend of yours over for dinner on Sunday. Call me!

I roll my eyes at the message. Oh, my mother the one and only Mrs. Lillian Dubley. The greatest women on the planet, my rock, my queen, whom I love and adore so very much, but she is so very annoying when it comes to my love life. A smile creeps across my face and I open my eyes and send back a reply.

Me: See you on Sunday!

I wasn't sure if I'd be going alone or not but I would definitely be there.

"Hey, Renea, I just talked to PR and some of the social sites and media outlets are asking if you'd like to confirm the rumors of a relationship with Dejuan Washington."

"What?" I turn and look at her. "You already know the answer to that."

"Of course, just thought I'd ask." She replies.

I stop and turn to face her noticing the change in her tone. "If you have something to say Kerry just say it," I say squinting my eyes at her.

A nervous smile appears on her face and then she said, "Well—I was kind of wondering myself."

I laugh and turn and continue towards the door. "Kerry you're not the paparazzi. If you want to know who I'm fucking I will gladly give you the juicy blow by blow." I say turning and moving my hands towards my mouth as if I'm giving a blowjob then wink at her and smile.

She gasps and puts her hands over her eyes as her mouth drops. Kiani laughs and puts her arm around her and walks into the elevator.

***

I fall back onto the cream-colored leather chair in Shanice's office letting out a long sigh. She looks at me with her lips pressed into a thin line trying not to laugh at the ridiculous expression on my face.

"I see someone had a long day," she says sitting her pen on her notepad and leaning back in her chair.

"Yes, girl I'm exhausted."

"I think we should go to the spa and relax. What do you say?"

"I say let's do it. I'd rather be working my kinks out another way but seeing as how someone is MIA, I'll have to settle for a message." I poke out my lip pouting.

"Awe is your boo too busy to come give it up."

"Yes," I cross my arms in front of me and poke my lip out a little more.

She laughs loudly. "You are crazy. Come on I need to get out of this stuffy office anyways, I've been up to my eyeballs in paperwork all morning." She said as she walks over and grabs her purse and jacket from the hook.

"We should get Mani & Pedi's as well," I say, as I pick up my purse and follow her out the door.

"Sounds good to me."

We arrive at the Salon and Spa in Beverly Hills it's one of Shanice's favorite places. A very pretty Japanese woman greets us once we get inside and after discussing what all we would like done she shows us to the back where we change out of our clothes and into our robes. A couple of minutes later another lady enters the room and shows us to the massage room where we went our separate ways. After we were finished with our massages we would meet up in the salon for our Mani & Pedi's.

"Good evening, I will be catering to you this evening. Have you chosen the type of massage that you would like to receive?" Asks the massage therapist.

"Yes, the relaxation massage."

"Excellent choice ma'am. I'm going to step out and collect a few things, and while I'm gone I will need for you to remove your robe and lie down on the table for me. I will return momentarily."

Once he steps out the room I slide off my robe and place it on the chair then climb on to the massage table and lay flat on my stomach pulling the sheet over the lower half of my body.

"Are you ready?" he asks, knocking on the door before entering.

"Yes, you can come in," I call out to him.

He enters the room and places his things on a stand beside the bed that looks to be filled with different essential oils. He places a bottle in a small warmer for a few seconds then removes it and rubs it on to his hands and rubs them together then begins massaging my legs and working his way up the rest of my body.

I close my eyes and relax I could feel all the stress and tension melting away as his hands worked their magic. I let my mind drift off to the night Dejuan and I hooked up. The memory was so vivid and clear in my mind. The way his hands felt as he caressed my body and the way it hurt so good when he pressed his long and thick cock inside of me.

I must admit I was a little nervous when he dropped his boxers and I saw the size of his dick, it was kind of intimidating. I'd never had anyone that big before and I'm sure he could tell from the tightness of my lady soul and on top of that, it had been a long time since I'd had sex with anyone.

"Miss Dubley we're all done. I will step out so that you can get dressed." He said, pulling me from my thoughts.

I sit up on my elbows. "Omg, thank you. I feel so much better." I reply.

"I'm glad you enjoyed it, ma'am," he smiles then turns and heads out of the room.

I sit up on the edge of the table and twist my neck around and roll my shoulders back and forth. I was amazed, he was really good, and my body felt so relaxed. I jump down from the table and grab my robe and slide it on tying it tight around my waist before walking out into the hall. Shanice waves to me and I join her in the sitting area.

"So how was your massage?" she asks, grinning from ear to ear.

"It was so relaxing. I'm going to have to come here more often," I reply, taking a seat in the plush white chair beside her. "And that grin on your face tells me that yours was ten times better."

"And very much needed," she said with a laugh.

We talk until they come and let us know that they're ready for us. The lady comes and shows us to our seats and we sit down and place our feet in the water letting the bubbles massage our feet.

I close my eyes and get comfortable so that I could enjoy this much-needed break and pampering.

I arrive at home a little after 7 pm and I take a quick shower then put on a pair of yoga pants and a tank top. I grab a glass of wine and snuggle up on the sofa and surf the net for a bit, post a few photos on Instagram, and spend a little time on twitter. But after about an hour my stomach starts growling so I head into the kitchen to grab something to eat.

Being the left-over queen that I am I'm sure I'll find something that I can toss into the microwave and heat up. I look through the fridge not finding anything that I wanted so I decide to just order take out. I head back into the living room and settle back in my spot picking up my phone and ordering some Chinese from my usual spot.

I hang up and place my phone on the cushion beside me and pick up the remote. I'd browse through the channels trying to find a good movie or something to watch until my food arrives. I come across the movie 'Brown Sugar' it was one of my favorite movies, so I was content with that.

I hear the doors to the elevator open and I assume that it's Francisco our Euro bringing my order up, but I turn around and see Dejuan walking in.

"Did someone order take out?" he said smiling at me holding the bag in the air.

I leap off the sofa and rush over to hug him and he stumbles back a little wrapping his arms around me and hugging me tightly. He kisses me and hands me the bag as we walk towards the kitchen.

"So, do all of your delivery men get that same reaction?" he joked.

"Only the sexy ones," I reply, winking my eye at him.

"Well, in that case, where's my tip?" he said, as he walks over and pulls me closer to him.

I stand on my tippy toes and wrap my arms around his neck and pull him in and kissing him hard. I feel myself falling for him more and more each time that I'm in his arms, but I don't want to move to fast.

"We should eat,' he said as we release one another.

"Yes, we should," I said, smiling a half smile at him. "what would you like to drink?" I ask, opening the fridge.

"a soda is fine."

"Cool a soda for you and a glass of wine for me. Is a grape ok?"

"Sure."

We go into the living room and sit in front of the tv choosing a movie to watch while we eat our dinner. I cuddled up to him resting my head on his chest once we were finished eating, and towards the end of the movie, I noticed his breathing slow into small shallow breaths he had falling asleep.

I pull my throw from the back of the couch and place it over him and head down the hall towards my studio room. I go inside and power up my laptop and the rest of the equipment then begin working on some music, going over a few tracks and writing a few verses for songs that I'm going to be featured on.

I hear a noise coming from behind me and I jump in my seat turning around to see what it was.

"I'm sorry, I didn't mean to scare you." He said standing in the doorway.

"Omg," I say grabbing my chest. "it's ok, come in." I push the seat over his way.

"Your voice is incredible," he said as he took a sit and pulling his seat closer to mine.

"Thanks," I replied feeling my cheek flush.

Why does this man make me feel like I'm back in high school talking to my crush for the first time?

I can't help to have butterflies and blush every time he comes near me or compliments me. I play him one of the songs that I'm going to feature on and sang my verse for him. He listened and then gave me some feedback and I needed an honest opinion and he seems like a very honest and upfront person for the most part.

"So, I have a question and you can say no there is no pressure."

"Ok," he agrees with a curious look on his face.

"Well, my mom invited us over for Sunday dinner," I pause and close my eyes before finishing. "And without thinking I kind of said yes."

I scrunch up my nose and hold my eyes shut tight waiting for him to answer. I peak out of one eye after a couple seconds of silence to make sure he was still there and hadn't bolted for the door. But he hadn't left thank god, but he was staring at me with a silly looking grin on his face and I let out an uncontrollable laugh.

"What?" He asks.

"Nothing," I respond shaking my head. "So, what do you say?"

"Sure, I'd love to meet your parents."

I let out a deep breath then relax back in my chair, but he was still staring at me with that same expression on his face when I looked back over at him.

"What? You're creeping me out." I giggle pushing his chair away with my foot.

"So, does that make us official now that I'm getting the chance to meet the parents and all that."

I tilt my head to the side and stare at him with a raised eyebrow. He rolls his seat back over to mine and pulls me onto his lap and begins kissing my lips, neck, and my ear then whispers your mine in between kisses.

"Am I?" I muttered.

He stops and looks me in the eyes. "I want you to be—and if you say yes you will be."

"Yes," I whisper softly before leaning in to kiss him again.

He kisses me back slowly smiling into the kiss then lifts me up as he stands from his seat and carries me out of the studio room and down to the hall to my bedroom.

He lays me on the bed and takes off his shirt, and then his shorts as I scoot to the middle. He climbs on to the bed and lays flat on his back pulling me on top him and I lean in to kiss him moving from his lips to his chest, then his stomach, letting my tongue run across his abs as his dick slides between my breast. I cup my breast and squeeze them together and began to move up and down letting his erection slide between my breast. He lets out a low growl deep in his throat when I lick the tip of his dick each time I slide down moving my tongue in a circular motion while sucking his head a little.

I wanted to feel his tongue on me, so I turn and straddle his face.

"kiss me," I moan softly.

He smiles and begins to flick his tongue over my clit and my legs start to tremble. I moan on his dick as I continue taking him in deep throating his dick. I began to slowly grind my hips riding his tongue while I talk to him.

"Yes, baby, right there." I moaned.

I feel myself getting closer, so I move from his face and straddle him easing myself on to his dick then slowly begin to rock back and forth.

"Oh fuck," he groaned through a clenched jaw as he grabs my waist.

I move a little faster when he begins to thrust his hips upward pushing deeper inside me. My pussy tightens around him and I feel my juices run down his dick as I reach my climax all around him.

"Yes, beautiful come for me."

I through my head back and allow my orgasm to take over as he continues to move in and out of me. He holds me in place while he thrusts deeper and harder slamming into me and then I feel him erupt inside of me pushing me over the edge once again.

I fall on to the bed beside him out of breath. I've never felt this comfortable with a man, or not to the point where he brings out the freak in me.

"Beautiful, I see you've been holding back," he says with a breathy laugh.

I roll over on my side and lay my head on his chest as he lifts his head a little to kiss the top of my hair while he runs his fingers up and down my spine. I close my eyes and smile into his chest.

Nae T. Bloss

Chapter Eight

Dejuan

I let my eyes adjust to the light blinking them a couple of times then I turn and look over to my side. Her hair was slightly covering her face and she was laying on her stomach with one leg stretched over mine. My lips part into a smile as I gaze at her, she was even more beautiful sleeping. Fuck, I'm starting to love waking up next to her and her face being the first thing I see and feel her body next to mine. She moves a little and I turn over onto my side as her eyes flutter open. She blinks a couple of times then smiles at me.

"Good morning," she said, brushing her hair out of her face.

"Morning Beautiful."

"Did you sleep ok? I've been told that I snore and move around allot." She said, rolling on to her side and proper herself up with her arm.

"I slept great," I reply. "And no, you don't snore." I chuckle, and she smiles.

"I think someone's broken into your place and made breakfast," I say playfully.

She giggles. "That would-be Maria my chef."

"Oh, I see," I reply sitting up in the bed and stretching.

"I'd better go and tell her I have a guest—"

"Yeah, I think you mean boyfriend." I cut in and she rolls her eyes at me.

70

"Well boyfriend," she repeats in a sarcastic tone. "I have to go and inform her that you're here so that she fixes enough for the both of us."

She lays back and gives me a quick kiss on the cheek then hops out of the bed and hurries out of the bedroom. I lay back on the pillow placing my hands behind my head grinning like a kid on Christmas morning that received the exact gift that he wanted.

A couple of minutes go back and then she dashes back into the room and jumps on the bed holding out my phone towards me.

"Ok, let me explain," She begins, "I promise I wasn't snooping and I didn't mean to answer it, it was totally an accident and my finger pressed the button." She said, with a shaky voice.

I laugh and take the phone from here. "Hey, calm down it's cool."

"Ok, well it's someone named Maylan and breakfast is almost ready so come join me when you're finished."

She kisses me on the lips and then disappears out of the room and I take a deep breath before unmuting the call and putting the phone to my ear.

"Why the fuck is you calling me and how'd you get this number," I ask, in a bitter tone.

"We need to talk can you meet me," he said, his voice rattled.

"We don't have anything else to discuss. Whatever you need, get it from Montez."

"That's just it this is something bigger then Montez. It's something I have to have your approval on."

"What?"

"Meet me later, I'll send you the address in a few." He replies, then hangs up the phone.

I take the phone away from my ear and throw it onto the bed beside me. He must be out of his mind trying to set up deals behind Montez's back he must not realize that fool with cancel his ass with no hesitation. I rub my hands over my face and shout "Fuck," then I remembered where I was, and I sat up and looked towards the door waiting to hear her footsteps coming towards the room.

When I was sure she wasn't coming I picked my phone back up and sent Jerome, Lavon, and Montez a text. Just as I hit send my phone chimed and the message came through from Maylan with an address. I copied the address and sent it to the fellas and told them to meet me there at 7 sharp and I sent Maylan the same message to be there at 7 PM on the dot.

I got out of the bed and slipped on my shorts and headed to the kitchen. I could smell the aroma in the air bacon, eggs, pancakes, fried potatoes, and I think hash browns. I walk into the kitchen and Renea` was seated at the breakfast nook sipping on a cup of coffee.

"Good Morning Mr. Washington," Marie greeted me with a thick accent.

"Morning Maria, and you can call me Dejuan," I reply, and she smiles.

I kiss Renea on her cheek and take my seat at the table and grab a plate and pile it full of pancakes. I could feel the both of their eyes on me, so I look up and look from one to the other.

"That's a lot of pancakes you sure you can handle all of that." Renea` said picking up her mug and taking another sip.

"I'll manage," I wink at her and pick up the syrup pouring it over top.

I spend the rest of the day hanging out with Renea` before heading home and packing a few things before I head out to Long Beach to find out what kind of shit this bitch Maylan's gotten us into now.

***

I arrive at my spot around 5:45 pm and the fellas meet me there so that we could ride over together rather than separately. We pull up at the warehouse parking along the street so that we could scope out the place, we see Maylan's car parked out front and a little red convertible parked beside it. I look around but there was no one outside no other cars, no security, nor did we have a clue who he was inside with.

"Yo, I don't like this shit man," Lavon said.

"Yeah man, we don't know what we're about to walk into," Jerome speaks up agreeing with Lavon.

"We strapped, so if anything pops off just start dropping bodies. You feel me." Montez said turning and looking back at the fellas.

"Alright, enough bullshitting let's get this shit over with," I say motioning for Tez to pull forward.

We pull up to the front and the doors to the warehouse open and out walks Maylan and a woman with long black hair, mid-height, and a slim figure.

"Aye man," Jerome says tapping me on the arm. "I knew this damn address sounded familiar." He said pulling out his gun and loading up.

"What are you doing bruh?" Montez asks.

"Dejuan, are you telling me you don't remember this place?" Jerome asks, with a serious expression on his face.

"Should I?" I ask confused not understanding what he was trying to say.

I look closely at the young woman and Maylan as they continue walking towards the SUV stopping just a few feet away.

"Hold the fuck up—is that?" I say as a wave of alarms rushes over me.

"Yeah, bruh now you hear me," Jerome said.

"Who is she?" Lavon asks.

"Aw fuck that's Olivia Stevens in the flesh. Damn!" Montez said, holding his fist over his mouth.

"Is this a fucking joke. Why in the hell is Maylan hanging around with the Stevens?" I barked now angry.

We all step out of the SUV and walk over closer to where the two of them were standing waiting for us. I look at Olivia and then to Maylan before holding out my hand gesturing for this fool to talk because if they were setting us up it was going to be too dead motherfuckers stretch out in front of us. There is no way in hell that Olivia or any of the Stevens for that matter would have Maylan's no good ass around their family after he killed her father. Unless they don't know.

"Hello, Dejuan, it's been a long time." She said, breaking the silence.

"Olivia," I reply with a nod.

"So Maylan why are we here?" Jerome asks demanding an answer.

"I can answer that," Olivia replies before Maylan could get anything out.

We all turn our attention towards her waiting for to explain and all I know is it better be good because this was definitely not where I wanted to be right now. I wanted to be where my heart was and that was lying next to my woman and making love to her.

"I ask Maylan to set up this meeting with Montez because I have a proposition. But then Maylan mentioned that I would need approval from you, Dejuan." She said looking back to me and I could see the effect that I was having on her the way she said my name and the lust that filled her eyes. Even now after all these years, she was still in love with me.

"What makes you think that we'd even be interested. We don't exactly push the same kind of product." Lavon said.

"Well, that's just it. Maylan told me that you all were looking to expand and I'm sure that if we agreed it would benefit us all." She said then turned her attention back to me. "But Dejuan I didn't know you were back in the game." She says, giving me a flirtatious smile.

"I could say the same," I tilt me to the side. "No, wait actually I never knew that you were," I reply sarcastically.

"Well, after my father passed away," she begins and we all cut our eyes over to Maylan and he quickly looks away. "I decided to take over the family business that is until my brothers are prepped and ready to take over the ranks." She finishes.

"Look I don't know what the fuck Maylan told you or what he promised you but no thanks. Were good." I said, nodding my head to the fellas letting them know that we were done here.

She comes over and grabs my arm but loosens her grip running her hand over my shoulder and back down my arm. She leans in and kisses me on the cheek and I see Maylan's jaw tighten up as he clenched his fist at his side and my lips part into a smile.

"It was good to see you Dejuan," she said, "I hope this isn't the last time give me a call if you change your mind." she licks her lips then turns and walk back towards the warehouse.

Maylan watches us walk back over to the SUV and climb back inside before turning and walking away. So that's it he's fucking her, fucking the daughter of the biggest drug lord that the worlds ever known or seen and whom he killed in cold blood. This fool was beyond psycho and I needed to get rid of his ass before one of us ended up laid six feet deep.

Chapter Nine

Renea

I wished the day never had to end and that he didn't have to run off to Long Beach once again. I felt like he was hiding something from me all the phone calls and private conversations he has when he's around. And anytime that I mention or ask about his business in Long Beach he never answers he just changes the subject or fucks my brains out until it's no longer a thought.

My phone rings and I look over at the caller ID and I see that it's my dad calling.

"Hey daddy," I say with noticeable excitement in my voice.

"Hey, baby girl. How are you doing?" He asks, and I could hear the smile in his voice.

"I'm great. How's everything with you? Mom said you'd been working late here recently when I stopped by."

"Yes, we've gotten a few new successful clients so that's keeping us busy."

"Sounds good, congratulations dad. Anyone, I know?"

He laughs. "I don't think so sweetheart."

"Hey, you never know. I'm a pretty popular person." I tease.

"Oh, that I do know baby girl." He replies as he lets out a roar of laughter.

My dad's construction company was soaring, and I was so proud of him. He's finally living his dream and doing what he loves. His whole life he wanted to own his own construction company, but he was stuck working for other people. As soon as I made my first million I bought him his own company and there was no better feeling than seeing the look on my father's face when I handed him the keys. I think my mom cried for a whole week after that.

I talk with my father for about an hour before we say our goodbyes. He told me how excited he was that I'd found a young man that I was willing to give a chance and he was as equally excited that it was Dejuan. He'd been his biggest fan ever since the day he'd been drafted to the NBA. And when my mom told him that we'd both be joining them for dinner on Sunday he was ecstatic.

I hear the elevator doors close and footsteps in the foyer.

"Hey sis, where are you?" Shanice calls out as she enters the living room.

"I'm in here," I respond.

"What are you doing you should be getting dressed."

"I was waiting for you," I said getting up from the sofa giving her a hug.

We walk back to my room and into the walk-in closet. She helps me chose something to wear for tonight, we'd decided to go out with a few friends and I invited Kiani to come along with us. I hadn't been out in a while, so I needed to let loose and enjoy myself.

I change into my clothes and then we head back into the front room just as Kiani comes through the foyer with a huge smile on her face sitting her purse on the edge of the couch. She looked really pretty I didn't get to see her dressed up too often, but it was good to see her all done up and looking relaxed.

"Hey, you all ready to go." She asks, as she came over and hugged Shanice then me.

"Yes, let me just grab a jacket."

Francisco and Euro meet us out front, we hope into the Lincoln Navigator and wait patiently for the guys to get take their seats. I enjoyed spending time with my girls and here lately I haven't had much time to just hang out. With all the meetings, photo shoots, recordings, commercials, and the press for the new album. I'm shocked that I have time to breath, but I'm grateful I get to live my dream and make a lot of money doing it plus I learned long ago that if you are blessed to do what you love you'll never work a day in your life.

Although I do get tired and want to just take a break from it all it still never really feels like I'm working for a paycheck. And I always feel like I'm where I belong doing exactly what I love.

"Hey are you ok, Renea?" Kiani asks reaching over and placing her hand on top of mine.

"Yes, I'm fine," I say returning a smile.

"Missing your man, huh," she looks at me with a knowing smile.

"a little," I say softly feeling my cheeks blush.

"It's ok to miss your man. Besides every minute of every day seems like a century when you first get together." She said, "I say enjoy the feeling because it just might one day fade."

Is she right? Will this feeling one day fade away because I never want it to? I want to continue to feel this way forever, I want us to always enjoy being in each other's presence.

We pull up and hop out the SUV and head inside. The line was full of people waiting to get inside and as soon as they noticed us and that we were going inside the once calm and quiet crowd was now anxious and impatient. The dance floor was crowded and so was the bar, people were shouting trying to get the attention of the mixologist and there were several fellas hanging around spitting game to the females waiting for their drinks.

Francisco escorted the ladies over to the VIP area as I head up to the DJ booth with Euro by my side. DJ Roxy is a good friend of mine, so I always make sure I stop in and say what's up. She sees me just as I reach the top of the stairs and a huge smile appears on her face as she spins the record starting her next mix.

"What's up baby girl? How you been?" she asks, coming over and wrapping her arms around me hugging me tight as she rocks from side to side.

"You know me busy." I smile back at her returning the embrace.

"Of course, as always." She said playfully before releasing me and turning back towards the crowd. "You want to get in on this." She asks, grabbing the mic and holding it out to me.

"It's like you can read my mind," I say taking the mic from her. "Aye… it's your girl Renea` Dubley and I'm in the building. Are you guys having a good time tonight."

"Hell Yeah," the crowd screams back at me.

"Is my girl DJ Roxy giving to you all right tonight."

"HELL YEAH," the crowd roars.

Roxy does a little spin and then the beat drops and I rock the mic giving the crowd a little piece of my new single. I spend about an hour on the mic and then I had it off to Roxy and let her finish doing her thing. I give her a quick hug then head back to the VIP area with the ladies.

"Yo ma' you killed that." A very attractive gentleman says to me stepping in front of me blocking my way.

I wink at him, "Thanks."

Euro slides in front of me blocking my view telling the guy to back away. I go around him and continue towards the booth stepping inside the ropes where Shanice and Kiani were enjoying glasses of champagne with a few of our other celeb friends. We dance awhile then hangout blowing through bottles of wine and taking several shots until we'd all had more then we could handle.

Kiani even got a few numbers and clicked with one of the guys that made their way into the circle.

I was loaded by the end of the night I don't even remember when or how I made it into the house and into bed, but I woke up in a blacked-out room and just a glare of light coming from the master bathroom, I was still dressed but my shoes had been removed and I was laying across my bed. I roll over and glance at the clock it was 3:34 am so I rolled to the end of the bed throwing my legs over the edge and sitting up slowly. I see a glass of water and a pill bottle sitting on my nightstand, I'm guessing whoever put me to bed placed them there for me to cure my hangover in the morning.

I get up and stumble into restroom then change out of my clothes and into my pj's and climb back into bed pulling the cover up around my shoulders and closing my eyes drifting off to sleep.

***

The music begins, and I walk over to the stairwell as my father greets me, taking my arm and placing it around his.

"You look beautiful sweetheart." My father says smiling at me with tear-filled eyes.

"Thank you, daddy," I say trying to hold back the tears that begin filling my eyes.

We look straight ahead at the wedding planner waiting for her to tell us when to begin our walk. We walk down the stairs and through the double doors. We stop at the entrance watching as everyone rises from their seats. I look straight ahead and lock eyes with Dejuan, he looks back at me with a huge smile on his face as he mouthed the words "WOW".

Jingle, Jingle, Jingle

My alarm clock goes off startling me, causing me to jump and sit straight up in the middle of the bed. I place my hand on my head and then my chest feeling my heart pounding into my chest. I shut off the alarm and pick up my phone glancing at the screen. There was a text from an unknown number and I sat staring at the message for a moment contemplating whether or not I wanted to open it or just delete it. But I let my curiosity get the best of me and I clicked on the message.

Unknown: Hello Renea, I hope that your morning is going well. You must have quite the hangover after all those shots you had last night. But I have a question for you, do you know what your boyfriend was doing last night?

Me: Who is this?

Unknown: There'll be plenty of time for questions later. But first, you should probably check on your man and see how it's going with his illegal drug business.

I look at the message again with a confused look on my face, I couldn't believe what I'd read. "This has to be a joke," I say to myself this must be a prank there was no way that Dejuan was involved in anything illegal. Was he? I mean he did mention getting hung up with the wrong crowd when he was in his teens, but no I don't believe it. My phone chimes again with another text this time it was an address to a house in Long Beach.

I set my phone on the nightstand and pop open the bottle and shake out 2 pills and pop them in my mouth taking a few sips from the glass of water to wash them down quickly. Then something dawns on me. How did they know about my hangover? Or that I was out drinking last night, something wasn't right I could feel it in my gut.

Do I have a stalker or does he?

I decide to go and check it out, so I call up Shanice and tell her about the texts I received and that I was going to check it out, and she insisted that she come with me just in case it was a trap or something, but I refused. I needed to do this alone I didn't want to put her in harm's way and I didn't need to put myself in harm's way either. But I needed to know that Dejuan was safe and that what this person was saying wasn't true.

"You better call me as soon as you get there and let me know what's going on as soon as you find out, you hear me? I need to know that your safe or I'll call Francisco and tell him everything." She demands, in a serious tone.

"Okay," I reply.

"Promise!"

"I promise. I will call as soon as I get there and after don't worry," I assure her.

I threw on a pair of yoga pants and a t-shirt and slid my sneakers on in record time. Before I knew it, I was racing to the elevator and then sliding into the driver's seat and putting the key into the ignition speeding out of the garage and into the early morning traffic.

"Please let this all be a joke," I repeat to myself over and over again.

It took me about twenty minutes to reach Long beach and arrive at the address. It was a beautiful one story single family home it looked as if someone with a small family lived there. I stop in front of the house next door and put the car in park sitting and watching before I make my next move. My heart sank to the pit of my stomach at the thought of Dejuan having a whole other life here, maybe he'd lied about the divorce maybe he was still living with Jaylyn and they're still married.

I see a Cadillac Escalade pull into the driveway and a Mercedes follows behind it. Three guys get out and walk up to the door and begin knocking and after a couple of minutes the door swings open and I see Dejuan. He greets the three men with a huge smile on his face giving them fist bumps as they enter the house then he closes the door behind them.

A tear streamed down my cheek, I knew right then that even if he wasn't still married and raising kids there was still something that he wasn't telling me. My sadness quickly turned in to anger and I jerked the keys out of the ignition and got out of the car and headed up to the front door.

"You are caught," I say quietly to myself before banging on the door as hard as I could.

The laughter that I'd heard when I first walked up stopped and it got quiet.

Chapter Ten

Dejuan

"HEY, MY BABY!" my grandmother says as she steps out on to her front porch, with her arms extended."

I walk up and hug her tight closing my eyes and breathing in her scent. Being at my grandmothers was home for me, my brother and I spent most of our time as a child with my grandmother because my mother was always working late. That's where I met Montez and Jerome, we were clicked tight from the moment we met, it was more like a brotherly bond that connected us.

"Hey Gamma," I said kissing her on the cheek.

"My baby, hold on step back and let me look at you," She said laughing that laugh that only my grandmother has. "You are looking good my baby. Look here come on in this house I got a pot of greens on the stove."

"Thanks, Gamma," I said as I followed her inside "You got it smelling good in here what else are you cooking?" I asked taking in the sweet and delicious aroma.

"When you said you were coming I put on you and your brothers favorite. And I know you need it I can hear your stomach rumbling from over here. I guess all that fancy foods not filling you up." She said placing her hand on her hips.

All of the different smells brought back memories of my childhood. They flooded my mind as I took my seat and watched my grandmother move through the kitchen with such ease preparing each dish. My brother was away at college he'd gotten a scholarship to play football and hopefully, in two more years, he'll be drafted into the pros after he graduates.

"Have you spoken to your brother lately?" She asks, looking over her shoulder at me.

"Yes, ma'am. I got to talk to him a couple of days ago."

"Good, I'm glad the two of you are still communicating I know the two of you are so busy nowadays and I'm so proud of you boys." She smiles a beautiful and contagious smile and I find myself grinning like a little boy back her.

"Thanks, gamma. Oh yeah, I also have some good news for you to gamma."

"Really and what's that?" she asks, curiously.

"I just signed 2 endorsements and my divorce has been finalized."

She turns to me and throws her arms in the air. "Thank you, Jesus." She shouts, "Woo—child I'm so glad you got rid of that no-good girl." she leans down and hugs me.

"Yes, it's finally over and I'm moving on with my life."

"As you should and congratulations baby on your endorsements and your championship win. I'm telling you Gods got allot more in store for you just watch." She smiles placing her hand on my face and kissing my forehead.

She made our plates then sat down at the table and we continued to talk as we ate. I loved talking to my grandmother there were no other conversations that could compare. I told her about my goals and about my new relationship with Renea and I could see the happiness in her eyes as she listened to me attentively as I talked.

Once we finished I help her clean up the kitchen and washed the dishes for her while she dried. We got a little dance into some old school jams. She cut me a slice of sweet potato pie and wrapped it up so that I could take it with me, I kissed her cheek and hugged her goodbye and she returned the embrace and the kiss before I headed out the door. I wave at her once more after taking my seat in the car then pulling away.

***

"What's good bruh?" Montez said, answering his phone.

"I don't know, you tell me. How'd your meeting with Olivia go last night." I ask, in a stern voice.

The line goes silent for a couple of minutes. Rome had called and let me know that Montez had gotten a call from Olivia yesterday and set up a meeting and instead of turning it down or getting at me he accepted and went alone.

He took a deep breath and let it out. "Which one of those bitches ran back snitching and shit." He said in a nonchalant tone.

"What," I pull the phone away from my ear for seconds then replace it. "What the fuck you mean snitch? Look, Nevermind all that why the fuck is you meeting up with her after I clearly told her ass there would be no business done between us."

"Man, calm down it wasn't even about that. She called me up on some other shit."

"Like what?"

"Like your dumbass. You couldn't tell that bitch is still feeling you?" he asks. "And she didn't mention the business deal again, of course, telling me to talk you into it, but I shut her ass down."

"Good," I said, relaxing on the sofa.

"I told you, man, you need to trust me I got this. She was hinting at you hard, but I told her she was wasting her time, but she still wasn't trying to hear it. Shorty look like she was getting wet just mentioning your name." He laughs.

"Yeah ok. Look I'm still in long beach hit up the fellas and ya'll come through."

"Bet. Just let me finish up with shorty."

"Shorty—dude get your ass over here now." I demanded.

"Alright man chill, damn." He said before ended the call.

About an hour later these fools finally show up, I open the door and stare them down for a couple of minutes before letting a smile break out onto my face.

"I see you took your sweet time getting here," I say dapping it up with each of them as they enter.

"These two fools are always knee deep in some pussy and you know it takes they dumbass about three hours to fall out." Lavon jokes.

"Fuck you," they say in unison.

"You just mad cause you not getting any," Tez says calling him out.

"Oh. No. my brother I gets mine all the time." Lavon replies.

We all laugh and head inside taking our seats and they continue clowning on each other. My phone buzzes and I pick it up from the coffee table and see a message from an unknown number. I slide my finger across the screen and open it.

Unknown: Have you told your new girlfriend about your business? Or have you been lying to her about that part of your life as well?

Me: Who the fuck is this?

Unknown: I'll take that as a NO. Well... Looks like you'd better perfect your story now because your covers been blown in 3...2....1!

A loud bang on the door causes me us to jump and the room goes silent. I sit frozen on the couch as we all look towards the door, Lavon turns back and looks at me, Jerome reaches for his gun, and Tez jumps from his seat pulling his 9mm from his waist and walks over to the door.

"Who the fuck is it?" Jerome asks.

"Yo bruh snap the fuck out of it," Lavon says panicked and waving his hand in front of my face.

"Dejuan, are you expecting someone?" Tez asks.

I try and speak but it felt like someone had glued my mouth shut and my breath was caught in my suffocating me. I hear a bang on the door and I release my breath and slowly rise from my seat.

"Yo man what the fuck," Lavon said.

"Aye, man it's a female," Tez whispers "she looks like oh girl—uh the singer. What's her name? The fine ass one." He says rattling on.

I stop mid-step and look at him "Renea`."

"Yeah, man Renea` Dubley." He said. "Yo I think this really her what the fuck is she doing here?"

"Get away from the door and put that shit away," I tell him as I place my hand on the knob.

"Fuck all that. I will when you tell me what's going on." Tez replies.

"Get the fuck away from the door and put that shit up," I say again with a little more base in my voice.

I knew I was caught and there wasn't anything I could do about but man up and take responsibility for my actions. Although I didn't know how well it was going to go seeing as I've left things out before but this, this was a whole other ball game. I was going to tell her the truth because she deserves it and hopes she doesn't walk away leaving my ass broken and feeling dumb.

I unlock the door and open it slowly. "Hey, beautiful." I smile at her.

She stands there for a second silently staring at me with disbelief in her eyes and I could see that she was angry it was all over her face. I swallowed the lump in my throat and began to speak again.

"Don't," She puts her hand up stopping me, "What the hell is going on Dejuan?" she asks walking past me stepping inside.

"Baby look let me explain before you—." I began.

"So, you've been lying to me all this time. Keeping what you're doing here from me?" She said, cutting me off as tears filled her eye.

I reach out to place my hand on her shoulder trying to console her, but she moves away from my touch.

"Don't touch me," she says hastily.

She steps away from me and looks around the room at the fellas and all the guns and product sitting on the table. She looks back towards me with a disapproving expression on her face and folding her arms in front of her chest. I swallow hard once again trying to get the lump out of my throat before speaking.

"Can we please go talk in the back," I ask softly trying to keep it together but my voice cracks.

"Why, so you can just tell me more lies." She counters.

"Me lying to you is for your own safety."

"Oh, so you are lying to me to keep me safe?" she asks.

I take a deep breath and run my hands over my face. "I'm sorry, would you just—please just come to the back so we can talk," I begged.

"Fine," she spits out in anger then storms to the back.

I let my hands fall to my side then turn to the fellas as they stare back at me with a smirk on their faces. I shake my head and throw up my hands and walk away.

"Bruh are you fucking Rene Dubley?" Tez asks, raising his eyebrow.

"Ugh… not now man. Give me a minute to get her straight and Tez keep your fucking eyes to the ceiling bruh. Yeah, I peeped you." I reply.

"Aye, Yo leave the door open so we can hear man," Lavon calls out.

I stick up my middle finger at him as I disappear down the hallway towards the master bedroom. I walk in and close the bedroom door behind me then walk over to the middle of the room where she was standing waiting for me.

"Can we sit down please"

"No, I'd rather stand," she snaps. "So, talk." She demands.

"Beautiful, please try and understand why I had to keep this from you. I was trying to keep you safe."

"And you think not telling me was going to keep me safe?"

I step closer to her I needed to hold her feel her in my arms. I wanted her to look at me the way she did before not the way she was looking at me right now with anger and fear in her eyes. But she backs away from me again not wanting me to touch her and she looked at me with such disgust it made my stomach turn.

"I'm sorry, I thought I was doing what was right."

"So, what is all this. Are you a drug dealer Dejuan?"

"I used to be. But I'm not anymore, I promise."

"Then why are you here Dejuan? If your no longer apart of all this, please explain to me, why are you here?" She asks. "Because I want to believe you and I don't want to lose you, but you are clearly lying to me. Why?" She said choking back tears.

"I promise you, I'm not lying to you beautiful. Something, or maybe I should say someone from our past popped up and I'm just helping the fellas handle the situation and once it's over, it's over. I'll never go back to this life again."

She places her hand over her mouth as tears begin to flow. "I want to believe you, I really do, but I can't. You've lied to me twice now when you should have just told me the truth and we could've moved past it. But you didn't you showed me just how easy it is for you to be dishonest. Dejuan, how can I ever trust anything you say ever again after this?"

She steps closer placing her hands on my face searching my eyes for an answer and waiting for me to speak, but I had no words to offer her. She was right I had felt like lying to her was easier rather than trusting her the truth because I didn't want to have her walk away from me. I close my eyes and place my hand over hers kissing her palm I feel he move closer to me and her lips press against mine.

"I'm sorry Dejuan, but I can't do this."

"Renea, please don't go," I reply reaching out to her.

"Goodbye Dejuan," she said walking past and opening the door.

I call after her again, but she doesn't answer me she continues down the hall and after a couple of seconds I hear the door slam and fall back into the chair. I could feel my heart crack in my chest and the pain in my stomach felt heavy. I'd really fucked up this time and now she's probably gone forever. I lean forward in the chair placing my hands over my face wiping the tears that stained my eyes away and after a couple minutes had gone by I composed myself and heading back into the living room.

"Aye, Dee you alright man?" Jerome asks.

"Looks like you fucked that up." Tez jokes.

"Come on man," Lavon turns to Tez throwing up his hands.

"I need to find out who's been contacting her. Because I didn't tell her about this place and the same person that hit her up sent me a text right before she showed up."

"You thinking it was maybe Maylan or Olivia?" Jerome asks.

"I don't know but whoever it is, they just started a war with the wrong fucking one."

Chapter Eleven

Renea

It's been a couple of weeks and I was finally getting back into my regular routine and spending a lot more time in the studio clearing my head and doing some writing. I've been trying to relieve myself of all these overwhelming emotions that are flowing through me. Ever since the day I left Dejuan's place I've been asking myself two questions, "Why is he so comfortable lying to me, and If I'm really that naive that I didn't see this coming?" He didn't tell me about having a wife and probably wouldn't have if I hadn't mentioned it that night so why was I so surprised to find out he was hiding something else.

Today was different though I pulled the cover over me and laid back on the bed. I picked up my phone and checked my text messages first then I listened to a few of the voicemails. It'd been three weeks and I hadn't been very vocal with anyone. Only sucking it up and putting on a brave face whenever I'm out in public so that no one can tell how I'm really feeling. I was actually getting kind of good at being a robot for the camera's which is a little scary.

Dejuan tried to get in contact with me a few times, but I ignored him. I didn't have anything to say to him and my wounds were still fresh that he slashed into my heart. My phone chimed, and I contemplated not answering it at first, but once I saw Shanice's number I answered.

"Hello," I said, with a heavy sigh.

"Hey, love. How are you feeling?" she asks, concern in her voice.

"Like someone ripped my heart out of my chest and fed it to a pack of wolves before replacing it."

"Awe babe. Do you want me to come over when I leave the office? I'll go home and grab my jammies and bring wine, lots of ice cream, and candy. We can just have a girl's weekend how does that sound?" She asks her voice a little more upbeat.

"You're not spending the weekend with Jonathan," I ask.

She was silent for a few moments not saying anything and I knew that it was something about Dejuan, but she was trying not to mention home.

I let out another sigh. "Just say it?"

"He really misses you and if it makes you feel any better he's just as miserable as you are."

"Good he should be," I say in a sharp tone.

She sighs. "Come on Renea` you know that man loves—," she starts to say then stops before finishing her sentence. "I mean he really cares for you."

I sit up straight on the bed leaning back on the headboard. "Why would you say that? Did he tell you that?"

"I'm sorry it slipped out—please don't say anything. I overheard him talking to Jonathan the other night and he said it."

"But how can he love me and lie straight to my face," I ask, as my eyes tear up once again, but I quickly brush them away with the sleeve of my sweatshirt.

"Listen Renea' after talking to him I can understand where his mind frame was." She begins.

"Wait you've been talking to him. Oh, great so he's taking my best friends too." I cut in before she could finish.

She laughs. "No one could ever take me away and you know that. We are ride or die, sis, but I can also understand where he's coming from. You do things that don't make sense to others when trouble comes, and it may not be right or feel good, but you know in your heart that you have to protect them, so you do what you have to."

"Sounds like you're speaking from experience," I huff.

"That's because I am," she said then cleared her throat before speaking again. "Do you remember when I told you that my family had to go away for a while a few years ago."

"Yes, when you all went on that very long unusual vacation."

"Yes, well that was a lie."

"What?"

"I never really left California we were still here. My father was assigned to a case to take down a notorious drug lord and some things got crazy and terrible things started happening, so my family and I were taken away to a safe place where we had to stay. And I had no choice but to lie about everything to protect you and my other friends as well as our family members and the only way to do that was for them to know nothing."

I blinked away tears as I continued listening to her tell the story of the worst day of her life. Back then I'd known something was wrong when she said they were taking a vacation in the middle of the school year, and they never said goodbye before going they just packed up and left in the middle of the night without saying a word. I remembered asking my mom if they had lied and really moved away after two months had gone by, but she'd said that they had extended their trip and were staying a little longer.

And even though I could understand the reason she'd lied I still couldn't understand his reason for lying, especially when the situation could be avoided. If he wasn't a part of that lifestyle anymore then why was there a need to protect me and why does this person want to harm him after all these years?

"I'm sorry Nesse. I wish you would've told me."

"I had planned to one day, but I wanted that day to stay buried." She said, "Hey I have to go I'll be over as soon as I'm finished here."

We say our goodbyes and end the call.

***

Everyone is up on their feet shouting, clapping, and singing along with the choir as they belt out the song. The usher escorts us to our seat and the room was jam-packed, so we were seated further to the back a little too far from where my mom usually sat. Shanice and I decided to join my mother for church this morning after spending most of our time in the house watching romance and comedy movies while stuffing ourselves with ice cream and junk food.

And even though I was feeling a little better the truth is I miss Dejuan and after thinking it over I realized that I was in love with him too. We sat down our purses and joined in singing with the rest of the congregation and I tell you the spirit was moving, and I could feel it in the atmosphere. By the time praise and worship were over, I felt allot better it was exactly what I needed to lift me up and get me out of that funk. We all took our seats as the pastor stood before us ready to preach his sermon.

"Good Morning saints. It sure is good to be back in the house of the lord." He begins.

"Amen," the crowd said.

"Can I have you all open your bibles and turn with me to Proverbs 19:1." He said, opening his Bible.

I look over to my mother she looked so happy with a big bright smile on her face. She must've noticed me looking in her direction because she turned and looked at me and her smile got wider. Maybe I'll talk to my mom about my situation with Dejuan. I haven't mentioned anything to her because I don't want her to worry but I really need some sound advice and my mother always has the best.

"Sweetheart," my mother whispers and I jump a little. "Are you ok baby." She asks, resting her hand on my knee.

I didn't want to take a chance at speaking and having my voice crack and giving myself away, so I just nodded my head and gave her a fake smile. She wraps her arm around me and pulls me close as she pats my shoulder, I could tell that she knew I wasn't telling the truth, but she didn't want to push well at least not right now anyway.

One of my mother's good friends, who was also one of the ushers came over and tapped me on the shoulder getting my attention.

"Renea, honey there's a young lady asking for you outside." She whispers into my ear.

"Oh, did she happen to mention her name?" I ask, a little curious about who would be looking for me at church.

"No, sorry she didn't. I can go find out if you'd like." She said.

"Oh, no it's fine. Thank you."

I turn to my mom getting her attention then pointing towards the restroom and she nods her head and mouthing ok. I stand up from my seat to scoot through the aisle and Shanice stops me.

"Where are you going?" She asks.

"I'll be right back someone's asking for me."

"Who?" she asks, with a confused look on her face.

"I don't know."

"I'm coming with you," she replies quickly and begins getting up from her set, but I place my hand on her shoulder to stop her.

"It's fine. It's probably Kerry or Kiani."

She slowly sits back down in her seat and I head towards the exit. I see Euro out the corner of my eye as he begins to move with me matching my pace, but I hold up my hand stopping him.

I step into the lobby area and there was no one there. So, I walk towards the doors and step outside looking around but there was no one there, so I turn around and begin to walk back inside the building.

"Hello Renea," I hear a woman's voice coming from behind me, and I feel something press into my back. "Don't say a word and don't turn around." She demands.

I nod my reply quickly then I do as I'm told and began walking towards the parking lot. I had no clue who this woman was, and her voice didn't sound familiar to me, but the scent of her perfume was Chanel No. 5 one of my favorites perfumes, a classic. Once we reached the end of the sidewalk and I looked to my left searching for the Lincoln Navigator that Francisco was in waiting for us. He wanted to keep an eye on the perimeter for any suspicious activity and I was praying like hell that he could see me. I wasn't sure of where he'd parked but I hoped that it was somewhere close so that he could stop us before we made it to her car.

"Keep walking," She ordered pressing a sharp object into my back.

"Where are we going," I ask.

"Shut up," she said in a strong and demanding voice.

"Who are you and what do you want?" I say.

"You don't follow directions very well, do you? I said shut up and keep moving." She replied raising her voice and I could hear the anger in her tone.

I do as she says and began walking faster she grabs my arm yanking me to the right of her and pushing me up against a metallic colored BMW. She presses her body up against mine and rubs her face into my hair inhaling deeply before pushing it away from my face and running her tongue up the side of my face as she whispers in my ear.

"So, he thinks that he can ruin my life, play with my emotions, and then tell me no," she said in a voice that made my body quiver with fear. "Well, let's see if I can be a little more persuasive and get him to agree once he finds out that I have his little bitch."

She twists her hand around in my hair and pulls my hair back and pulling me away from the car and opening the door and pushing me inside. I grab my head once she lets go of my hair and she slammed the door in my face before I could get a glimpse of her. My heart was pounding, and my stomach was twisted into knots and my hands were shaking. I watched as she gets into the driver's seat and starts the car I felt like the area around me was closing in on me and I couldn't breathe. She looked at me with a smile on her face as if she was enjoying the dear and panic that she was causing.

"Aw, don't be scared," she said, in a soft tone running her fingers through my hair. "I promise it'll be quick." She winks at me with a horrifying look in her eyes.

Fear shot through my body and I felt hopeless. I was going to die, and she was going to be the one to take my life. But why? I didn't know who the guy was that she was talking about and I wish like hell that I did. Why hadn't I let Euro follow me to the lobby or let Shanice walk out with me just to be safe?

"Why are you doing this?" I ask as a tear came rolling down my face.

"Ask your boyfriend," She replies.

"Wait, Dejuan? What does he have to do with all this?" I ask, but she doesn't reply.

She starts the car and begins to back out of the parking space when a black Navigator pulls up behind us blocking her in. I felt a wave of relief sweep over me once I saw Francisco jumping out of the SUV with his gun drawn. She slams her hands on the wheel screaming out loud as she swings her head around then relaxes and takes a deep breath. I could still hear Francisco yelling for her to get out of the car. She opens the glove compartment and pulls out a gun.

She rubbed her hands over her hair that was long and black and pulled back into a neat ponytail. She looked over at me and told me not to move then opened the door and aimed her gun at Francisco and began unloading the clip. I see Francisco run behind the SUV and duck down.

"Renea, get out of the car and run," he calls out to me.

I turn towards the door and reach for the handle, but I feel her hands in my hair as she grips it tight pulling me back inside. It felt like she was ripping every strand of hair out of my head, the door slams and I feel the gun pressed against my temple.

"Move and I will unload what's left in this clip right into your head," she hissed, removing her hand from my hair and putting the car in reverse, slamming into the SUV, then speeding towards the exit.

I didn't know what to do all I knew is that I didn't want to die, so I reached over and grabbed the wheel sending us crashing into the side of the building. The airbags descended, and it felt like someone had hit me in the face and the chest with a sack full of bricks. My breath caught in my windpipe and it felt like my ribs cracked as it hit sending my body back into the seat hard. I struggled to breath, and I could feel something wet dripping down my face, I hear movement on my left, and that told me she was still alive the car door opened on her side and I could see someone pulling her from the car.

I tried to speak but nothing came out finally someone was at my side and I could hear voices all around me, people shouting, and someone crying. Through the blur in my eyes I could see my mother's face she was afraid, and I wanted to tell her that I was ok and hug her, but I couldn't move all I could feel was an intense pain shooting through my entire body.

I could hear Euro calling my name as he and Shanice pulled me from the car placing me on the ground.

"Can you hear me Renea," he asks, checking my pulse. "If you can hear me don't try to move or speak just blink for me.

I did as he asks and blinked my eyes twice letting him know that I could hear him. I could feel Shanice's hand in mine, so I moved it a little trying to squeeze it.

"Omgosh, Renea you're ok," She said her voice hoarse and cracking.

I could hear sirens getting closer and tried so hard to stay awake, but I could feel myself drifting away.

"Try and stay with me Renea, try and keep your eyes open for me the ambulance is here," Euro called out.

I open my eyes and see a bright light that burns my eyes causing me to shut them quickly. I try opening them again this time blinking a few times until my vision was clear. I turned my head and I could see my mother standing near the window with her arms crossed in front of her and she looked tired like she hadn't slept in days. I called out to her, but my voice was so low that she didn't hear me the first time.

"Mom," I repeated.

She turned and looked at me then rushed over taking a seat in the chair beside the bed.

"Oh, sweetheart, I'm right here." she raises my hand and kisses the back of it squeezing it tight. "I'm so glad you're awake. We thought we'd lost you," she said, with tears in her eyes.

"Where's dad?" I ask.

"He went to tell the nurse that your awake baby, he'll be right back."

I try and take a breath but a sharp pain shoots through my chest and a stinging pain is in my throat that causes me to cough. The doctor rushes into the room with a few nurses following behind him, I see one of the nurses take my mom away as they all surround me hovering over my bed. After a couple of minutes, my eyes closed and once again everything goes dark.

My eyes shoot open again and I quickly scan the room looking for my parents and I see my mother asleep in a chair with the covers pulled up around her shoulders and my dad stretched out on the sofa asleep as well.

"Good morning Renea`." The nurse whispers softly.

My eyes shot over to my right and I see a short brunette dressed in scrubs standing beside me and I give her a weak smile.

"How are you feeling? Are you having any pain?" She asks, watching me attentively.

I shake my head no and she walks a little closer placing her hand on my wrist checking my pulse before hitting a button on the machine and the cuff tightens around my arm taking my blood pressure.

"Looks good," she said, after reading the screen. "My name's Shelly if you need anything just press that red button on your bed and I'll be right in," she whispers gently rubbing the top of my hand.

I look up at the tv and it was already set to my favorite channel and I'm sure I could thank my dad for that one. I relaxed and shut my eyes trying to force myself to go back to sleep, but I wasn't tired. All I could see when I closed my eyes were memories of that day flash back into my mind. Her face seemed so familiar, but I just couldn't place it. Now that I think about it Dejuan did mention someone from his past popping back up, she must be the one he was referring to.

"Hey baby girl," said my dad bringing my mind back to the present.

"Hey daddy," I replied smiling up at him.

He comes over and kisses me on the forehead then pulls a chair next to the bed and takes a seat placing my hand in his.

"You gave us quit a scare." He said his voice shaky.

"I know dad, I'm sorry."

"Oh, no, sweetheart it wasn't your fault. You didn't ask for this to happen."

I turn away lowering my eyes into my lap.

"Sweetheart, why didn't you tell someone about your troubles."

"I hadn't noticed—I mean I don't even know who she is, daddy."

He takes a deep breath and looks at me and his gaze softens. "Well, the police think that maybe she was a stalker who'd been watching you for a while just waiting to make her move."

I look up at him, but I don't say anything I couldn't tell him the truth. Because the truth was going to hurt him, and I couldn't let that happen. I had to make sure that my mother and father never found out what was really going on or why she tried to kidnap me.

"Do the police know her name?" I ask, and he looks back at me hesitant not sure whether to say her name. "Dad?"

"Her names Olivia Stevens."

And then it came to me her last name was Stevens she's the daughter of that drug lord that was killed several years ago. "But wait," she said that Dejuan ruined her life—what did she mean by that? Does she think he had something to do with it? I needed to talk to him and let him know what happened.

"Dad, has Dejuan been here?"

"Yes, he comes every day sweetheart."

"Did someone tell him what happened or mention the girl's name?"

"No. Only that there was a stalker and that you saved yourself by crashing the car."

So, he doesn't know, which means his life is still in danger. What if she has someone helping her? She did say "we" when she was talking about getting revenge. So that would mean the other persons still out there.

Chapter Twelve

Dejuan

I receive a call from Jonathan telling me that Renea was in an accident and that she's in the hospital. So, I drop everything and rush over to the hospital. The last conversation that I had with Olivia about meeting up with Montez behind my back it didn't end well, and as soon as Jonathan mentioned a female with long black hair tried to hurt Renea I knew it was her.

I wasn't sure how she'd found out about me and Renea because none of the fellas knew until the day she showed up to my house in long beach. And then I remembered the photos that the paparazzi took of us together, they were all over the internet and on the front of most magazine covers. I take out my phone and call Jerome.

"Yo," he said after the second ring.

"Aye, grab the fellas and get ya'll asses to this city asap and meet me at the hospital."

"Hospital?" he said confused.

"Now Rome!" I shout into the phone then hang up.

I get inside and go over to the front desk. "Renea Dubley, where is she?"

"And may I ask who you are?" she said with a bit of an attitude as her eyes ran over me."

"What room lady?" I snap at her.

She leans back in her seat and crosses her arms. "I'm sorry, but if you're not immediate family then you can't—sir, SIR." She calls to me, but I run towards the elevators.

I take out my phone and call Shanice and she picks up on the first ring.

"Hello, Dejuan, where are you?"

"I'm here what floor?"

"4th floor ICU."

I hang up the phone and step into the elevator pressing the fourth floor. I walk off the elevator and over to the waiting room where I find her family waiting. I notice her father and mother from pictures at her house. He was pacing the floor and her mother was seated tapping her foot. Shanice was sitting beside her mother with one arm around her shoulders and the other placed on her hand.

Her mother's eyes lift and connected with mine and a small smile forms on her lips as she slowly gets up from her seat and begins walking over towards me. Shanice looked over and meet my gaze then stood from her seat as well following behind Mrs. Dubley.

"Hello sweetheart," her mother said walking right up to me and wrapping her arms around me.

"How is she?" I ask as I return her embrace.

"We don't know. She was unresponsive when they took her away from the church."

Tears burn my eyes, but I quickly blinked them away. I couldn't allow myself to fall apart or get emotional I needed to stay strong and help her parents get through this, and then I'd make sure that Olivia and Maylan paid for what they'd done. I help her mom back to her seat and say a few words to her father before Shanice pulls me by the arm and over to a corner away from everyone else.

"What the hell is going on? And don't lie to me because she told me everything."

"I don't know."

"Who is Olivia Stevens?"

I turn my head to look away, but she reaches her hand up and pulls my face back around to meet her gaze then releases me. She shakes her head at me placing her arms across her chest.

"This is all your fault," She said snarling at me then walks away.

I reach out to grab her arm, but she pulls away from me and walks back over to join Renea's parents. Jonathan comes through the door and walks over to Shanice hugging her and then Renea's parents. She was right this was my fault, but I wasn't going to let them get away with it, I was going to fix this by any means necessary.

Jonathan walks over taking my hand and pulling me into a half hug patting me on the back.

"You good man?"

"Yeah, I'm fine."

"What's going on bro talk to me." He said, "Why is Olivia Stevens trying to hurt Renea?"

I couldn't lie to him and he already knew my past and he knew all about the Stevens family as well. Everything that happened seven years ago when Maylan killed Olivia's dad, and how we all almost went down for Maylan's fuck up. He was there through it all and helped me out of it so that I didn't have to bring my mom and step-dad into it.

"Olivia popped up a few weeks ago along with that fool Maylan. She's been trying to get me to work with them."

"And you told them to fuck off right? Man, don't mess around and lose everything."

"I'm not," I shout causing everyone to turn and look at us. "I'm not. I didn't even know that Montez was fucking with that bitch Maylan, or that Olivia was even in the game," I reply trying to speak in a calmer voice.

"So, what you're telling me she did all of this because you turned her down on a partnership?"

"Yes, why else?" he shoots me a look. "Come on man I wasn't fucking her I just told you I didn't even know she was back in LA," I reply then I start to turn and walk away letting out a frustrated breath because I can't handle that shit right now.

"Ok, alright, I believe you." He said grabbing my arm. "But Dejuan I'm telling you right now let it go. You hear me, LET IT GO!"

"You know I can't do that man," I reply in a strong tone, "I have to go, call me when she can have visitors." He tries to stop me again, but I hold up my hands and walk away.

"Dejuan," he calls outs after me.

I nod to Shanice and Renea's parents before heading back to the elevators and down to the lobby. I step off the elevator just as the fellas come through the door they see me and rush right over to me.

"Bruh what's going on?" Tez asks, holding his hands out.

"Renea's in ICU."

"What?" Jerome shouts.

"What the fuck happened bruh?" Lavon chimes in.

"Oliva happened. She tried to take Renea, but she crashed the car and got away."

"Wait, hold up, why would she do that?" Tez asks.

"To force me to agree to her fucking demands." I fumed. "Let's go find that nigga Maylan so I can get to the bottom of this shit," I say shooting a death stare Tez's way.

He holds his hands up as to say, "Lead the way."

We pull up to the warehouse where we met up with Olivia and Maylan last and hop out the SUV, stomping towards the front entrance. The door swings open and out walks Maylan holding his hand out in front of him.

"Ok, wait—wait I didn't have anything to do with what happened to your girl. I had no idea that Olivia was going to do that."

"Then why are you stuttering like your ass is guilty," Jerome said, rushing towards him but Lavon holds his arm out stopping him.

"I promise man," He says taking a step back. "All she said is she has a plan that would get you all to join us. I didn't know she was going to hurt anybody. Plus, I didn't even know that you had divorced her sis—," he stops short realizing that he'd said something he wasn't supposed to.

"What the fuck did you just say?" I asked with my fist balled up as I walk up a little closer towards him.

"Nothing man," he says and steps back from me putting more distance between us.

"No, you were going to say her sister. Jaylyn right, she Olivia's sister."

He doesn't say anything he just backs away a little more, looking back as though he's going to break and run if he gets an opening. Before I could get the next word off my lips Montez breezes past me knocking Maylan to the ground and begins smashing him in the face with his 9mm.

"Stop, stop, please. I'll talk!" Maylan cries out.

"You mark ass bitch you think this shit is a fucking game, huh?" Tez spits out in anger hitting him one last time before pointing the gun at him. "You two must be the dumbest motherfuckers in the world if you thought you'd get away with this."

I walk over closer to the two of them. "So, you were saying?"

"Look, I heard about you and her sister getting married a while back. That whole begging you to take her back and rushing you to marry her was all planned by the two of them. She was supposed to talk you into taking over the family business, but once you were drafted to the pros Jaylyn told her that she wanted out, she didn't want to be a part of this lifestyle and neither did you."

"So, you're telling me none of it was real," I ask.

"No, it was all Olivia man." He replies.

"What about her dad?" Rome cuts in.

"She doesn't know it was me," He smirks and Tez presses his gun into the side of his head harder. "She thinks it was you and Tez that took him out."

"So, this was all about revenge? And you taking over their family's business like you'd planned to in the beginning." Lavon said.

"Yes," He said sitting up and spitting the blood from his mouth onto the ground. "If she'd succeeded in taking the two of you out then I wouldn't have any other problems."

Everything was suddenly clear. The way Jaylyn had changed right before spring break and then after a year she suddenly out of the blue wanted to reconcile and get married. She'd broken it off with the man that she was in love with, so she could help her sister get back at me. The thought made me laugh as I ran my hands over my head.

"And Darron who is he?" I ask, and he looked up at me shocked, he didn't know that I knew Darron.

"That's her fiancé. The guy she was with before her sister made her get back together with you—wait how do you know Darron?"

"Fuck," I said taking my phone out of my pocket and calling Jonathan.

The phone rings several times then goes to voicemail, so I hang up and try again after the fourth try he finally answers.

"Hey Bro, where are you? I've been calling you for hours, Renea is awake and they're allowing her to have visitors now," his voice was a little more upbeat than it was earlier.

I take a deep breath then say, "That's great, man, I'll be back there soon. But listen, Jon, I need you to do something for me asap and it's important. I can't explain everything right now, but I promise I'll tell you everything late."

"What happened Dejuan?" Jonathan asks fear in his voice.

"One of your security guards, his name's, Darron Reed."

"Yeah, I know Reed. Why are you asking about him?"

"I need you fire him immediately, deny all access, I mean completely ban him from your building."

"I can't just fire him without a cause or any explanation."

"Trust me, man, you don't need one. He's bad news just do it now."

"Ok, I'm on it." He said, "But you better hit me back and tell me what the fuck is going on."

"I will man. I promise."

I have Tez tie up Maylan and put him in the SUV while I discuss our next move with the fellas. The first thing we need to do is find a way to let them know that we're not the ones responsible for their father's death and after that, we'll figure out how we're going to handle the rest of this bullshit. Coming after us was the wrong move and trying to hurt my woman was definitely a mistake and anyone involved was going to get dealt with.

Chapter Thirteen

Renea

I press the button on the morphine giving myself a double dose because the pain was becoming unbearable.

"I can't believe Dejuan got me tied up in this mess," I said looking over at Shanice as she tapped away at her keyboard. "Are listening to me?" I ask.

"Yes," she glances at me for a split second then drops her eyes back down to the screen.

"If you were going to work the whole time you could've just stayed at your office," I say a little annoyed by her silence.

"Testy, are we? Maybe you should press that button one more time." She winks at me, and I give her the finger, but she just smiles at me and shakes her head. "I'm almost done." She said tapping a few more buttons before closing her laptop and turning to me. "Alright, I'm all yours madam. What is it that you would like for me to get you?"

"Well, you can start by massage my feet," I say giving her a sneering look.

"Cute," she replies, getting up from her seat and joining me on the bed. "You really scared me you know." She whispers and gently places her arms around me.

"Yeah, I scared myself."

I lay my head on hers and let out a heavy sigh closing my eyes for a second. I still couldn't understand, why me, out of all the people in his life that he loved and cared about why'd she come after me. I mean don't get me wrong I wouldn't wish this type of thing on anyone in his family, but what was her reasoning for coming after me.

"I had to ask myself who is Dejuan Washington really?"

I feel like I've never really known at all we're just getting to know each other and already things are going to hell, and just when I was really starting to fall for him. I mean I can understand him not mentioning his ex-wife the first night we were together because he thought he was just a booty call. I don't think I would've mentioned it either it's not really something you need to discuss if you're not planning on keeping the person around.

"Hey, should I come back later?"

I hear Dejuan's voice and my eyes shoot open. Why can't I control my emotions or my body when he's around, as soon as I hear the sound of his voice it seems to connect with me and every word that he speaks sends an uncontrollable wave of intense feelings through my body.

Shanice raises her head and looks at me waiting for my answer, I nod my head letting her know that it's ok and she gets up from the bed and walks towards the door.

"I'll be right outside if you need me," she says looking from me to Dejuan piercing her eyes at him.

She walks out of the room and closes the door behind her and he stands by the door with his hands in his pocket. I hope he's not waiting for me to speak first because I really have no words for him at the moment. But he should be full of apologies after getting me into all of this, and I didn't need his sympathy only an apology then he could leave and never come near me again.

He lowers his eyes looking down at the floor as though he was searching for the words that he wanted to say, so I took a deep breath and closed my eyes laying my head back onto the pillow.

"I...I'm sorry Renea," he begins. "I'm really and truly sorry. But this is the reason that I didn't tell you."

"Really," I say cutting him off. "If you had told me then I wouldn't be here, if you had told me I would've been aware and alerted my team, if you had told me then I would've known to be a little more cautious and on the lookout for fucking psychos," I shout, and my breath catches in my throat as I feel the sting of pain in my chest and I wince at the pain.

He rushes over to the bed and places his hand on mine and begins brushing my hair back with the other. "Calm down beautiful you don't need to get upset."

"Maybe you should leave then," I hiss at him then try and steady my breathing as the pain eases a little.

"No. Look you have every right to be angry with me but I'm not going anywhere." He said as he takes a seat in the chair where Shanice was seated before.

"Fine. Then tell me why Olivia Stevens is trying to hurt me and don't lie to me."

"She was trying to hurt you to get to me."

"But why me?"

"She's jealous. We dated back when we were in high school and I worked for her father."

"For a notorious drug lord?"

His eyebrow lifted. "How do you know—"

"Their kind of famous you know. He did have one of the biggest drug cartels in the world, that is until he was murdered."

"Yeah," he chuckled.

I eye him and his face falls. "You think this is funny?" I counter.

"No, I'm just surprised you know all of this." He replies.

"I don't live under a rock." I joke but then quickly wipe the smile off my face. "So why is she back I thought you weren't a part of that life anymore?"

"I'm not," he turns to me with a hard expression on his face. "She thinks I had something to do with her father's death."

"Did you?"

"No!" He said sternly.

We look at each other for a long time before either of us said another word. I believed him, there was just something in his eyes that he was sincere, and I could see that it was a burden that he was carrying.

"But you know the person responsible?"

"Yes," he said, in a muffled voice.

"So, what does she want?" I ask.

"Me, and the dream that she had for us." He said, with a small laugh. "She wanted us to go to the same college, graduate, and get married in hopes that I would take over the family business once her dad stepped down. But that's not the kind of life that I imagined for myself, it was fun and a fast way to make money when I was a kid and those things appealed to me, but as I got older I realized I wanted more."

"And your friends?"

"They're still living that life running what I built back before I got out. And they call me for advice and shit like that, but I promise you my hands will never get dirty again." He said placing his hand on mine.

I move my hand from his and look away. "I wish I could believe you."

"I understand." He said, "I just want you to know that I'm going to fix this I promise, and hopefully you can forgive me one day so that we can move forward because I'll never let you. I love you Renea." He stands and leans over kissing the top of my head then turns and walks away disappearing out the door.

I feel the tears as they stream down my cheeks on to my lips and I quickly wipe them away. He said it, he told me that he loved me, and I wanted to say it back, but I couldn't bring myself to let it roll off my tongue. I'd felt it a while ago but it all seemed to be happening so fast and I figured it was just one of those moments where the dick was so good to the point where I thought I was in love, but I really only fell in love with the way he'd dick me down really good after a long drought.

But now hearing him say it and looking into his eyes the feeling is just as strong as it was the first time I felt it. Even with the feelings I have now and being mad at him and wanting to give up and let go my heart is still filled with the same emotion. Because I loved him too!

***

After spending three weeks in the hospital I was finally cleared to go home, well to my parent's house that is. They insisted that I come and stay with them until my cast is removed, I didn't want to put a lot of pressure on them, and I tried hard to convince them to let me go home and have someone stay with me, but my mom wasn't having it. We pull up in front of the house and my dad opens the door and helps me out of the car.

"Slowly baby girl," he says lifting me up so that I could put my arm around his shoulders and put all my weight on him.

"I got it, dad."

He helps me into the wheelchair and rolls me into the house. He wheels me to the couch and helps me out the chair. I get comfortable and settle into the cushions propping my leg up on a couple of oversized pillows.

"Thanks, Daddy."

"Anything for my baby girl." He said with a wide smile.

He heads off into the kitchen to fix us lunch so that we can eat while we watch the football game. I'm such a daddy's girl and sports has always been our thing. My mom wasn't a huge fan of football or basketball, but I would watch the games with my dad and his friends when I was younger. My dad and I, we've always had this bond that was special and I'm sure my mom wishes that I'd been a little more of a girly girl and liked dolls and make-up, but I was a tomboy and I loved getting dirty.

My dad returned with a tray full of food and took his seat at the end of the couch. He picks up the remote and turns up the sound before grabbing the bowl of chips from the tray. My phone chimes and I look down at the screen and see a text from Dejuan, I ignore it and turn my attention back to the game. My dad looks over at me from the corner of his eye and lets out deep sigh placing the bowl in his lap back on the table and sits up straight turning to face me.

"Alright, baby girl, talk to me. Why are you ignoring that young man's calls?" He asks.

"I just want him out of my life," I say in a soft voice.

"Aw, baby, you don't mean that," he said, moving closer to me and placing his hand on my leg.

"He lied to me dad and look at what happened. It was all because of his dishonesty."

"Sweetheart, he can't control what other people choose to do. Even if he had told you about his past or about this young woman there was still no way of knowing what she was going to do."

"I know but he still—" I sigh placing my hands over my face and begin to sob into my hands and my dad comes over to comfort me kneeling beside me. "I'm so scared and confused daddy I don't know what to do."

"And it's ok to be scared, baby girl," he said rubbing my shoulder. "But you can't move towards your future if you're looking back in the rear-view mirror, and you know this." He pauses and gently wipes away my tears with his shirt. "Give him a chance to correct his mistakes. This thing between the two of you it's new and you have to give it time. I can see that you love him, and I can see it in your eyes even now, just mentioning his name makes you light up."

"OK… I'll think about it."

"Good, now let's get back to the game."

He picks up the bowl of chips and places it back in his lap and putting his feet on the ottoman. I pick up my phone and click on the last message from Dejuan and send him a reply.

Me: Thanks for checking on me, I'm feeling a lot better. Do you think that maybe you could come over to my parent's house so that we can talk?

Dejuan: Of course, just tell me when and I'll be there.

Me: If you're not busy now is good.

I place my phone on the table rolling my eyes at my dad once I noticed him staring at me with a weird and goofy look on his face.

An hour goes by and he finally arrives, my mother rushes off to answer the door and then I hear their voices in the foyer as they make their way towards the living room.

"Sweetie. I believe this handsome young man's here for you." My mother says with a huge smile plastered on her face.

My cheeks blush a bright red at the sight of my mother gawking over Dejuan. This was only one of the reasons I never let any of my dates pick me up from the house when I lived at home because my mom could never control herself. I cleared my throat and my mom jumps in place then turns and gives Dejuan a quick hug and exits the living room. I wish I could say it was to give us some privacy, but I know she's only going within earshot so that she can listen in our conversation.

"Hey beautiful," he says walking over to the couch stopping at the empty space.

I nod my head towards the empty spot assuring him that it was ok to sit, and he slowly sat down on the couch carefully trying not to touch my foot or move the pillow. The expression on his face and the way he positioned himself in his seat made me giggle and he quickly turned to look up at me with a look of relief on his face after hearing me laugh.

"Thanks for coming,"

"Did you think I wouldn't?" He asks, confused.

"I don't know—I mean I've been really hard on you lately."

He chuckles. "Yeah that you have."

I look down at my fingers, fiddling them around nervously trying to think of what I should say next. I'd had this whole speech prepared in my head of what I was going to say to him and how I was going to end it and let him go his own way, but as soon as his eyes met mine it all washed away, and my mind went blank.

"What's on your mind beautiful?" He asks breaking my concentration.

I pause for a second then bring my eyes to his. "I think we should—I mean I don't think this is going to work out Dejuan," I said, swallowing the lump in my throat.

"Ok, I understand."

"Wait, that's it just an ok?" I say searching his face for something, anything, but it was emotionless.

"I know this is hard for you and I understand your reasons as to why you've made the decision to move on. I appreciate you telling me to my face and not on the phone or through a text like most people would probably do in this situation."

"I'm really sorry Dejuan."

"You have nothing to be sorry for beautiful. I fucked up and now I have to live with it. Although I hope you've forgiven me because like I said before I'm truly sorry and I really was just trying to protect you."

"I did. I mean I do forgive you."

"Thanks," He said, "I still love you beautiful, so I'll be waiting for you to come back to me," he says as he rises from his seat and walks over to me lifting my lips to meet his and kisses me so slow and passionately that I want to tell him not to go, but I catch myself.

Honestly, I'd forgiven him the moment he apologized at the hospital. But I also need time to figure out whether or not I want to continue our relationship. He obviously has some things that he needs to straighten out and I think he should do that before we try and go any further. Who knows maybe in the future we'll cross paths again and things will be different.

Chapter Fourteen

Dejuan

"Yo, Dejuan meet us at the hospital man Tez's been shot."

I press replay and listen to the message again making sure I heard him right. Rome called me several times and left me several voicemails. I make a U-turn and head towards MLK and when I get there I pull into a spot and rush inside the ER and the lady directs me to the waiting room. I find Montez's mom and younger brother along with Jerome and Lavon. Their eyes shoot towards the door and land on me as I enter the room, and I begin walking over to them. His mother stands and gives me a hug first then his little brother. I pull the fellas to the side, so I could get some info on what went down and why they weren't keeping an eye out knowing that Maylan and Olivia were on some crazy shit.

"What the hell happened Rome?" I ask.

"I don't know. Honestly, man I think that was supposed to be you in there." He replies, with a pained look in his eyes.

"What?" I said, confused. "What's that supposed to mean?"

"It means that you should be happy that oh girl called you to meet up with her. Because he was leaving your place when he got shot."

My stomach twisted, and it felt like a punch to the gut. Was someone really trying to kill me? Maylan is locked up in a container at the port, Olivia's in jail, and Jaylyn, no, there's no way she would be capable of shooting anyone. Could she?

"Ms. Broadwick," we hear the doctor say and we all rush over to hear what he has to say.

"I'm here. How is he?" She asks, watching his expression closely.

After a brief silence, he says, "Your son is fine. However, there is a slight possibility of paralysis due to the damage to his spinal cord caused by the bullet."

"So, are you saying he may never walk again?" Lavon asks.

"Yes, as well as loss of other bodily functions as well. We won't know how severe it is until he's awake and can talk to us." He replies.

"Oh, my baby," his mother cries out falling against me, burying her face into my chest.

"He'll have a long road to recovery ahead of him. He'll need all the support and encouragement that he can get."

"Thanks, doctor," I say pulling his mom closer and wrapping my arms around her tighter. "It's going to be ok Ms. B he's tough he'll bounce back."

She releases me and gives me a soft smile placing her hand on one side of my cheek and kissing the other. She wipes away her tears and goes back over to her youngest son and lets him know that his brother is ok as she pulls him in for a warm embrace. After dropping Ms. Broadwick and her son off at home I head back to the city. I had planned to go back to my place in Long Beach but after what happened tonight I wouldn't be going back there for a while. Not until I do a little digging and talk to the cops because I knew they're going to call to question me.

***

I didn't get much sleep, and my mind is still a little out of it with all that was going on. I was worried about Tez and still feeling down after having Renea tell me that it was over between the two of us. I'd left her parents in a daze feeling as if my entire world had come crashing down. I was in love with her and I didn't want anyone else but her. It was crazy how in just a short time she'd become the air that I breathed, my other half, my rock. And now she was gone maybe forever I mean who knows what will happen in the future she could move on and find someone else or things could come back full circle for us.

"Hey man, you alright?" Cameron asks, lowering the speed of the treadmill to a slower pace.

"Yeah, I'm alright man," I reply

I continue running on the treadmill for about another hour then I head over to the court to do a couple of drills. I hadn't seen my teammates since the season ended so it was nice to kick it with them, plus working out helped relieve some of the built-up stress and tension. Once I finished up I hit the showers and then got dressed and headed over to meet Jonathan at his place.

I pull up to Jonathan's place out in Malibu and park. His house was one of those houses that people only dreamed of, 4.8 acres of land, 18,075 SQ FT, 10 Bedrooms, and 9 bathrooms, a huge pool, basketball court, tennis court, and it was overlooking the ocean. Once you're here you'll never want to leave.

As I approach the door it swings open. "Dejuan, OMG," Marsha runs out the door screaming as she runs up to me and leaps into my arms wrapping herself around me.

"Woo," I stumble back. "What's up baby girl?" I wrap my arms around her returning the embrace.

"I've missed you so much I'm glad you're finally home."

"I missed you too short stuff."

I place her on her feet and she put her arm around me as we walk into the house. Marsha was Jonathan's youngest sister of the three and he was the only boy, but he was the oldest, so they use to always want to follow us around when we were kids tagging along making our days long and annoying. They would always give any girl that we brought home grief making it impossible for us to keep girlfriends. No one was right for us in their eyes and it's still kind of that way even to this day.

"Hey, look who I found," she shouts getting everyone's attention once we got out to the backyard.

"Aye. Bro. Welcome to the party." Jonathan says, diving into the pool.

"Hello son, it's nice to see you." Says Mrs. DeClair walking up beside me leaning in and giving me a peck on the cheek.

"Hey mama," I say returning the kiss on the cheek.

I walk over and bump fist with his pops and join him at the table taking the seat across from him. His dad and I talked sports and watched the family swim and have a good time.

"There comes my sexy lady," Jonathan calls out. "Come on baby, get your sexy ass in this pool with me."

Shanice walks past me and heads over to the pool taking off her top and jumping in. She hasn't really had much to say to me after everything that's happening with Renea, which I expected they are like sisters, so it's only right that she would be equally pissed.

We all sit down for dinner talking, laughing, and joking having a good time and it was much needed. I ran into Shanice as I'm coming down the hall from the bathroom.

"Hey, can I talk to for a second."

"No," she said sternly and continues walking passed me.

I turn back and follow behind her trying to keep up. "Please, 5 minutes that's all I ask."

She stops and turns around walking slowly towards me then stops a couple of steps away, "Go ahead talk."

"Look what's with all the hostility?" I question.

"Well, let's see. You lied to my best friend, you brought a psycho into our lives, and you almost got her killed. Did I leave anything out?"

"You know that's not true. I had no clue that Olivia was capable of doing something like that, I haven't seen that woman since we were teens. And you know I would never do anything to intentionally hurt her or let anyone else for that matter. That's why I keep that part of my life to myself, on the hush. And you should know better than anyone that, that's what has to be done sometimes. You can't tell me that you've never lied to her to protect her."

She lets out a heavy sigh and rolls her eyes. "Fine, you're right." She said holding her hand up in front of her. "But that still doesn't take away from the fact that my friend—my sister is hurting both physically and emotionally."

"So, help me to help her understand that I only wanted to protect her."

She crosses her arms over her chest, huffs, and says, "Ok, I'll talk to her. But remember I'm on her side, not yours, and I'm only doing this because I believe you when you say you love her and I know she loves you too." She let her hands fall down to her side and walks away.

I head back downstairs and back into the living room to join the rest of the family they were snuggled up watching a movie that I'd never seen or heard of, so I found myself a spot and settled in.

***

I'd made plans with Jaylyn and Darron a couple of days before to meet up with me in Long Beach. She was hesitant at first and I expect that because I knew she was afraid that I knew her and her sisters little secret and she probably figured I was going to kill her boyfriend. Either way, she would be absolutely right.

After a few hours of torcher with a few of Montez's hell hounds, he told us their whole sick and twisted plan. Including the part where they were supposed to take me out the night, Tez was shot. See Darron was supposed to camp out near my place until I arrived back at home and then make his move once I got out the car making it seem like a drive-by so that when my past was exposed they would chalk it up as a revenge kill and case closed.

I squeezed every ounce of information out of that bitch before recording a confession from him, so the world would know who was really responsible for killing of Mr. Stevens.

When Jaylyn and Darron pulled up to the port the hellhounds snatch them up and drag them to the container.

"Tie them up and sit them over there," I said, walking behind them as we entered inside.

I motion for them to remove the bags from their heads. Jaylyn was frantic but Darron, he was calm. His breathing controlled, but you could see the fear in his eyes, even though his body language would make you think otherwise. Jaylyn struggles to free her hands from the rope, but soon realizes that she's never getting out of the chair that she's now confined to.

"What are you doing Dejuan? Why are you doing this?" She shouts looking around the container, and she gasps as her eyes lock on Maylan who was leaning slouched over in a chair a few feet away from them. "NO—OMG, Maylan." She screams.

"My darling ex-wife are we really going to continue to play this game?" I reply, with a sinister smile.

"What are you talking about, Dejuan?" She asks, in between sobs.

"Maylan told me everything. How you're a part of the Stevens family, about you and your sister's little plan for me to marry you so that you could trick me into running the family business."

"I'm sorry Dejuan—," she begins.

"No, you're not," I said, cutting her off. "I'm sure you're sorry you got caught, and on top of that you're probably sorry because your little boyfriend here didn't get the chance to take me out."

"What?" she says turning to look at him. "I didn't have him come after you. Darron?"

"It was your sister and Maylan that ordered the hit." He replied with a smug grin while keeping his eyes on me. "Look can we get this over with, if you're going to kill me just do it already."

Slash!

One of the hellhounds walks up behind Darron and slit his throat with one quick swipe across his neck. Blood sprays everywhere as his body convulses and jerks in the chair until he bleeds out gurgling in his last breath.

"Yo, what the fuck was that?" Lavon shouts.

"Don't worry mate, I actually did him a favor, the other thing I had in mind was much worse." He said, with a sly grin on his face and a laugh that was far more disturbing as he winked at us.

I don't know where Montez met the hellhounds, but they were ruthless and not afraid to take a life and they enjoyed doing it. But they were also loyal, so I guess that's why he keeps them around.

"What now? What are we gonna do with her?" Rome asks.

"Let her go," I reply.

"What?" they say in unison.

"After what she just witnessed she won't be a problem to us anymore," I say as I walk over to her and squat down in front of the chair with my arms resting on my knees. "Listen to me carefully. You're going to take this tape back to your sister and have the rest of the Stevens family look at it too."

"Why? What is it?" she asks.

"You know as smart as you and your sister seem to be, your also very naive. Maylan killed your father, and before you ask me how I know, well it's because I was there the night that Maylan set him up.

Your father threatened to kill him for betraying him and Maylan shot him twice once in the chest then in the head."

"Omgosh," she said as she hung her head and let out a loud cry.

"It's all here on this tape, he confessed. Now tell your family and your sister that we took care of your father's murderer and to stay away from me and my family because the next time I won't be so generous."

She shakes her head in agreeance and one of the hellhounds removes her from the chair pulling her out of the container and out to the car.

"So, what are we gonna do with these two motherfuckers?" Rome asks, standing in front of Maylan's lifeless body.

"Don't worry broda I'm going to feed dem to da pigs and there will be nothing left of dem when dem boys finish." The hellhound said, with a heavy accent.

I give him a nod then head back out to the car with the fellas leaving the hellhounds to clean up.

Chapter Fifteen

Renea

Two months of laying around having people wait on you hand and foot would be a wonderful thing for some people but for me not so much.

"How's that feel any tenderness here?" Dr. Tristan asks as he examines my leg.

"It feels great," I reply.

"Good. Now you should watch for any numbness or loss of feeling over the next couple of days. Your leg may feel a little weak at first and that's totally normal in such cases." He stands and pulls a pad from his pocket. "I'm going to have you see a physical therapist for about 2 weeks and if you start to have any pain give me a call. And Miss. Dubley no performing until your therapy is complete."

I put on a fake smile and nod my head at him then he turns and leaves the room. I let out a deep sigh then slide my sneaker on my foot before climbing down from the exam table. My mother stands in the doorway waiting to help me out, as I grab my crutches and head towards the door.

"It's going to be ok, sweetheart. I know it feels like the world is falling all around you, but you'll bounce back soon, and you'll be back to performing in no time." She said softly, placing her hand on my back.

"I know mom. It just gets kind of hard sometimes."

"You just have to stay positive and your father and I will be right here to continue to help you through it." She said, leaning in to kiss the side of my head.

We get into the elevator and head out to the front of the hospital and get into the SUV. My mom has spent the last week at my place with me while my fathers at work. She still worries about me. Even though I've assured her so many times that my security team is on top of it, and that she doesn't need to worry about anything, but she still refuses to leave my side.

I haven't heard from Dejuan in these last two months and I can't say that I blame him. I did tell him that I didn't want him in my life anymore, and I'm sure that hurt him to hear those words. Shanice has tried to talk me into calling him several times so that we could try and work it out, but I'm just not ready to have him back in my life again.

Shanice invited me to a party that Jonathan's hosting in a couple of days, but I didn't want to take a chance of running into Dejuan, so I declined. However now I wish I hadn't because I want nothing more than to get out of this house and be around other people. I would kill for a glass of wine, and good conversation. Also getting laid would be nice as well, after a couple of seconds of pondering I pick up my cell and call Shanice.

"Hey love, how did the appointment go?" She asks, excitement in her voice.

"It went great I'm finally free of that cast."

"Woo-hoo," she sings into the phone making me giggle.

"Although I do have to do a couple of weeks of physical therapy and I still can't book any performances until it's over." I sigh dropping my head back on the sofa cushion.

"Oh, girl two weeks will fly by and you'll be back rocking the stage before you know it. You just need to find something or someone to occupy your time."

"Why do you always think a man can solve all of our problems?"

"Because the majority of the time all we need is some good dick and a little advice from the male species." She said, sucking her teeth. "Okay, and you know I'm right."

I shake my head not wanting to get into that conversation with her at the moment because somehow, she always wins. I guess that's what makes her such a good lawyer.

"So, the real reason I'm calling is because I was wondering if I could still snag a ticket for the event on Thursday."

"It's already taking care of, I purchased one for you. I knew you would finally come to your senses and want to get out and party."

"Really, Omgosh, I love you so much," I say blowing kisses into the phone.

"You know I got you, girl." She said, and I could hear the smile in her voice.

"Alright, I'll see you on Thursday."

We say a few more words before ending the call and I head back to my room in search of the perfect dress to wear to the event. After about an hour of looking through my closet twice, I decided that my perfect dress was not hanging in there. So that only meant that I needed to go shopping. I shoot a quick text to Shanice telling her to meet me tomorrow so that she can help me pick out a dress and a pair of shoes to wear to the event.

This would be my first time being back in the public eye and my first photograph since the accident, so I had to be on my A game.

Chapter Sixteen

Dejuan

"Come on man, one more time, push through," He said, "There you go man, great job," Camren said patting me on the shoulder as I dropped the weights.

Today was one hell of a workout, and Camren being on his shit pushing me way outside my comfort zone and I could really feel it. I showered and grabbed my things before I headed out of the gym, I had a few things I needed to tend to before Jonathan's fundraiser event tomorrow night.

I was really hoping that Renea would be there, but Jonathan told me that she declined. And I wasn't surprised. I'm sure she'd figured that I would be there as well and decided not to attend so that she wouldn't be anywhere near me. I tried for weeks to get her to talk to me, but she wouldn't answer any of my calls or reply to any of my messages.

I've been going crazy without her and I really wish that there was some way she could give me another chance. She would never have to worry about another soul hurting her again I'd made sure of that. And as for Olivia and Jaylyn, I'm sure they now understand exactly what I'm capable of, and more than willing to do, to protect the ones I love. Even though Olivia was sentenced to five years, she would eventually be back and plotting her revenge, so I knew that I had to send her a clear message.

I walk into the clothing store and a very attractive young woman catches my attention. I watch her as she comes around the counter and makes her way over towards me with a little more stride in her step to ensure she reaches me first.

"Good evening Mr.—" She said, biting her bottom lip waiting for me to respond.

"Washington. Dejuan Washington." I say shooting her a seductive smile.

"Yes, I thought so. So, what can I do for you Dejuan? It is alright if I call you Dejuan, right?"

"You can call me whatever you like sexy."

She smiles a flirtatious smile. "What will we need to dress you in this evening?"

"I'm looking for a suit."

"Oh, and what kind of event are we attending?"

Catching on to the "we" that she kept throwing out there, I smiled at her letting her know that I knew exactly what she was getting at.

"Well, we will be attending a charity event on Thursday." I lick my lips and from the breath that was now caught in her throat and the expression on her face, I could only imagine how soaking wet her panties are.

She clears her throat and points towards the back. "Well—right this way sir."

"Ladies first," I reply.

She turns and begins walking in front of me leading the way and I could tell that she was putting more of a twist in her hips than usual because she was throwing that thing. Her ass jiggled from left to right and in my mind, I could picture her bouncing on my dick as she straddled me in reverse cowgirl just so that I could see all that ass.

She begins taking my measurements, pausing once she felt how low my manhood was hanging and seeing the thick imprint. After everything was all set we exchanged numbers and I invited her to be my plus one for Jonathan's Fundraiser and she was all too eager to except. I wanted to invite her back to my place so that I could get her on her knees and see how it felt to have her hot wet lips wrapped around my dick, but I decided to wait. There will be plenty of time for that tomorrow night.

Chapter Seventeen

Renea

"Renea, darling how are you doing?" Ralf said, rushing over and falling into a long embrace. "Honey you look fabulous, you don't look as if you've missed a beat."

"Hello Ralf," I said, embracing him back. "I'm doing great doll how about yourself?" I kiss both cheeks before releasing him.

Ralf is one of the top designers in the entertainment world. He's dressed and undressed some of the hottest celebs from the music industry as well as movie and TV. He's always my go-to guy and he's always dressed me in the finest gowns the worlds ever seen, so it was only fitting that Shanice and I come here.

"So, what can I do for you darling?" He asks, with his thick accent.

"We have a charity event tomorrow night and it's my first night back on the scene, so I need something sexy," I said snapping my fingers.

"Yass... I know just the thing—mm hmm come with me." He said, taking my hand and leading us to the back.

He puts me in a very sexy royal blue gown that crosses over the shoulder and flows at the bottom. I felt like I'd died and gone to heaven when I turned to look at myself in the oversized mirrors.

"Omgosh, this is perfect, Ralf," I say placing my hand over my mouth.

"I knew you'd love it. It's so perfect for your skin tone and the curve of your body."

"It is," I said turning and admiring how the dress clung to me.

Just as I take my last twirl in the mirror Shanice comes out in this over the top sexy red lace gown and she looks drop dead gorgeous in it. She stops noticing the look on my face.

"What? Is it too much?" She asks, nervously.

"Oh my, I don't think you'll make it out of the house once Jonathan sees you in that," I said, and her face relaxes.

She walks over to the mirror and looks at herself, her eyes begin to tear up a little as she takes in how beautiful she looks. We stand there quietly for a second not wanting to ruin the moment that she was experiencing as she spun around.

Then she shouts, "My ass looks amazing in this dress," and we burst out laughing.

"We'll take both dresses, Ralf," I say, stepping down from the mantel in front of the mirror.

We change back into our clothes and return to the front to pay for our dresses and then say our goodbyes to Ralf. We head over to the nail salon to get a Mani & Pedi so that we could relax, and gosh was I overdue for some pampering.

"So, have you given any thought about the situation with you and Dejuan?" She asks, hesitantly.

I roll my eyes and look over at her saying to myself, "Oh, no, not this again."

"Come on Renea you know you still love that man."

I sigh and lay my head back on the cushion of the chair trying to tune her out and focus on the nail tech that was massaging my feet. With a low growl in her throat she stares at me waiting for an answer but instead, I continue to ignore her until she throws a magazine at me.

"Really Nesse," I say turning and lowering my eyes at her.

"Stop ignoring me then heffa," she glares back at me.

The nail tech laughs and says something in Chinese under his breath and we both turn and look at him. He flinches in his seat then gets back to what he was doing.

"I'm not ready to talk to him and I know that he loves me but that doesn't mean that we need to be together," I replied.

"It's been two months, almost three and you're telling me you still haven't forgiven him."

"It's—" I begin but then I pause.

"What?" she asks. "He's willing to do whatever it takes if you'd only give him a chance."

"I don't know Nesse. I'm scared." I sobbed.

She looks at me with a sad look in her eyes as she reaches over to take my hand. I know that she wants me to pull myself up out of the mud and get back to life as usual but to be honest everything that's happened kind of changed me.

***

My makeup artist finishes up and I quickly slip into my gown, so that my hair stylist could finish up with my hair. I couldn't believe how good I look in this dress and I knew once Dejuan saw me, he would be falling all over me the entire night. I grab my clutch off the table and we head out to the SUV, climbing inside, and pulling away from the building making our way to the event.

The server offers me a glass of champagne, as I enter the room. I take one and thank her before drinking half of the glass. I spot Shanice and Jonathan standing in the middle of the room conversing with two older gentlemen, whom I'm sure is trying to impress so that they'll receive a very nice sizeable donation to the charity.

Jonathan started this charity for underprivileged kids. So that they too would have the opportunity to afford college and have programs to attend after school which would keep them off the streets. And it made a lot of sense, his father and Dejuan's stepfather are the reason that Dejuan and his brother made it out. My mind drifted off and thoughts of him came flooding into my mind, and I looked around the room to see if I could find him, but he wasn't there.

"Hey, Renea," Shanice calls out to me waving me over once she notices me standing at the entrance.

I walk over and join them, and Shanice introduces me to the two men that they were talking to before returning to their conversation. I stand there drinking from my almost empty glass of champagne, waiting for one of the servers to come back around so that I could get my hands on another glass. Why am I so nervous? I mean I knew that he was going to be here and it's not like this is our first time being in the same room together.

I turn my head just in time to catch a glimpse of him walking in the door. He was dressed in an all-black tux complete with a red shirt and a black bow tie and boy did it show off every bit of his hard-toned body. I look to his right and every muscle in my body clenched, my stomach ached, and I suddenly felt nauseous as I watched a pretty young woman walked up beside him and places hers around his.

I take in a shaky breath and both Shanice and Jonathan both turn and look at me.

"Are you ok, Renea?" Jonathan asks, placing his hand on the middle of my back staring me in the eyes then following them in the direction I was staring.

He takes a deep breath then exhales as his jaw clinches his jaw then Shanice turns and looks in the same direction as Jonathan and could finally see what had made me so upset. I swallow hard trying to get the lump out my throat, but it was stuck, and I felt like I couldn't breathe.

As he searched the room his eyes finally met mine and he smiled and began walking over towards us. I wanted to turn and run away but my feet were glued to the floor and my body wouldn't move.

"I'm so sorry, Renea I forgot to tell him you were coming. Do you want to go?" she asks, in a nervous tone.

I shake my head no and take a deep breath and exhale before they reach us.

"Good evening everyone." He said, greeting us once he was standing in front of us.

"Hello," the two older gentlemen say before walking away to mingle.

"What's up bro," Jonathan said, giving him a manly hug and whispering something into his ear before releasing him.

"Hello Dejuan," Shanice said in a cold tone then her eyes shoot over to the woman next to him. "Who is this lovely young lady."

"Hi, I'm Jill it's nice to meet you all." She speaks up before he could say anything.

She extends her hand, and everyone shakes it but me, I was still frozen in place unable to force myself to move. She drops her hand with a confused look on her face as she glances over at Dejuan and he smiles back at her giving her that look that he used to give me.

"It's good to see you out Renea. I'm glad you're doing better." He said.

After a couple of seconds of silence, I finally find my voice. "Nice see you too," I say then clear my throat. "Um...can you all excuse me."

I turn and walk away quickly not knowing where I was going I just had to get away from them. I finally find the bathroom and run inside, into one of the stalls, slam the door, and lock it. I couldn't believe he'd moved on I begin to breathe in and out trying to calm myself with my back against the wall inside the stall. He said he loved me, he said he wanted to marry me, yet it only took him two months to have another woman on his arm and probably in his bed.

"Renea," Shanice calls out to me as she enters the bathroom.

"I'm in here," I shout, choking back the tears that I refused to let fall for him.

"Omg, love I'm so sorry. I didn't know that he was seeing someone or that he was bringing a date."

"No. it's fine. It's my own fault right, I pushed him away."

She doesn't answer but her silence was all the answer I needed. Instead of trying to move past it and working it out I pushed him away, so I guess that made me the blame for her being on his arm instead of me. We sit quietly saying nothing for about 10 minutes then there was a knock on the bathroom door.

"I think we'd better go," Shanice said.

"Yeah, I'll be out in a minute."

"Ok, take all the time you need." She gives me another hug then heads out of the bathroom.

I walk over to the sink and clean my face up doing what I could to fix the blotchy mess I'd made of my make-up. I take a couple of deep breaths and put a smile on my face before I head back out into the party. After an hour of conversation and working the room we all head to the tables and take our seat as the fundraiser begins. There were a couple of keynote speakers and a few of the young men that were a part of the foundation that was now college graduates who shared their stories.

I tried to focus on what they were saying but my eyes were drawn over to the two of them as I watched her fall all over him, seated close, giggling, and laughing with each other. My heart sank from my chest and hit the floor. He hadn't looked at me twice the whole night, all of his focus was on her. It was like I didn't even exist to him anymore.

When the night came to an end I said goodbye to Shanice and Jonathan then headed out to the SUV and headed home letting the tears flow freely during the car ride.

Chapter Eighteen

Dejuan

"Fuck," I said to myself once I noticed Renea across the room talking to Shanice and Jonathan.

They told me she wasn't going to be here tonight, so why is she here? I take a deep breath and straighten my tie and fixing a smile on my face. I never would've brought big booty Jill with me tonight if I'd known, this can't possibly end well. She turns, and our eyes connect, and she smiles at me at her face glowing, but it quickly drops, and the smile fades away, when Jill joined me and placed her arm around mine. My heart dropped from my chest and I begin to regret this moment even more. Once we made our way over to the group and I introduced Jill, I didn't see Renea for a while after that. She'd run off so quick and I wanted to take off after her, but I didn't. I mean why should I? She said she didn't want anything to do with me anymore and that I should move on, so I'm only doing what she asked of me.

"Ladies would you excuse us for a second," Jonathan said, nodding his head motioning for me to step aside.

"What's up man?" I ask.

"Bro, what are you doing man?"

"I didn't know she was going to be here you both said she declined the invite." I snapped back.

"I left you two voicemails last night telling you that she would be here."

"Oh, damn. I didn't get a chance to check my phone last night. I was trying to make sure everything was straight for tonight."

"You know you just fucked up any chance you had, right?" he said.

I let out a heavy sigh before and shook my head at him and after a few minutes of talking quietly in away from everyone, we walked back over and join the ladies. Jonathan and Shanice headed off to talk to the rest of guest and do their thing. I grab Jill's hand and pull her towards the bar because I needed a much stronger drink. I ordered a glass of scotch and she gets a shot of tequila.

"So that was your ex, huh?" She said, with a devilish grin on her face.

"What?" I ask.

"Renea`. She's your ex-girlfriend, isn't she?" she asks again.

"Yeah, she is—or was."

"I thought so," she laughs. "it was obvious from the clear shade she'd thrown when I offered her a handshake." She said, quickly downing the shot. "So, what happened between the two of you? Was she too much for you to handle?"

I cut my eyes at her and she shrugs her shoulders, "I don't want to talk about." I finally reply.

"Fine by me," she turns and picks up the second shot glass and throws it back.

If this were any other time I would've been impressed, but at this particular moment, my mind was on Renea and the pained look that was on her face that I'd once again caused. We finished up or drinks and when it was time to be seated we found our seats and joined the others. Renea also returned and joined us at the table. I'd noticed her watching us a couple of times, but I tried not to make eye contact with her so that I wouldn't sour her mood.

She'd looked like whatever she was feeling before had passed as she smiled big and bright while listening attentively to the speeches and stories. I wanted to tell her that she looked gorgeous in her dress and the way it clung to her every curve made my dick twitch. I wanted to take her home and rip that dress right off her and fuck the shit out of her until she screamed my name.

Jill reached over and wrapped her arm around mine and whispered in my ear. Then reached my hand under the table and pressed it between her thighs as she whispered in my ear again.

"Watching you crumble in front of your ex is kind of turning me on. I would love to feel your finger fuck my pussy while she watches."

I move my hand from between her legs and she laughed laying her head on my shoulder rubbing her hand up and down my arm.

After the event was over I tried to catch Renea before she left but I was too late. Jill and I made our way to my Mercedes and we climb inside, I drop Jill off at her place and let's just say she wasn't very happy when I declined her invitation to come inside. I'd already made one unwise decision and I wasn't going to make another or make it worse by sleeping with Jill now that I know Renea still wants to be with me.

***

I waited a week before deciding to stop by Renea's place to see if we could talk. I mean it was time for us to either move on or work it out. I arrive at her building and I first greet nick then head over to the elevator, step inside, and press the button for the intercom. After a couple of seconds, her voice comes over the speaker and my heart pounds in my chest.

"Hello."

"Hi, it's me. Can I please come up so that we can talk?"

She didn't reply and for a second, I thought she had walked away and I had an empty feeling come over me. I close my eyes and let out a heavy sigh then open them and begin to walk out of the elevator, but she finally says something.

"Sure, come on up."

I don't know what I would've done if she hadn't responded. I knew that I was going to be heartbroken all over again and this time it was my fault. The doors open, and I step off the elevator and head down the foyer and into the living room where I find her seated on the sofa with her legs tucked under her and a glass of wine in her hand.

She sits her glass on the table and turns to look at me. I guess waiting for me to speak but I didn't know where to begin or what to say first, so I just went with the first thing that came to mind.

"I miss you beautiful."

She chuckles. "Really, so I guess fucking another woman is how you show someone you miss them nowadays, huh?" she said, her voice cold.

"I didn't sleep with her she was just my date to the event and that's it I promise," I reply.

"What do you want Dejuan," She asks, picking her wine glass back up from the table.

"You. That's all I've wanted from day one." I say in the sincerest way I possibly can.

Her eyes began to fill with tears, so I move closer to her, but she holds up her hand stopping me before I could get up from my seat. Why is she being so stubborn I know she still loves me I can see it in her eyes.

She looks down into her glass and says, "I'm scared."

"Of me?" I ask, confused.

"Of all the skeletons and baggage, you bring. I could have died Dejuan, that woman could have killed me, and for what, all because of all your past."

I run my hands over my face and let out a long breath through my nose. "I know beautiful and I'm sorry. I don't know how many times you want me to say it-- a million. Because I'll say it for the rest of my life if you want me, and I promise you I'll do any and everything to make it up to you whatever it takes."

She slowly gets up from her seat and walks over to me and presses her lips to mine kissing me passionately, I pull her onto my lap and deeper into the kiss. I lift her up and walk over to the sofa and lay her on her back, sliding in between her legs, pressing my body against hers. She begins to grind her hips underneath me as she kisses me harder and more feverishly, but I pull away and sit up quickly.

"What's wrong," she asks, still breathy from the kiss.

"Renea, I want this to be about more than sex."

"And it is," she said, "I love you Dejuan and I don't want to be with anyone else other than you."

She places her hand on my arm and pulls me back over to her and I lean in and kiss her again as we fall back on to the sofa. "Make love to me, Dejuan"

Chapter Nineteen

Renea

The next morning, I awake to his voice whispering from a distance. I sit up in bed and stretch my arms as I look around the room and I see him standing near the window naked. His back was turned to me and he was on a phone call, so I wasn't going to disturb him, I scooted back and rested against the headboard watching him begin to pace back and forth.

His body truly is sculpted to perfection. I sat back and watched his dick as it swung back and forth each time he passed back and forth, and his ass flexed with each step. I giggled, and he turned in my direction his eyes meeting mine. His lips parted into a small smile as he began to walk over to me. He leaned onto the bed, kissed my cheek, and whispered, "good morning beautiful," in my ear before placing the phone back to his ear. My pussy pulsed as his breath brushed over my neck and I could feel her getting moist responding to his touch. I thought that it was the end of us the other night when I saw him with that other woman, and for the first time in a long time, I was jealous. At that moment I could see her having the life that was supposed to be mine, with the man that I loved, and defeat filled the brim of my stomach. I sat on the sofa sulking in a pit of emotions, sipping on a glass of wine, and hoping that it would help ease my pain.

When the sound of the speaker filled the room, I'd thought it was Shanice coming to comfort me, but I was surprised when I heard Dejuan's voice. I was shocked, and I felt an overwhelming flood of emotions come over me, but I knew I had to contain myself. That is until he was right in front of me again. I was hoping that he'd come to apologize and beg me to let him back into my heart, but I also feared that he was here to give me closer and tell me to move on.

Even if he had I wouldn't have let him, I was determined to have him, to move forward and leave the past in the past.

"Hey beautiful," he said, hanging up the phone and sliding under the sheets beside me. Pulling the cover up and over the lower part of his body.

"Good morning handsome." I reply with a grin.

"I hope I didn't wake you," he says, leaning in, kissing my neck, and trailing them up to my lips. I smile at him and put my arms around his neck.

"No, you didn't. But you can put me back to sleep." I whisper softly.

"Mm… Tempting. But first I think we should grab some breakfast." He said, giving me a quick kiss on the forehead and getting up from the bed, looking around searching for his boxers.

I poke my lip out and pout as he walks into the bathroom and returns a couple minutes later with my toothbrush hanging out of his mouth. My mouth falls open and I jump out bed and over to him trying to grab it out of his mouth, but he playfully pushes me away. I jump on his back and he carries me into the bathroom then places me on my feet in front of the sink. He reaches over and grabs my toothbrush from the cup and hands it to me.

I smile at him and say, "oops," while batting my eyelashes at him and he lifts me up off my feet and tries to kiss me. "NOO… STOP! You have toothpaste all over your mouth, please stop." I shout.

He shakes his head no and leans in once more and plants a big kiss on my cheek. I wiggle free and wipe my face with the back of my hand, walk over to the shower, and turn on the water grabbing the shower head.

"Oh, you better not." He said, "Renea. Put it back on the handle, now."

I shake my head no smiling at him with a devilish grin and he rushes towards me, I hit the button and water sprays everywhere. After a couple of seconds, he was soaked and so was the bathroom floor. He grabs the sprayer out of my hand and tosses me over his shoulder smacking my butt. The spanking was kind of turning me on and I let out a loud moan with every smack to my backside.

"You like that don't you?" He asks, putting me down after we enter the shower.

"Yes," I lean in and try to kiss him, but he moves.

He backs me up against the wall pinning my body to it and lifting my arms above my head, holding them together above my head and using his other to slip out of his boxers. He turns me around and pushing me into the wall giving my ass another smack and I cry out as the stinging sent pleasure waves throughout my entire body. He places his hand on my ass rubbing it gently for a second and then SMACK, his palm hits my ass. My lady soul was leaking and my juices spilling down my thighs. He releases my hands and bends down lifting my leg up, placing my foot on the shower bench.

He kisses my ass gently then lets his tongue slide over my slit parting my lips with his tongue circling my clit. I gasp at the warmth of his mouth as he licks up my juices, sucking, and putting pressure on my pearl with his tongue.

"I want you inside me, baby."

"No. You've been a bad girl and bad girls don't get what they want." He says his voice deep and intense it sends chills down my spine.

He teases my clit over and over again sending another wave of orgasms ripping through my body. I couldn't take it anymore I wanted him inside of me, I need to feel him pushing deep into my walls sharing in the pleasures, but when I tried to turn around he stands up swiftly turning me and pinning me to the wall with my hands above my head all over again.

My breathing was faster, and my heart was racing as he ran his fingers through my hair pulling and tilting my head back exposing my neck. He let his tongue make small circles on my neck before kissing down to my breast, kissing the top of it before he began sucking, nibbling, and kissing on my nipples.

"Dejuan, baby please," I begged, my body trembling under his touch.

He smiles into my mouth as he kisses me, and he knew he had me and that I was powerless, and he was the one in control, and I must say I liked this side of him I like the feeling of him having complete control of my body, being aggressive, and telling me what to do. In my life, I'm always in control, every day that I wake up making decisions and telling people what to do and when to do it, so it was nice to have him dominate in the bedroom.

He turns me around again and places his hand on my back gently pushing me forward. I lean over and arch my back resting my arms on the bench then he lifts my ass in the air taking his dick into his hand and rubs the head of his dick between my pussy lips letting it brush my clit. I let out a moan and move my hips a little, but he stops taking his hand and smacking my ass harder this time.

"Be still," he says in a hard sexy tone and I do as I'm told.

He begins again and then pushing himself deep inside of me then pulls out doing it over and over again.

"Baby, I'm sorry, please I need you." I plead with him.

He smiles down at me then pushes into and pulls out one last time before pounding into me. He grips my waist and plunges deep inside me, fucking me hard and fast and I scream out as another orgasm rips through me and my pussy tightens around his dick.

"That's right baby come for me." He groans.

I throw my ass back matching his speed and rhythm hearing my ass clap every time we connect. My pussy tightens around him once again as I go over the edge and he pushes inside of me hard once more and I feel him as he erupts inside of me filling me with his seeds. He pulls out of me and rests his back against the tile and I fall onto the bench trying to catch my breath.

"So, umm we should probably grab that breakfast now," I say breathy, breaking the silence.

He turns and looks at me for a second and then we both burst into laughter. He takes my hand and pulls me up from the bench and into him squeezing me tight.

"I love you," he said kissing the top of my head.

"And I love you more," I reply.

***

Everything was finally going great. I was head over hills in love with my man, my career was back on track and I was finally on the road traveling for my tour and I was genuinely happy with how everything working out.

Basketball season was back and in full effect which meant that Dejuan was on the road allot as well. We tried hard to make time for each other and if we ended up in the same city then we would meet up or share a hotel while we were there, and he and his teammates had even come to a couple of my shows.

I sat in my dressing room as people were spilling in and out of the room as I was getting ready for tonight's performance. My make-up artist was beating my face when Dejuan and two of his teammates walked into the dressing room.

"You look gorgeous," He said as he walked over and kissed the top of my head.

"Baby you made it," I said, waving her away so that I could give him a hug.

I give him a long embrace then release him and turn back towards the mirror. My stylist clears her throat and looks over at Dejuan with a "no you didn't" expression on her face and he smiles at her.

"What's up ma." He says giving her a quick embrace and a kiss on the cheek.

"Mm-hmm... don't act like you not going to speak." She said waving the make-up brush in his direction. "And um Introduce me to your friends." She said, smiling seductively at the tall light skin guy.

"This is Braxton and Jay two of my teammates."

Braxton was the tall light skin one he reached out and took my stylist hand kissing the back of it and for a moment I thought she was going to pass out or fall to the floor the way she got weak in the knees.

"We're going to go over here and take a seat and let you finish getting ready." He kisses me again then heads toward the sitting area.

Once my makeup was finished I jump from my seat and run over to wardrobe and then I hurried to slip into my performance attire and head towards the stage. We all gathered together and said a quick prayer before heading out to the stage. We walked down the long hall finally reaching the stage after a couple of minutes. My dancers all fall in places and I made my way under the stage; the music begins, and the stage director turned to me and said, "you're up".

I step into place and slowly rise to the top of the stage as the lights began to flash and the crowd goes wild. They were singing and clapping their hands as they belted out the chorus of the song.

"Hey…. Let's go" I shout into the mic as I walk down to the center of the stage, joining in on the choreography with the rest of my dancers.

We performed 10 songs before closing out the show and after we get off the stage I congratulated my dancers, band, and background singers on a job well done tonight as well as the crew.

Dejuan and I make our way out to the car and head to the hotel. I wrap my arm around him and lay my head on his shoulder snuggling in real close and closing my eyes.

"Hey beautiful, let me ask you something."

"Sure. You can ask me anything." I reply.

"What do you think about getting a place together."

I raise my head meeting his gaze, "What?" I ask with a raised eyebrow.

"I'm just saying, look, I'm either at your place for weeks or you're at mine. And honestly, I'm tired of packing things back and forth, so why not move in together?"

"Hmm…" I say then shrug my shoulder. I lift his arm and place it around me, snuggling into his chest.

He chuckles and kisses the top of my head, "Just think about it beautiful."

I nod my head and close my eyes drifting off to sleep.

Chapter Twenty

Dejuan

The crowd roars in the arena as they cue the music and the intros begin as we head towards the entrance ready to make our way to the court as our names are called.

We put in work and ended strong, home 109/visiting 86. Once again, we walked away with a win and my team was hype about how our season's starting off. Our coach was happy with all the hard work we'd put in during the offseason and it was showing on the court. The team was focused and bringing their A-game and even I was impressed with how some of the guy's skills had improved.

"Yo that three from half court was amazing man," Parker said, imitating my shot with a whoosh sound.

"Yeah, that was pretty dope, huh," I replied bumping his fist and then shoulders.

"Yeah... man." He said as we headed into the locker room.

I take my phone out of my locker and send a message to Renea letting her know that we'd won tonight's game. I knew she wouldn't respond right away because at this moment she was probably tearing down the stage with her performance.

Our relationship has gotten a lot better and our love is stronger. A lot of people said that once we were back to our individual schedules and they began to clash that everything would fall apart, but I think the distances actually brings us closer.

I scroll through my contacts then press on Montez's name and listen to the line ring.

"What's up man?" Montez said after the second ring sounding a little winded.

"Yo, you good bro?"

"Yeah, I'm good. Shorty got me over here going hard in the paint."

I chuckle "Good that means she's doing her job. Tell Shannon I said hello and to push harder."

"Nah man, come on, she's killing me over here already."

I hired the best physical therapist in the business to help Tez get back on his feet and so far, he's making really good progress. I talked to Tez for an hour then we ended the call so that he could get back to his session. I hated seeing him down and I wish that I could have changed all that happened. I also know that Tez is strong and that he'll bounce back better than he was before.

I slept most of the plane ride as we head to the next state for tomorrow night's game. Once we arrived at the hotel I put my things in my room and changed into my workout gear then headed to the hotel's fitness center. I turned my music up in my headphones and get to work doing 5 miles on the treadmill and three sets of crunches on a swiss ball with plates.

My legs and my abs were on fire once I was finished with my workout, so I headed back up to my room to take a hot shower and relax before dinner. The guys and I were going to get together and grab something to eat after everyone was settled in and had some time to relax.

I touch my key card to the door and go inside kicking off my shoes at the door once I was inside. I walk towards the bedroom and when I rounded the corner I see a naked female lying on my bed and I stop mid-step.

"Mm, you look even sexier when you're sweaty." She said, moving from the middle of the bed and crawling towards the end on her hands and knees.

"Jill. What—how the fuck you get in my room." I ask, my voice rugged from all the heavy breathy.

"Oh, so you do remember me," she says in a sarcastic tone. "I told them that I was your fiancé and I wanted to surprise you."

She lays flat on her stomach staring at me seductively and waving me over with her finger. I run my fingers through my hair and then walk over to the end of the bed scooping up her clothes and throwing them at her.

"What are you doing?" she asks, confused.

"Get your clothes on and get out." I snapped.

She sucks in her teeth and scoots to the end of the bed sitting her clothes beside her and crossing her arms over her breast.

"So back in LA you wanted to fuck me and now you want to act all brand new. What's up with that?" She fumed, and I could hear the hurt and anger in her voice.

"Look I just got back with my woman and I'm not about to have you or any other broad fuck that up for me, so you've got to bounce."

"Oh. Ok. So, I see now." She grins "Well you know she could always watch while you're away and then join in when we're together back in LA." She smirks as she stands up and walks towards me stopping in front of me and rubbing her hand over my chest.

"No," I say in a stern voice, placing my hands on her shoulders and moving her away. "Look, you need to go and don't try and pull this shit again because the next time I won't be so nice."

She rolls her eyes and steps back. "Fine, but if you ever change your mind you know where to find me."

She walks back over to the bed and picks up her clothes sliding them on before going over and grabbing her purse from the chair in the corner of the room and then I walk her to the door. After she's gone I call down to the front desk and have them send up the manager, once he arrives I explain to him what just happened, and I ask him to bring me two new keycards for the room.

It's crazy how easy it is for a female to just walk in and say that they are your spouse or significant other and get into your hotel room. You would think that the hotel's security would be up on that shit and at least double check when there are so many psychos out there trying to get at celebs and ball players.

After he brings me the new keys and resets the locks to the door of my room I go shower and get dressed. I head down to the lobby to meet up with the fellas and they were all gathered at the entrance waiting for me. I walk over and dap it up with each one of them before we head out to the SUV and pull away from the hotel.

**

Renea and I walk along the beach to get to our cabana and I could feel every eye that was on us. The men were watching Renea as she walked alongside me, and the women they were watching the both of us. I don't blame though her breast was sitting up nice and perky and her ass jiggled to the rhythm of her walk, every bounce made my dick twitch. The team is in Miami for a couple of days, and she has two shows here. So, we decided to spend our time here together relaxing in the sun and doing a little swimming in the ocean.

"I love it here it makes me feel so relaxed and free." She says as we walk slowly into the water.

I take her hand and pull her close to me holding her in my arms and kissing her from her neck to her lips. She throws her arms around me and pulls me into the kiss and for a moment we lose ourselves then she breaks away.

"What?" I asked looking into her eyes as she smiles up at me.

"I want it to be like this always. You and me traveling the world together swimming in every ocean, experiencing life together, trying new things, and making new memories." She replies, looking up into the sky with a huge smile on her face.

"And we will beautiful, all of that and more. I want to grow old with you, make babies with you, and live my best life with you."

She snaps her head back to meet my eyes and I let out a loud laugh. I knew exactly what she's thinking and the look on her face was so cute that I can't help but to hold it in just a bit longer.

"Dejuan?" She said my name in a way that made it sound like a question.

"Calm down, I'm not proposing or anything. I just want you to know how I feel about you and that I see a future with you."

Her eyes light up and she pulls me in for another kiss, but I pull her under the water and she let's go and swims away from me, and I chase after her. We take a break from swimming and get some sun not that I really need any, I'm already chocolate enough.

"Baby, I'm getting hungry."

"Ok, maybe we should head back, and order room service."

"Sounds good, let's go."

We pack up our things and head back to the hotel and I place our orders while she showers. I'm glad she agreed to the room serves because I wasn't ready to share her with anyone else and lately going out to eat or being in public period was like stepping out on to the red carpet. Her fans were everyone and there seemed to be a camera flashing at every turn.

"Are you going to shower?" she asks drying her hair with the towel as she walked out of the master bath and taking a seat on the bed.

"Yes, I'm going now. Room service should be here any minute and I ordered you your favorite."

"Thank you, babe," She said reaching over and smacking my ass as I got up from the bed.

"Hey, watch out now," I say with a wink.

The hot water felt great on my body I was tired, and my muscles were tense. I was in need of a full body massage to relieve the stress but for now, the shower jets were doing the trick. I heard a knock at the door, so I cut off the water and dried off, wrapping the towel around my waist and head out of the bathroom.

"I'm starving beautiful, was that the…" my voice trailed off as I walked into the bedroom and seen Jill standing in the doorway and Renea beside her with her arms crossed.

"I guess your side piece got her days mixed up," Renea said, tilting her head to the side walking over and taking a seat on the bed staring at the both of us.

"Jill. What the fuck are you doing here?" I ask, anger streaming from each word.

"Well… hello to you to Dejuan." Jill smirks.

"Renea—" I start but she puts her hand up silencing me.

"What is this?" she asks, "You know what, Dejuan, I'm getting really tired of you and all of this basic bullshit." She said, running her hands over her legs then getting up from the bed.

"Let me explain."

"Explain what?" She said, whipping back around and facing me. "There is nothing to explain, Dejuan. You need to choose or I'm leaving and once I'm gone it'll be forever."

"Beautiful, I told you I don't want anyone else but you. The only reason I fucked with her is because I thought it was over between us."

She takes a step back from me. "So, you lied to me. You told me that you didn't fuck her." She shouts, her eyes wide.

"NO," I shout back, "I never touched her… I mean I was going to, yes, but it didn't happen. I promise you beautiful it never happened."

Jill laughs getting our attention. "So, you didn't tell her that you had me naked in your bed a week ago."

"What?" She shouts.

"Are you fucking serious?" I snap at Jill. "Don't listen to that bitch baby she's lying."

How in the hell is she finding out where I'm staying and why the fuck is she so obsessed with me? I didn't even touch the girl and she's bringing chaos? I turn to Renea again and walk closer reaching out to her, but she takes a couple of steps back away from me. I could see in her eyes the hurt, the anger, and the sadness that lingered, and I knew that she was about to break down and I knew once that happened there was no going back.

"Tell me you didn't?" She says shaking her head at me. "Please, tell me you didn't have sex with her in your hotel room in Dallas and then called me up like nothing happened."

"No. Baby, I didn't. I promise you nothing happened. She was in my room when I got there. She told the front desk that she was my fiancé, so they let her into my room to surprise me, but I put her out and called security. I spent the entire night out with the guys."

She watched me closely for a moment just staring into my eyes and then she turns and walks over to the bed and picks up her phone and walks back over to me. She puts her hand on the back of my neck and pulls me in kissing me passionately and I could hear Jill sucking her teeth and mumbling something under her breath.

"I believe you," She said releasing me and then she walks over to Jill. She snaps a picture of her before walking up to her and stopping directly in front of her barely leaving any space between them. "Ok.

Bitch. listen to me and listen to me well. What I need for you to do is turn around and walk your ass out of our hotel room and don't look back. He doesn't want you, so your desperate attempts are pathetic and it's really not a good look for you."

"I know you didn't just—"

Renea holds her hand up stopping her. "Yes, I did. And trust me you don't want these problems, you see I'm beyond the description of crazy, so don't tempt me." Renea says with a laugh and a look on her face that kind of scared me, to be honest.

"Are you threaten me?" Jill asks with a nervous giggle.

"No, of course not," She whispers, "I don't make threats only promises. So, are we clear?" She said her tone hard.

Jill looks over at me as I stand by the door with a smirk on my face. She rolls her eyes and grabs her purse and stomps out the door almost knocking over the guy who was waiting to bring in our dinner. I look at Renea with a raised eyebrow and a small smile appears on her face, and I shake my head pushing myself from the wall walking over and giving her a quick kiss on her forehead. I give the young man a tip and walk him back to the door before joining Renea in the living room.

We sit quietly and eat our food and I wanted to let her be the first to speak but she said nothing for the rest of the night. We cuddled in bed watching movies until it was time for her to leave out for her show and at that time I helped her get what she needed together and walked her down to the lobby.

I pull her in and kiss her lips softly. "Beautiful we need to talk about this."

"No…we don't." She said "I told you I believe you and I trust you, so let's just leave it at that. I'll see you later tonight." She gets up on her tippy toes and kisses me one last time before getting into the SUV.

I watch as they pull away and disappear into the distances. I walk back into the hotel with my mind racing, I was happy to hear that she trusted me, but something just didn't seem right, something seemed off. But I decided to shake the negative thought from my mind. I step into the elevator and I head back up to my room and once I was back inside I pulled off my shirt and walked into the master bedroom throwing myself on to the bed.

I close my eyes and let out a deep breath before closing my eyes.

Chapter Twenty-One

Renea

The nerve of her showing up to my man's hotel room thinking that she was going to get a taste of what's mine. But I made sure I checked that bitch and let her know to never cross my path again. Even after she left the hotel that night I had my team throw a couple of reminders her way just, so she doesn't forget. And just because I'm kind and sweet doesn't mean that I won't throw down with the best of them if needed.

"Hey, you ok?" Kiani asks, staring at me with a curious look on her face.

"Yes, I'm fine," I reply putting a reassuring smile on my face.

"Are you sure?"

I shake my head at her, "Yes"

"Alright, if you say so." She said still not convinced but she decided not to press the issue, "Well I have some not so good news. One of the dancers is out of tonight's show so there's going to be a couple of changes to one of the sets."

"Oh no, what happened."

"She's sick poor things being throwing up all day."

"Aw, ok. Well, I'll be there in a second and we can go over the changes."

"Alrighty then," She said pulling the door shut and leaving me in the empty room alone once again.

I settle back into the sofa and close my eyes getting back into my zone. Tonight's show was the last one and we were back in LA and I was happy to be home and happy to have completed a successful tour. Every show was sold out in each and every city and every crowd were amazing. I had a lot of fun and I enjoyed being on the road with my team and my whole crew once again, but all things must come to an end.

After I finished my meditation I headed out to the stage where my dancers were going over the dance routine that's being changed for tonight's show. I immediately join in and after about thirty minutes and two tries we nailed it. I felt comfortable with the changes, so everyone headed back to get dressed and ready to hit the stage in a couple of hours.

***

I stand in the middle of my closet trying to figure out what to wear to tonight's game. I'm going for something cute but not too sexy, I don't want to distract Dejuan or any of the other players from the game. I laugh just thinking about it, I could see it now the front cover of every magazine and the top story on every social media site blaming me for the teams losing streak because I couldn't keep my ass and tits covered up. I giggle once again and shake the thought from my head. I grab a pair of ripped jeans and a white t-shirt and head over to my shoe closet. Heels? No, not tonight. I think I'm going to go for the more comfortable look, so I grab a pair of sneakers off the shelf.

I get dressed then chose a purse that compliments my look best then head out. I get down to the lobby and I see Francisco waiting for me by the door.

"Good evening, Renea," He said.

"Hello, Francisco," I wink at him and he smiles back at me.

He opens the door and I get inside and take my seat, Shanice, Jonathan, and Kiani was joining me this evening for the home game. We stop at Kiani's first to pick up her and her son. As soon as we pull up Brandon runs out the front door and over to the SUV jumping up and down in place. Francisco got out and walked around the front of the car and over to the door to open it for him. He hops inside and over on to my lap wrapping his arms around me screaming.

"G-ma we're going to the game, we're going to the game," I wrap my arms around him and squeeze him tight giving him a great big hug.

When Kiani found out that she was pregnant she asked me to be her son's godmother and I happily excepted. I love kids, but I've never been in a rush to have any of my own mainly because I wanted to do it the right way, you know, to be in love and with a man that's going to stick around and raise his child.

Kiani came out the door a couple of minutes later and got inside with a huge grin on her face as she watched her son bounce up and down on my lap I returned the smile and leaned over to give her a hug once she was inside the car.

"Ah, you're squishing me," He says wiggling out from between us and we laugh. I rub the top of his head and he jumps into the back set and puts his seatbelt on.

"I'm ready now Mr. K, let's go!" He yells from the backseat with his hands raised in the air.

"Alright, little men it's time for takeoff," Francisco says looking back at him through the rearview mirror then pulls away from the building.

Once we arrive we find our seats and I look around to see if I could spot Jonathan and Shanice, but they hadn't made it yet. So, we take our time and order drinks, popcorn, and other snacks for Brandon. About 20 minutes later the two of them come strolling in and hurried over to take their seats giving us a quick hug along the way.

"Aunt Nesse come sit by me," Brandon says jumping in his seat.

"Hi, sweetheart," Shanice says taking a seat beside him, leaning over and giving him a big squeeze and a kiss on the cheek.

The lights go down and the music fills the room as the pregame intro begins. Brandon jumps from his seat dancing to the music and yelling "Oh yeah," but his mom pulls him back down in his seat and we all laugh.

My man is so fine, and I can't begin to explain to you how moist I get watching him run up and down the court as sweat drips down his body. Every muscle in his body toned and on display, his arms as he shoots the ball, the way his ass looks in those shorts.

"Girl you look like your about to take him down right here on the court," Shanice leans over and whispers interrupting my thoughts.

"Hmm... what are talking about," I say turning to look over at her.

"Mm-hmm... you know what I'm talking about," She says before mouthing the word nasty at me then laughing

I roll my eyes at her and turn my attention back to the game with a smirk on my face, she knows me too well and I swear it's almost like she can read my mind.

The buzzer sounds, and our team takes the win. Everyone jumps from their seats and rushes over onto the floor, I get up from my seat and look around for Dejuan. After a couple of minutes, I see him pushing through the crowd coming towards us smiling from ear to ear.

He grabs me lifting me off the floor giving me a big sweaty kiss and I start to squirm in his arms. He laughs and puts me down and I wipe my mouth with the back of my hand.

"Congratulations baby."

"Thanks. I'll see you soon beautiful." He said before giving Brandon a fist bump and then jogging off towards the locker room with the rest of the team.

The rest of us head over to the restaurant and wait for Dejuan and a few of teammates to join us along with their wives. The food was great, and the conversation was flowing between everyone for a moment until one of the wives got a little catty and decided she was going to try and read Shanice, but she quickly shut that down. I guess they were embarrassed about how things ended because they decided to leave early, and no one was complaining about it. We were all actually relieved to have the negative energy leave the table.

Everyone said their goodbyes after dinner and headed off.

Chapter Twenty-Two

Dejuan

I step onto the porch and ring the doorbell then wait patiently for Montez to let me in. I hear a lot of commotion inside and the sound of things falling over on to the floor, so I knock again and call out to him through the door.

"Hold up bruh, I'm coming." He shouts.

Finally, I hear the latch and then the lock and he slowly opens the door but not wide enough for me to see in. He looked like he was preoccupied with something or someone and he was naked and using only one crutch to hold himself up.

"Yo, you alright?" I ask, trying to glance inside but he pulls the door closed.

"Yeah man…um," he stops and glances over his shoulder. "this isn't a good time for me right now."

"What? Man get out the way, I didn't drive all the way over here to stand in the door." I said pushing past him.

I walk in the living room and I see Shannon standing in front of the massage table naked with handcuffs dangling from one arm. I turn back and look at Montez and he was standing behind me with his hand over his face shaking his head.

"Mm-hmm... so this is what I'm paying for?" I ask with a chuckle. "Um, Shannon, sweetheart I'm paying you to fix my man not give him a happy ending."

"Ah… come on man." He says embarrassed.

"Hey, there's nothing wrong with a little of both." She said biting her bottom lip and winking at me.

I smile back at her and turn to head back towards the door. "I'll hit you up later man. Shannon, try not to hurt him, babe." I wink at her then leave.

I get back in the car and head over to my place in long beach. I haven't been there since the shooting happened, but I figured it was about time that I made my way there. I pull into the driveway and put the car in park and I see someone open the door and movement on the porch, so I wait. A second later my mom pops her head out and waves to me grinning when she notices me. I get out the car and start towards the porch and the front door opens, and my little brother walks out.

"What's up big bro?" Jamie asks, jogging down the sidewalk meeting me halfway.

I give my mom a hug and then my brother. I hadn't seen him in a while and he'd gotten taller, almost as tall as me and he's put on some muscle too. I guess all the training and working out was paying off because he was not my scrawny little brother anymore.

"What's up little bro? Man look at you, you are getting all buff and things." I say as we bump fists.

"Yeah, the coach has me on this crazy workout."

"I know the females are lined up trying to get at you," I say with a smile as we bump fist.

"Humph, he better be in between the pages of them books and not between some female's legs. We don't need him ending up like you marrying some no-good thot that's only after what he's got." Mom said placing her hand on her hips and rocking side to side as she spoke.

"Dang…Ma, you just going to shade me like that." I said, "And do you even know what a thot is?"

"Yes. I. do. Don't try and treat me like some old fart boy, I know the meaning of the little slang words you youngsters use nowadays." She snapped.

"Come on ma lets go inside before you get your blood pressure up," Jamie says taking my mother's hand and leading her in the house as he looks back at me with a smirk on his face.

I shake my head and follow them inside closing the door behind us. My mother Ella Washington-Taylor was always the type to tell it like it is and she never held anything back and she would always let us boys have it. When my father passed away she took it hard, she didn't know how she was going to raise two boys on her own, but she did it. Working two jobs, getting us into sports, after-school programs. And we didn't turn out too bad. My brother and I are lucky to of had two strong women in our lives and we will be forever grateful for out stepfather coming in and stepping up and treating us like we were his very own.

"Where's pops?" I ask.

"Oh, he's working. You know that man has to be doing something productive with his life or his day just doesn't go right." She laughs, "How about you come and sit down and tell me about that beautiful new woman in your life." She pats the seat beside her on the couch and I sit down beside her.

"What can I say she's everything I could ever want in a woman. Talented, smart, beautiful, a voice like an angel, and she makes me want to be a better man."

"Well, that is lovely baby. You make sure that you hold on to her she sounds like a pretty amazing young woman and you look so much happier." She said patting me on the knee.

"Thanks, ma and I am."

"So, when do we get to meet her?"

"Yeah bro when are you going to bring her to meet the fam?" My brother asks with a broad smile on his face.

"Soon ma. She just came off tour, so let's give her a little time to relax and then we'll do dinner."

"Sounds good to me. I'll let your grandmother know and we can get together at her place."

I lean in and kiss her on the cheek. "I love you ma."

"And I love you, my son." She says, smiling up at me.

Chapter Twenty-Three

Renea

After months of pondering I finally agreed to move in with Dejuan and last week, we began searching for our first home together. We'd talked about moving from the city before but now that we were serious we really needed to make up our minds. I want to buy a house in Malibu and he wants to move to Bel-air or Long Beach, so we've been looking in all three areas instead of choosing one so that we can let the home and the area pick us.

The homes that we'd gone to in Long beach were single-family homes nothing to big. It was a perfect suburban neighborhood where you would see kids out playing in the front yard and riding their bikes in the street, you know one of those nice quiet places where nothing ever happened. And honestly that wasn't what I was looking for and neither was he. Although it was the place where he'd grown up our lifestyle now required a little more security then these homes could offer, so we moved on.

We looked at a few penthouses and condos in the city and there wasn't any real spark, but by the third try we'd finally found the one and it was perfect. A Balinese-style oasis with a panoramic view to the Santa Barbra Islands, a private entrance to the beach, 5 bedrooms, 7 bathrooms, a custom pool, waterfall spa, studio, theater, and a basketball court inside.

The luxurious spa-like bath in the master suite was wonderful with full windows so that you could look out onto the ocean and I must say it as a very relaxing view. I'm sure that this will be the place that I come to unwind after a grueling day or after coming back from tour.

We put in our offer and was waiting to hear back from our real estate agent. Two days later my phone rings and she let us know that we were the new owners of that amazing home and that beautiful piece of land. We were both excited about the move, but when the day came I was left to do all the hard stuff because basketball season was still in full effect and he was still on the road. After we were all settled in and living life or maybe I should say adjusting to our new life things were slowly coming together for us.

"Where are you beautiful? Daddies home," I hear Dejuan say as he enters the house.

I get up from the sofa and run into the foyer and leap into his arms planting kisses all over his face. He carries me into the living room and sits me down on the sofa, but I move to his lap and straddle him as I pull his shirt up and over his head. I unbuckle his pants and carefully unzipping them and freeing his semi-erect penis. I stood and quickly removed my shorts and climb back on top of him.

"Slow down beautiful," he said grabbing my waist.

I sit back on his lap and stroked his dick until it was hard and ready for me. I positioned him at my opening and slowly eased down on top. I let out a soft moan as I slide on his dick taking it all, staying still for a second to let my lady soul adjust.

He leans up and pushes my hair from my neck and begins kissing me from my neck and down to my breast cupping each one with his hands as he sucked on each of my nipples, gently biting them sending an intense rush of pleasure to my groin. He places his hand around my neck pushing me back as I rest my hands on his knees. He lets out a groan as I start to move up and down slowly riding him as he looked into my eyes.

I could feel my juices running down his dick. I tilt my head back and began moving faster placing my feet flat on the cushions to support myself as I squeezed my pussy tighter and bounced on his dick a little faster.

"Ah. Yes. beautiful. You missed riding your dick didn't you baby," He says pulling me forward as I place my hands on the back of the sofa.

"Omg, yes," I scream out as I feel myself getting closer and closer.

"Cum for me baby, I feel you, cum on your dick."

He sits up holding me tight around my waist and begins pounding into me harder. The pain of him being so deep inside of me sends me over the edge and my orgasm rips through me as my pussy tightens around him and I feel him let go deep inside of me causing me to crumble all around him again and again.

I lean into his chest breathing heavily as he falls back onto the sofa trying to catch his breath. We sit quietly for a while not moving I just lay there listening to his heart pounding in his chest.

"I love you Renea," He says breaking the silence.

I smile into his chest then lift my head so that I can look into his eyes. "I love you too, Dejuan," I say then lean in and kiss his lips softly.

"How about a shower I think we might be able to squeeze in round two," he says with that sexy smirk then lifts me up and carries me to the master bathroom.

It's been an awhile since I've been this sore from sex. My legs ached, and my body was hurting all over, a whole three days of rough sex had worn me out and he was like the energizer bunny. I walked slowly into the bathroom and turned on the water filling the tub then adding some scented oils to relax and ease some of the pain.

I slid into the tub and laid my head back on to my cushioned pillow and let the jets massage away the pain from my body.

"Are you ok beautiful?" he asks.

I turn and see him standing in the doorway. "Yes, I'm great," I reply with a smile.

He walks over to the tub and kneels at the side leaning over to kiss me. I love the way his lips taste I just can't get enough of him, I reach up and place my hands on the nape of his neck pulling him into the kiss deeper, but he pulls back from the kiss and smiles down at me.

"I think you're trying to start something," he laughs reaching his hands in the water and splashing me. "I think we both need a break."

And he was right we really did need to take a break and the expression on his face let me know that his body was just as tired and pained as mine. I sit up and scoot forward in the tub then turn to him and lean my head to the side motioning for him to join me. He stands up and removes his shorts and climbs in behind me and I relax my body against him once he gets comfortably positioned.

"So, my family thinks that it's time that they get to meet you. What do you think about that?" He says rubbing his hand over my hair.

"I think they're absolutely right, it is time. You've met my parents, and I would love to meet your family."

"Alright, then that's settled I'll call my mom and my Gamma and let them know where coming to Sunday dinner."

"Great. I hope I leave a lasting impression."

"They're going to love you beautiful."

Chapter Twenty-Four

Dejuan

I put on a brave face and suck a little breath in and quickly exhale before getting out of the car and rushing over to open Renea's door.

It was 6 pm and I knew that they were all anxiously waiting for us to arrive. My Gamma was usually finished cooking by this time and was setting the dinner table with my mother trailing behind her. It'd been that way for as long as I could remember, Sunday dinner with the whole family sitting around the table sharing how their week had gone and what the goals were for the next week.

I turned the knob on the door and Renea's arm tightened around mine.

"Relax, beautiful," I said, with a smile and she shook her head with a nervous smile on her face.

I open the door further and we step inside. All the different smells hit us as we walked in the door and our nostrils flared up as we took in a deep breath savoring each and every one of them. My Gamma knew what she was doing when it came to a home cooked meal and she sure could throw down in the kitchen. My stomach growled as I thought of biting into a piece of her fried chicken and scooping up a big helping of Mac & cheese that was made from scratch.

I opened my eyes just as my mom was coming into the living room from the hall. She jumped a little once she noticed the two of us standing there quietly in the entryway.

"Oh my gosh, you scared me, baby, I didn't know the two of you were here already. Come here and give me a hug." She said walking towards us with her arms extended out in front of her.

She walks over and hugs me first squeezing me tightly in a bear hug and then turns to Renea staring at her with a doting look on her face with her hands clasped together over her mouth.

"My darling you are ever so beautiful. I'm so happy to finally meet the young woman that is bringing so much joy to my son's life." She said, before leaning into a big warm embrace.

Renea put her arms around my mother and returned the embrace and I could see her body relaxing and her lips turn up into a small smile. My brother came strolling into the living room just as my mother and Renea released each other and if I didn't know any better I'd think my brother was star struck. He froze in place with his mouth practically hanging to the floor, so I cleared my throat trying to get him to snap out of it before I introduced the two of them.

"Hey, big bro you made it." Jamie said after finding his voice.

I walk over and give him a manly embrace then step back so that I could introduce him to Renea. But before I could get the words out of my mouth he'd already scooped her into his arms hugging her tight. I held back a laugh as I watched the surprised expression on Renea's face when my brother lifted her from the ground.

"It's so nice to meet you." He said holding her in the air.

"Alright, that's enough bro put her down." I said.

He released her and placed her feet steadily back on to the ground and she straightens her dress before she turns and gives him a big loving smile.

"Come on, I'm sure you two are starving I can hear your tummies all the way over here." my mom said, waving us towards the kitchen.

Renea took my hand and I kissed the back of it before following my mother down the short hallway to the dining room.

Chapter Twenty-Five

Renea

His family is so loving, and his grandmother is hilarious. We sat at the table laughing, talking, and enjoying our time together. After dinner, his mother and grandmother were telling me stories about Dejuan and his brother when they were kids. I'd never laughed so hard in my life, but his grandmother had me gripping my stomach. She held back no punches and I could see the embarrassment on the two of their faces as she told a few stories that had even me blushing a little. But his family was beautiful, and I could see that his mother was proud of her boys by the way she spoke of their accomplishments and how excited she was about their future.

"So Renea how did you and my brother meet?" His brother asks.

"Well—," I hesitated not knowing if I should give the complete story. "It was at the finals last year. His best friend and my best friend are a couple and they introduced us as we were heading to the team's celebration party."

"Oh, Dejuan, you didn't tell me that Jonathan has settled down." His mother said, shooting a surprised look in his direction.

But he remained quiet picking up his glass from the table and taking slow sips from his cup, trying hard to avoid eye contact with his mother and everyone burst into a fit of laughter. We continued our conversation and then Dejuan and Jamie took our plates clearing the table as his mother grabbed dessert.

She came out of the kitchen with a tray in her hand and placed it on the dining room table. She sat the apple pie in the middle and then handed each of us a small bowl that was filled with Vanilla ice cream. The smell of the cinnamon and baked apples filled my nostrils making my mouth water I couldn't wait to dig into a slice.

After dessert, we head into the living room to relax and unwind and after all that good comfort food we needed a good stretch. I cuddled up next to Dejuan on one end of the sofa while his mom sat on the other end. His grandmother sat across from us in an old rocker and his brother in a chair opposite of her on the other side of the room.

She sat rocking back and forth humming an old song that sounded very familiar, so I closed my eyes and let the soft sound of the melody fall over me. I began to remember the words to the old church hymn that my grandma used to sing to us as she cooked dinner and the words began to flow out of me.

As I finished singing the last part of the chorus I opened my eyes and found everyone in the room was staring at me with their eyes wide and at that's when I realized that I'd started to sing out loud and not only in my head.

"You have a very beautiful gift, my dear." Said his grandmother with a soft smile.

"Thank you," I said, returning the smile as my cheeks flushed.

She started rocking in her chair again and this time singing instead of humming. Her voice was so big and powerful and when she got to the chorus she nodded my way for me to join in. We sang together in harmony as the others closed their eyes and listened enjoying the beautiful melody.

***

My agenda for today is jam-packed so I know that it's going to be a full day of chaos, and I need to have my morning coffee before it all begins. I walked into the Coffee shop with Euro alongside me in my usual get up that most days does an excellent job of hiding my identity.

"Good morning ma'am, what can I get you?" the bistro asks with a pleasant smile on her face.

I give her my order and she punched it in, I swiped my card before she could say the total of my order then she tore off my receipt and I quickly walked over to the pick-up area and found a place in the crowd of people waiting. Kiani had insisted on picking up my morning cup of jo on her way over but I liked getting out every now and then. It was nice to be out in the world doing what everyone living a normal life had the opportunity to do each and every day.

Once I receive my order and we get back into the SUV, Euro pulls into the early morning traffic and heads into downtown LA. I have two photoshoots today with two amazing photographers that I adore, and then it's off to the Elan show to do the pre-tapping.

"Kerry wants to know if you're going to be walking the runway this year?" Kiani asks walking with me trying to keep up with my pace.

"Tell her, yes, but I have a few requests," I reply.

"Okie dokie and noted."

I slip my shoes off as I walk in the door picking them up and holding them by my side as I walk through the foyer heading towards my room when I hear voices followed by laughter in the kitchen. I turn on my heels and head in the opposite direction leaving Kiani and heading towards the kitchen. The voice didn't sound familiar to me, so I took my time walking down the hall so that I could listen to their conversation.

I find a gorgeous brunette sitting at the kitchen island with her head tilted back laughing and Dejuan standing on the other side of the island laughing as well. She was first to notice me, and her smile got bigger as she starred at me with her big gray eyes.

"Hello," she said.

"Hi," I say in a confused tone.

"Hey, beautiful your home early." He said walking over to me and pulling me into an embrace and kissing me. "I missed you."

"I missed you too—," my voice trailed off as I looked from him to her and back again.

It took him a moment to catch on to the reason the room fell silent. But after a couple of seconds, it was like a light bulb had gone off in his head and he took my hand leading me over towards the brunette.

"Beautiful this is Shannon. She's a physical therapist that works with the team and right now she's working with Tez on his recovery in more ways than one." He said, with a wink and her cheeks turn a light shade of pink.

"Yo, the bathroom is huge," Tez said, as he walks into the kitchen. "Aye, shorty what's up."

I remembered him from Dejuan's when I'd caught him in Long Beach. He walks over and kisses me on the and I turn to look at him a little shocked that he was acting as if we were great friends. He walks over and puts his arms around Shannon pulling her in close.

"She must be one hell of a therapist," I say to myself as I watched him press his lips to hers kissing her erotically and I turned to look at Dejuan my eyes wide.

"Yeah, so I'm going to go and change," I say.

"Ok beautiful," he says and leans in kissing my cheek.

I say goodbye to Kiani then head down the hall, I walk into the master bedroom and throw my shoes in the walk-in closet. I'm too tired to go over and put them in their correct place. I pull my shirt over my head then slip out of my jeans. I left them in a pile on the floor and went into the bathroom to run a hot bath once the tub was full I put a few drops of lavender-vanilla in the water. I close my eyes and relaxed allowing the water to massage away the tension in my muscles.

I step out of the tub and onto the plush carpet before grabbing my towel and drying off, I wrap myself up in the towel as I walk over to the chair and take a seat. I remove my hair clips letting my curls fall down around my face as I looked at myself in the oversized mirror. I really need a hair appointment and a trip to the spa for a facial.

I take some of my body cream and rub it into my palms and began massaging my shoulders working the cream over my skin.

"Let me do that for you," Dejuan said walking into the bathroom and placing his hands on my shoulders.

I close my eyes and let my head fall forward as his masculine hand's work out the kinks in my neck and shoulders.

"I just came back to check on you. I thought maybe you'd falling asleep since you never came back to join us."

"I was enjoying a hot bath, I'm a little tired," I reply with a deep sigh.

Coming home to this man made me feel so complete, grounded, and happy.

Chapter Twenty-Six

Dejuan

"After you," I say opening the door for my mother and Shanice.

We walk in the jewelry store and an older blonde lady greets us. We say hello and ask her to point us in the direction of the engagement rings, she walks us over to a huge display case filled with rings of all shapes and sizes. My mother gasps in excitement as she stares into the case admiring all the beautiful pieces that were displayed.

"So, best friend, what does she like?"

"She's in love with Halo rings," Shanice shouts as her lips turn up into a smile.

"Alright," I said turning to the sales lady. "We'd like to look at the Halo rings, please."

She shakes her head and leads us over to another display case with an array of different Halo rings all varied sizes and designs. My head starts to swim as I feel overwhelmed by all the choices and I was happy that I decided to bring them along with me.

My mother and Shanice walk back and forth pointing to the rings and chit chatting as the lady pulled each of the rings from the case and handed them over. After 20 minutes they call me over to the end of the case where they have 4 rings set out in front of them.

"These are our top picks and we think she would love either of them, but the final decision is yours." My mother says gently running her hand over my arm.

I take a deep breath and step up to the case so that I could get a closer look. I'd learned over the past year that she wasn't hard to please, and she didn't really stress over material things. She liked the simple things and even though she's wealthy and could have it all, anything that she wanted, she was still happy with the simple things.

And at that moment I realized that I didn't want to buy just any ring. I wanted it to be special and the ones that sat before me were all beautiful, but I wanted to make it irreplaceable. So, I ask to speak with the designer and luckily, he was onsite today so the sales lady left us to go and retrieve him from the back.

"Dejuan Washington, what a pleasure it is to meet you." Mr. Nile Lance said as he approached us with his hand extended.

"It's a pleasure to meet you as well," I say taking his hand and giving it a firm shake.

Nile Lance is the top jeweler to the stars he's made about every A-list celebrity engagement and wedding ring. And now was my chance to have him design the perfect engagement ring for me to present to Renea.

"So, what can I do for you this evening?" he asks.

"I'm going to be proposing to my girlfriend—," I began.

"Ah, yes, the beautiful Renea Dubley." He says

"Yes. And I want to design a special piece for her. Not to say that the rings you have here aren't amazing I just want it to be," I pause searching for the right word and he holds up his hand.

"No need to say anything further I get what you're saying, and I couldn't agree more. Come with me we're going to go right this way and we'll get started."

He takes us back to a room where we sit and discuss all of my ideas and my mother and Shanice throw in a few as well. After an hour he held up a sketch that was the perfect image of the ring that I had once only imagined in my mind. I shake his hand and thank him before heading back down to the sales lady and giving her my information and then we head out of the store.

"Hello Dejuan," I hear a familiar voice say.

I turn and see Jaylyn a couple of steps away from us.

"Mrs. Taylor," she says then glances over at Shanice and rolls her eyes before she turns her head back in my direction.

My mother turns and looks at me. "Don't even bother addressing this—"

I stop my mother before she could finish what she was going to say because I knew what was coming next if I allowed her to go on.

I take my mother's arm and we turn and continue walking towards the car as Shanice followed alongside us. I could hear her devilish giggle as she walked away, and I turn my head shooting her a look that made the smile on her face disappear immediately.

***

I watched as the event planner guided and instructed the decorators and the rest of her team around the backyard as they put everything in place making sure that every detail was exactly the way I had described it to her.

Renea had healed a heart that was once broken and changed me from the man that I was once was. I was cold-hearted, emotionless, and just a pure asshole that didn't care about anyone or anything other than my mother, my brother, and the fellas. And today I was going to ask her to make me complete, to close the void that I was feeling in my heart and become my wife.

"So, Mr. Washington what do you think? Is everything to your liking?" Samantha asks, rolling her hand out in front of her.

I glance around the yard. "It's perfect."

"Good. So, I'm going to have the ring tied to the puppy's collar and when she walks through the doors and into the yard you'll be standing here."

"Sounds good."

She calls out to a young lady in the yard telling her to hurry up because time was almost up. The ladies took Renea out to get pampered so that she would be out of the house and they could keep tabs on her and have her come back at just the right time.

I'd invited all of our family and friends over to celebrate with us and be a part of this special moment. Renea's real big on family so I wanted to make sure that her mother and father were here when I proposed. Although after I ask her father's permission he insisted that it wasn't necessary for me to do so, it felt right to be that he is the most important man in her life.

Mr. Dubley, Jonathan, and my stepfather had come over after the women left to help out around the house, but we really just sat around drinking beer and watching the workers decorate.

The guest began to arrive, so I knew it was close to the time for ladies to return to the house. We cleaned up the mess that we'd made and straightened the area up then I placed the big gift box on the table.

Once everyone had arrived I sent them all out to the guest house to hide out until it was time for them to surprise her. My phone chimed, and I swiped my finger across the screen then pulled up the message from my mother.

Mom: 5 minutes away!

My heart pounded in my chest and the calm demeanor that I once had was gone. I rushed towards the backyard to take my place and make sure that everyone was clear from my site. As I stepped out the door and looked around, I was amazed by how everything was just how I'd pictured it. All of the little extra things that my mother and her mom, as well as Shanice, had requested were added and looked great.

"Perfection!" I whispered.

MY DREAM MAN

Chapter Twenty-Seven

Renea

I let out a relaxed breath, today was exactly what I needed I got to hang out with my best friend, my mother, and my bonus mom. We went to the salon and spa then we did some shopping because you know a little retail therapy is a great way to unwind, and seeing my mom hit it off with Mrs. Taylor was so heartwarming.

I wave to them as they pull off and around the long driveway and head back towards the gates. I'd ask them to come and have a glass of wine, but I think we'd done enough damage with the three bottles we'd had earlier at the spa.

I walk into the living room and I see a box sitting on the coffee table with a big red bow on it and a card.

"Dejuan," I call out but no answer. "Baby are you home?" still no answer.

I sat down my purse and my shopping bags and took out the card.

I have a question for you!

I read the card again then I place it on the table. I reach over and remove the huge bow from the box then take the top off and look inside, I place my hands over my mouth as my heart fills with excitement and joy. I take out the puppy holding it tight to my chest as he wiggles around in my arms, "he bought me a puppy" I say to myself. I looked him over checking his collar to see if he had a name but all I found was a ring dangling from his collar, I wasn't sure exactly why he was wearing a ring, but my eyes began to tear up as one thought came to mind so I got up from the sofa to go find Dejuan.

"Baby, where are you? Dejuan, come on stop playing and come out," I say, as I walk through the house.

After checking our room, the media room, and the den I finally make my way through the kitchen and out to the back of the house. I open the doors to the backyard and I see all of the beautiful roses and the decorations.

"Hey Beautiful," He says popping out startling me.

"Omg, baby what are you doing?" I say throwing arm loosely around him.

"I see you found one of my surprises," he says smiling at me

"I did. Thank you, baby, I love him. What's his name?" I ask, looking down at him.

"Whatever you want to call him."

I hold him up in front of me and look at him thinking of a good name to give him. "I think I'll call him Marley," I say kissing him and snuggling him once again.

"Nice, I like it." He replies leaning in and kissing the top of my head.

"Come with me, I have one more surprise for you," he says taking my hand and leading me out further into the yard.

I notice a trail of red roses leading out into the yard along with tons more filling the yard. They were in the shape of a heart with something spelled out in the middle.

"Dejuan, baby, what is that?" I ask heart begins to thump in my chest and tears filled my eyes.

"Go take a look," he says letting go of my hand.

I walk over to the oversized heart made of roses filling our backyard and looked inside, 'WILL YOU MARRY ME' it read. I turn back to face him, and I see him kneeled on one knee with the puppy in one arm and a small red box in his other hand.

I slowly walk back over to him as tears rolled down my face.

"I can't go another day knowing that I haven't placed a ring on your finger or made it official. We are two souls that were lost and wandering trying to find our way back to each other. And now that I've found you, my soulmate, it's only fitting that we take the next step. So, Renea' Dubley will you do me the honor of being my wife?"

I find myself crying even harder and unable to get the word out, so I just shake my head yes then run over and fall into his arms kissing him over and over again.

As he helps me up I see something out the corner of my eye and when I turn I see our moms and Shanice walk out into the yard with huge smiles on their faces and tears streaming from their eyes.

He winks at them then mouths the words. "she said yes," giving them a thumb up.

They all let a squeak and run back towards our guesthouse and a few seconds later the rest of our family and friends come walking out into the yard clapping and cheering. I fall into him and the waterworks start up again as I watch them flood our backyard. He'd planned this whole thing with our mothers and Shanice without me knowing. So not only did I get a proposal, I walked right into my engagement party as well.

The ring was huge and a perfect and so was he.

I was so overwhelmed with emotions and nonstop tears that it seems like the night had gone by in the blink of an eye. Everyone began to slowly make their exit and finally, there were only a few of us left his gamma, our parents, Shanice, and Jonathan.

"I'm so happy for the two of you," Shanice said as her eyes started to tear up again.

"Oh, please, don't cry. I don't think I can handle another crying session." I say, and everyone laughs.

My eyes were tired, my voice hoarse from all the crying, and my cheeks hurt from smiling so much. This was the best day of my life and I really didn't want it to end or see my family go but it was late, so we walked them to the door and waved goodbye as we watched the cars disappear one by one.

"Well future Mrs. Washington are you ready for bed?" He said, putting his arms around my waist and pulling me close.

"Well, Mr. Washington, I think the real question is, are you?" I reply smiling up at him gazing into his lust filled eyes.

I run my tongue slowly across his bottom lip and he leans in and scoops me up into his arms.

I could feel the connection, the intensity, and the need to have me, as he pushed deep inside me as he made love to me slow and passionately. I could feel every unspoken word with each stroke and when we reached our climax it was as if our souls connected and we'd become one.

Chapter Twenty-Eight

Dejuan

I sit patiently waiting for my agent to finish up his meeting. He called me a few days ago to discuss business, but I told him whatever it was it was going to have to wait. I didn't want anything to interfere with my proposal to Renea.

"Hey, Dejuan, how are you, my man?" Harlan says as I walk into his office.

"I'm doing great Harlan. What's up?" I reply, taking the seat in front of his desk.

"I just got a call from one of the top men magazine and they want you to be on the cover?"

"That's great. Set it up."

"Another thing I've been getting calls asking me to confirm that you and Miss Dubley are engaged."

"I'm letting her decide whether or not she wants to share that with the rest of the world. So just hit them with a no comment or a simple no."

"Got it," he stands and extends his hand out to me and I take it giving him a firm handshake.

I walk out to the elevators and press the button and wait for one to arrive. The sweet aroma of Chanel No. 5 gets my attention and I look around trying to find the body wearing the fragrance. But the elevator dings and the doors open so I step inside after everyone has exited the elevator. A faint voice calls out "hold the elevator," and I quickly press the button as the sound of the heels click faster and the woman rushes to the doors.

"Thanks."

"No problem," I say look up from the buttons.

And there she was dressed in a pair of stilettos, a romper dress that clung to her every curve, and her long black hair pushed back into a ponytail that hung down to the middle of her back.

"Olivia? How the fuck did you get out?" I ask, anger building inside of me as she looked at me smirking.

"It's nice to see you to Dejuan."

"Don't fucking act like you—" I say stepping over to her and she pulls a gun from her handbag.

"tis, tis," She said shaking her finger at me, "Settle down boy, let's not do something you'll regret."

I step back and press my back against the wall as I watch her with a grin on my face. She looks confused by my sudden calm demeanor. I cross my arms across the front of my chest waiting for her to continue saying whatever it was that she'd come to say. But she remained quiet not saying a word just starring back at me with a snarling look on her face.

"You don't scare me Dejuan. Because unlike your fiancé I know all about you and what you're capable of, so I'm well prepared to do what I have to." She says stepping closer.

I remain still and calm. She tries to hide her panic in her eyes once she realizes that her words are having no effect on me. The elevator sounds, and the doors open, and I extend my hand for her to go first, she places her gun back in her purse and then turns and walks out the elevator being sure to keep her eyes on me.

We walk out the on to the street and I head over to where Maverick is parked waiting for me. She looks at me for a second and then turns to head the other way, but I reach out and grab her arm pulling her in the direction of the SUV. She whips her head around and tries to jerk her arm away, but I squeeze tighter. She fixes her mouth to say something but quickly changes her mind noticing the look on my face. A familiar look, one she's seen plenty of times before, so she knew not to fuck with me.

I shove her into the back of the car and then I climb in beside her. Maverick shoots me a look of confusion before taking his place in the driver's seat and sitting silently waiting for my directions.

I reach over and slide my hand down her ponytail and her body tenses. "You've either turned into one hell of a psycho bitch or you have a death wish," I say wrapping her ponytail around my hand and jerking it back.

A breath catches in her throat and I feel her body began to tremble, she was afraid, and she was right to be.

"Dejuan, let me go," She said, swallowing hard. "You don't want to start a war with me."

I lean in closer and whisper in her ear. "The war began the moment you sent your sister's boyfriend to take out me and my crew. So, unless you want to join your boyfriend in the afterlife you might want to shut the fuck up and sit real still."

A tear rolls down her cheek and I release her hair.

She sits up and straightens herself in her seat. "You took everything from me." She said in a hard tone.

"I took nothing from you, Olivia," I reply.

She quickly wipes the fresh tears from her face before she spoke again. "You broke my heart and then you took away the one man that ever truly loved me."

"No, Olivia, that was Maylan. The man that you let into your bed, the one you were fucking every night, that's who killed your father." I spit the words out at her.

"That's not true," she said shaking her head.

I turn and look at her studying her face for a moment and then it hit me. "Where's Jaylyn? When's the last time you saw her?" I ask.

Something wasn't right I'd handed the video over to Jaylyn with Maylan's confession on it. So why was she still playing the victim and acting as if she didn't know what was going on?

"Before my court hearing. Why?" she asks her face a ball of confusion.

I chuckle and run my hand over my mouth. "She never showed you the fucking Video," I said, hitting the seat in front of me and she jumped. "Let's go Maverick, Long Beach."

"Video. What Video?" she asks.

We pull up to the house and go inside.

"Have a seat," I tell her pulling my phone from my pocket and sending a message to Rome, Tez, and Lavon to meet me at the spot ASAP.

Was Jaylyn following me? Is that how she knew where I was going to be the day she appeared outside the jewelry store. Maybe we'd gotten it all wrong because I'm getting the feeling that Jaylyn's the one that was calling all the shots and lying to her sister to get her to go along with it.

I'd only spoken of Olivia once when we were in college and that was when we were discussing our exes and past sexual partners. There is no way she could have figured out the exact Olivia that I was referring to on her own unless she already knew it was her.

"You want to let me in on the conversation you're having with yourself over there." She asks, right as the fellas knocked at the door.

I unlock the door opening it quickly and ushering them inside. Tez steps in first and throws his hands in the air and Rome pulls his gun pointing it directly at Olivia.

"Oh, come on bruh. Not this crazy bitch again." Tez shouts.

"Isn't she supposed to be locked up?" Lavon asks, looking back and forth from me to her.

"Rome put your gun away," I say, motioning towards him with my hand.

"Hell, nah man this bitch is on some other shit bruh. Dejuan, Yo how the fuck did she get out anyway?"

I take a deep breath and slowly exhale pressing my fingertips to the top of my nose between my eyes as I walk over to the couch and sit down. Tez and Lavon do the same, but Rome remains standing with his gun still aimed at Olivia. He doesn't trust her, and I understand his reason, but we needed to figure out the truth so that we can handle the situation.

"So, Olivia your sister never came to visit you before your sentencing?" I ask.

"No. I told you the last time I saw her was that day in court." She replies.

"Yo, this bitch is lying man. Let me take her ass out right now."

"Fuck you, Jerome." She spits back in a venomous tone.

Rome tightens his grip on the gun moving his finger to the trigger. The tension in the room was thick and heavy and I knew that if Rome didn't put his gun away things weren't going to end well for any of us. And on top of that, I wasn't letting anyone get killed in my house, this was my mother's place and she loved it, it's the one thing that's truly been hers.

"So, you didn't see the video of the confession?" Lavon asks.

"No, I didn't." She said confused.

"So, you don't know that Maylan and Darron are both dead?"

"What," she says shooting up straight in her seat. "They're dead? Omg, I think I'm going to be sick."

She jumps up from the couch and rushes towards the bathroom slamming the door behind her. I start to go after her, but I notice that she didn't take her purse with her, so I decided to give her a minute before I go and check on her.

My phone chimes and I pull it from my pocket checking the message, it was from Renea she wanted me to call her. I punch in a quick reply telling her that I was still with my agent and that I would call her once I was finished then locked my phone and slid it back into my pocket. Here I was lying to her once again and I wish I didn't have to, but until I knew what was really going on here I couldn't let her know. I promised to protect her and that's what I'm going to do.

She's just going to have to trust me.

Chapter Twenty-Nine

Renea

I hadn't heard from Dejuan since this morning and I was anxious to hear what it was that his agent needed to discuss with him. I'd never really thought about what would happen if the team traded him or how that would affect our lives.

Would I be willing to leave LA and start over somewhere new?

I took a big gulp of wine swishing it around in my mouth before swallowing it. I don't know if I want to have to adjust to life without my family and being so far away from my mother that would be hard on her and my dad.

I take another sip and then push the thought to the back of my mind. I'm just hoping for good news I mean it's probably another endorsement deal or something much bigger, maybe an award, or maybe a chance to grace the front cover of a magazine. Either way, I'm not going to stress about it anymore. I set my glass on the table and get up from my seat heading towards the bathroom when the doorbell sounds, and I turn back and rush through the foyer.

I open the door and see Kiani jogging in place.

"You ready to go?" she said, her ponytail swinging from side to side as she bounced from one foot to the other.

"Yep. But come inside for a second I need to use the bathroom before we go." I say opening the door wider for her to come in.

I run off to use the bathroom and return a couple of minutes later then we head out to run our 3 miles. Euro followed along behind us keeping watch for paparazzi they've been going to extraordinary lengths to get a shot of my engagement ring and a picture of me wearing it.

I haven't really thought about who I was willing to share the news with then again, I actually don't really want to share it with anyone other than the people who already know. And when I go on interviews or talk shows I could just leave the ring at home so that they'll just skip over the question once they see there is no ring on my finger and eventually let it go.

"So, how did it go with your date the other night," I ask, as we slowed our pace switching from jogging to speed walking.

She rolls her eyes and says "Ugh, it was horrible. I'm beginning to think I'll never find the right guy or maybe there is no such thing as the right guy."

"Wow. He must've been a real asshole."

She laughs. "Oh, honey let me tell you when the check came he pushed it over to me and said, 'were not fucking tonight, so dinners on you'. I wanted to reach across the table and knock his ass out, but I kept my cool."

"NO!" I said, my eyes wide. "Please tell me you didn't pay that bill Kiani."

"Hell no. I told him I was going to the restroom and walked myself right out the front door."

"That's my girl!" I said, giving her a high five as we both laughed.

Dejuan's been acting strange ever since he got home a couple of nights ago. He'd told me about his meeting with Harlan and that he was going to be on the cover of a magazine and he sounded excited, but his actions didn't match the tone of his voice. And whenever I ask him if he wanted to talk about it he would say it was nothing and change the conversation or walk away claiming he needed to handle something.

So, the next morning when he left the house I decide to follow him. I'd borrowed my mother's car because I didn't want to take the chance of him recognizing my car. An hour later he pulls into the driveway of his childhood home in Long Beach and I park on the street at the house next door.

Someone opens the front door just as he steps from the car, but I couldn't really see who the person was that was in the doorway. As he gets closer to the door the woman steps out a little further to greet him as he steps on the porch then they both walk inside.

I felt my chest get tight and my throat felt as if it was going to close and I was going to suffocate. Unwanted tears stung my eyes and I blinked them away quickly turning my focus back towards the house. Maybe it's not her, maybe it was someone who looked just like. I mean she kidnapped me and tried to kill me there is no way that they would let her out after all of that.

I take a few deep breaths to calm myself before stepping out of the car. I walk quickly cutting through the bushes and around the side of the house until I found a window that I could look inside. I ducked behind a bush that was right in front of a small window on the side of the house that gave me a clear view into the living room where they were all gathered.

Dejuan sat in a chair with his back towards the window and Olivia and Lavon were seated on the leather couch. Tez was directly across from the others sitting in an old wooding chair and he was the one talking but I couldn't make out what he was saying. I reached up and placed my hands on the wind giving it a little push checking to see if it was unlocked. Luckily it was so I pressed a little harder and the window seal squeaked.

"Shit!"

I got down as far to the ground as I could and stayed there until I was sure that no one was coming to check it out. I crawled around to the back of the house then stood to my feet and dusted myself off.

"That was close," I said myself blowing my hair out of my face.

If I wanted answers I wasn't going to get them by sneaking around or listening through the windows. I walk up to the door and lift my hand to ring the doorbell but then a moment of hesitation took over me and I dropped my hand back down to my side.

What was I going to say? I couldn't tell him that I'd followed him here like an insane stalker or maybe I could. Because the fact is I am crazy, and he's the one making me crazy, lying to me and sneaking behind my back instead of telling me the truth.

I let a heavy sigh then turn to walk away from the door, but it swings open.

"Renea?" Tez said, turning and looking back at Dejuan.

I look from Dejuan to Olivia and back to Tez and he shakes his head at me with a with a doleful expression on his face. Olivia rises from her seat and I step forward but Tez puts his arm out in front of me stopping me from entering.

"I promise you, Renea, it's not what you think." Said Tez as he moves forward placing his arm around my waist and pulling me back out of the door.

I push his arm away from me and he holds his hands up in the air, but he doesn't step back he stays close to me.

"So, you can look me in my eyes and honestly tell me that he hasn't been lying to me, again?"

"I was going to tell you beautiful," Dejuan said, getting up from his seat and walks over to me grabbing my arm and pulling me into the house.

We walk into the master bedroom and close the door behind us and I pull my arm away from him.

"How did you know I was here?" he asks.

"Really, you're questioning me?" I reply.

 He runs his hands over his head letting out a frustrated breath. "Why do you have to be so damn stubborn?"

"I—,"

"I've told you about my past and you know that whenever these people want to get back at me they do it by hurting my loved ones." He says cutting me off.

"But you can't just—"

"Let me finish," He says sternly. "I'm trying to protect you Renea, why won't you let me do that? You say that you trust me, so I need you to start believing me and know that I would never lie to you, but you have to understand that some things are better left unsaid."

I drop my hands down to my side, "I'm sorry."

"Damn it Renea," He said, "Come here baby," he pulls me close and puts his arms around me kissing my forehead. "I love you beautiful, and I wouldn't be able to live with myself if something ever happened to you, so I need you to stay away from all this, please." He whispers.

"I love you too and I'm sorry baby."

He agreed to fill me in but only on a need to know bases, discussing only the things that were necessary, and I was fine with that. I don't like being in the dark but like he said I have to start trusting him and the decisions he makes so that he can protect me as well as our future.

But deep down I still felt the need to be by his side facing it head-on in a true Bonnie & Clyde fashion.

Chapter Thirty

Dejuan

I was happy that Renea followed me and that she now knew the truth, but at the same time, I was still upset with her. I don't want anything to happen to her, so I need her to stay far away and stop putting herself in harm's way and let me handle things.

The fellas spent the night at my place so that they could keep an eye on Olivia and so that I could head home to Renea. Now that Renea is calm and everything is good between the two of us it's time for me to figure out what the hell is going on.

"Olivia, I gave your sister a video of Maylan confessing to killing your father. And a message for you as well, a warning, for you back off or the same thing that happened to your boyfriends was going to happen to the two you."

"So, you killed Maylan and Darron?"

I shook my head no and she lowered her eyes staring down into her lap. I can't imagine how hard it would be to hear that you were sleeping with the man that killed your father, but I had no sympathy for her. After what she had done to Renea and the fact that she was willing to kill an innocent woman made her just as sick as he was.

After we finished explaining things to her about the night her father died she let us in on a few things as well. Like how her sister paid one of the guards to let her out of the jail so that she could get revenge for her father's death. Also, that Maylan was the one that set up the hit on me and not her because he needed me out of the way.

"So that motherfucker thought he was going to take you out and then take control of what we'd built. Yeah, that fool was sho-nuff crazy." Tez said, chuckling.

We ask her a few more questions and she answered them all truthfully and then she tried to apologize, but I wasn't really trying to hear it. She just wanted to clear her conscience and she was going to have plenty of time to do that while she sat in her cell.

Tez called up his hellhounds to take Olivia back to the prison and while they were there he wanted them to take care of the guard that let her out. I had to clean up this mess and fast because I was getting too comfortable and in no way, do I want to get pulled back into this world that I want no part of.

Things were going great for me and I'd finally found the perfect woman, my soulmate, and we were happy and in love. And getting back into this world would only complicate things between the two of us, and I'm not willing to risk losing her.

I walk in the front door and Marley runs into the foyer barking and circling around me, so I bend down and pick him up.

"Marley, where's your mama?" I say rubbing the top of his head then sitting him back down on the floor.

He barks and takes off into the livingroom stopping until he sees me then continues to the master bedroom. Renea was lying in bed with the lights low watching T.V. with a bowl of ice cream beside here.

"Hey beautiful," I said, leaning in and kissing her lips and sucking the ice cream off and she smiles.

I climb on to the bed and Marley starts barking at me because he's too small to jump on the bed by himself. So, I reach down and scoop him up and put him on the bed and he run right over to Renea and snuggles up beside her.

I rest my head on the pillow and close my eyes, but I feel her gaze on me, so I open one eye and look over in her direction and see that she's staring at me.

"So, you're just going to come in and not say anything?"

"What do you want me to say, Renea?" I ask.

She sits up and scoots back on the bed resting her back on the headboard and placing her bowl on the bedside table.

"Where is Olivia?"

"She's back at the prison and I promise you there will not be any more surprise visits from her."

I kiss her on the cheek and get up from the bed and head to the bathroom to take a hot shower.

"What do you think about taking a vacation?" I ask, walking over and sitting on the edge of the bed.

"And where will our destination be?"

"Anywhere you want to go," I said, scooting close to her and kissing her neck.

"Mm... So somewhere with white sand beaches and clear blue waters."

I roll over and pull her down on to the bed spreading her legs and sliding in between them kissing her softly.

"If that's what you want."

***

We pull up to the airstrip ready to board our flight to the Caribbean Island. Renea loves Jamaica so we agreed on Montego Bay and I invited Jonathan and Shanice to join us.

"Good evening Mr. Washington," the pilot said. "I'll be your pilot this evening and if there's anything you need Malorie here will assist you." He points in the direction of the stewardess.

"Thanks," I reply walking onto the jet and taking my seat.

"Can I get you something to drink?" Malorie asks, looking from me to Renea.

"Yes, please," Renea replies.

She takes our drink request and heads off to prepare them. I hadn't told her that our friends would be joining us, I wanted it to be a surprise and I'm glad that Shanice didn't spoil it. The two of them cannot keep a secret they tell each other everything, but at least she kept her word this time.

"Finally, I didn't think the two of you were going to make it," I say giving Jonathan a manly embrace then hugging Shanice.

"Dejuan, you didn't tell me they were coming," Renea says excitedly as she leaps from her seat to hug the two of them.

We take our seat and prepare for takeoff.

Once we're in the air we all relax and kick our feet up and enjoying a good conversation. Vacation had officially begun once we touched down in Montego Bay and we stepped off the jet. We climbed into the car that was waiting for us and headed to the resort. An older woman and man came out and greeted us, as two other young men grabbed our luggage and took it inside the villa.

"Welcome to Jamaica my name is Alethia and this here is Agwe. Anything you need just let us know and we will be here for you throughout your stay." She says in a thick Jamaican accent. "Inside you will find some refreshments waiting for you in the kitchen if you would like to grab a bite to eat before you freshen up."

"Thank you, Alethia," I say, and she nods.

We walk into the villa and look around getting to know the place. The doors in the living room lead out to a huge balcony where there was a radically awesome view of the ocean. The living room was huge and had a modern feel to it, a crème leather sofa, two oversized red chairs, and a 50' T.V. hung on the wall. Each bedroom was complete with a king size bed, flat screen, and each suite had a master bath.

After we looked around we headed into the kitchen and noticed all the different foods spread across the dining room table waiting for us, so we all chose a seat and dug in.

Chapter Thirty-One

Renea

We eat up then retreat to our rooms to rest for a while before we freshen up for dinner. I walk out onto the balcony to take in the view of the ocean, it's so beautiful, the way the sun bounces off the still waters that are so crystal clear that you can see right through it.

"Baby, come look at this view, it's amazing," I shout into the room to Dejuan.

He walks out on to the balcony and put his arms around me "Wow, it's almost as beautiful as you." he says leaning in and kissing my cheek.

I Lay my head on his chest and close my eyes, the wind was blowing, brushing across my face, as the sun kissed my skin. I inhaled a deep breath and slowly let it out.

"I could stay here in this moment with you forever," Dejuan whispers into my ear and my lips part into a smile and I pull his arms tighter around me.

The sun sets as we dine out on the beach and it was the perfect setting for a romantic dinner for two. I initially thought that we would be dining together, but the fellas had other plans set in motion that we knew nothing about.

"This is so beautiful," I say unable to wipe the smile away that's been on my face since we'd arrived.

"I'm glad you like it. I wanted to spend our first night alone since everything back home has been so chaotic lately." He replies then reaches across the table and takes my hand. "Dance with me," he says helping from my seat.

I hear a piano begin to play and he pulls me close to him, wrapping his hands around my waist and I place my arms around his neck. Our bodies began to sway as we move slowly to the soft melodies being played.

"I love you Renea. You've helped me open my eyes and my heart, showing me that life is about more than taking, but that it's also about giving," he says, as he looks into my eyes.

"Aw baby, I love you too," I reply, and he leans in and kisses me. I must admit I'm so gone in the brain and I fall deeper in love with this man every day.

When the music ends we go back and find dessert waiting on the table for us. After we finish with our dessert we walked along the beach, hand in hand, enjoying the sounds of the ocean. I could see a small cabana that had rose petals sprinkled across the white lining and candles lit all around it.

I look over at him and giggle, "I see you've been busy." I say, letting go of his hand and walking over to the bed climbing on top and stretching out across it.

He pulls his shirt off and places it at the end then joins me. This was like a dream, I'd often fantasized about having sex on the beach and now I was experiencing it for the first time with my soulmate. And I'm sure this is only the first of many that I'll get to share with him.

***

The last four days have been the best that I've had in a long time. Spending time with the love of my life and our friends, soaking up the sun and being able to just let loose has been very relaxing. I'm happy that he invited them to join us on this trip and I could tell it was much needed and I mean that for all four of us.

I wish that it could continue for a few more weeks, but I know that it's back to reality for all of us in a couple of days.

"So, what's on the agenda for today?" Dejuan asks.

"I think we're going to go jet skiing, right ladies?" Jonathan said.

"You are absolutely correct," I reply, getting up from my seat to grab another cup of coffee. "We're spending the night on the Yacht so make sure you all pack a few things before we head out."

We'd done pretty much every activity that there is to do on the island and now we were going to spend some time on the water. I love being out there something about it is so serene and I just feel so peaceful and free, and I would love to one day just travel and go where ever the water takes me with Dejuan right by my side.

"Are you going to sit there daydreaming or are you going to come join me," Dejuan shouts, sitting on his jet ski out on the water.

I walk down to the deck and grab a life jacket and put it on, Jonathan and Shanice were already a few feet away from the boat with Dejuan.

"Come on move those pretty little legs a little faster," Jon yells out to me.

I throw up my middle finger at him then hop on my jet ski and ride out to where they were waiting, but before I could get there they speed off.

"Oh, so that's how you all want to play," I yell out as I shoot across the water racing to catch up with them.

We were all tired and my jaws were sore from laughing at Dejuan and Shanice. He fell off the jet ski at least five times and Shanice kept pulling out her emergency stop pin so hers kept shutting off. Jonathan thought that he could take me on and challenged me to a race and he had his ass handed to him not once or twice but three times.

We spent the entire day out on the water so for tonight we planned to chill out and have a few drinks and watch movies on the huge screen on the deck.

***

I can't believe this is our last night here. Relaxing on a Yacht, jet skiing, beautiful ocean views, it must all come to an end. But I loved every moment of it and I can't wait to do a little partying with the locals tonight.

"You ladies ready?" Dejuan asks, poking his head in the bedroom door. "Almost, we'll be out in a second".

I finish applying my make-up then lean my head forward shaking out my hair and flipping my head back up.

"Perfect," I say to myself.

"How's this look?" Shanice ask as she twirls in place.

"You look hot," I reply.

She wore a silver sparkly dress that stopped mid-thigh and draped around her neck, that was backless and complete with a pair of red bottoms. My girl was really killing it tonight and I was glad that she was feeling better. She'd gotten sick when we arrived back on the island and we all figured it was something she ate on the boat that upset her stomach.

I grab my clutch and my phone then we head downstairs to join the fellas. They were seated on the sofa waiting for us and we walked into the room they both stood as they looked us over.

"Damn. Baby, baby, baby, I see you trying to get something started tonight, huh?" Jonathan says leaning in to kiss her.

"Un-uh, back up before you mess up my makeup." She says playfully pushing him away.

Dejuan walks over and spins me around and slaps me on the ass, "mm, mm, mmm... maybe we should skip the club and just head back to our room."

"No," I said pushing his hand away.

"How in the hell did we get so damn lucky bro? We have two successful women and they are two of the finest woman in the entire world." Jonathan calls out from behind us, and I look over my shoulder and wink before blowing him a kiss.

We fall into the Escalade and take our seats as Jonathan tells the driver our destination and then he pulls away from the villa.

"So what kind of club are we going to?" I ask.

"One of the hottest clubs on the island, it's a place for all styles of music. I think you all will like it." Jonathan replies.

I could hear the music on the outside as soon as we stepped out of the car. Our security detail waited until we were all outside of the car before escorting us inside the club. We were seated in the VIP area and there were a variety of alcohol beverages waiting for us.

"We're going to need to them bring us something nonalcoholic for Neese," I shout over the music getting Jonathan's attention. He nods his head and calls for one of the security to have someone bring over some sodas. I didn't want her getting sick on us again.

The music is blurring, and the dance floor is packed and so is the VIP section. They bring us over the drinks for Shanice and the waitress takes one look at both Dejuan and I and almost spills it on us.

"Omgosh your—your Renea' Dubley!" She shouts as she sits the drinks down on the table in front of us. "Can I please get a picture with you?" she asks and begins to walk towards us when one of the security guys grab her before she could approach us.

"Hey, No, It's alright. She can come over she just wants a picture." I shout to the bodyguard and getting up from my seat walking over to the young woman.

I take her hand walk back over to the sitting area with her. I could see that she was a little shaken up, so I apologized for what had happened and let her know to wait for the ok next time before approaching. We took a couple of pictures with her and a video for her social media then she scurries off grinning like a kid on Christmas morning.

"You just can't hide anywhere can you, Miss International." Dejuan joked.

"Well you know?" I say flipping my hair with a playful grin on my face.

He laughs and takes my hand, "Come on, let's see what you got."

He stands up and leads me to the dance floor.

We step out onto the dance floor just as Rhianna's 'Work' comes blasting through the speakers and my body instantly begins to move to the beat, as I grind and twerk on Dejuan. He grips my waist and works me from behind and just as we get into it I see people out the corner of my eye with their phones out taking pictures and videos of us.

"I guess we'll be the topic of discussion tomorrow morning" I whisper into his ear, and he looks at me with a raised eyebrow, so I nod my head towards our audience.

The song ends and Drake's song 'Controlla' begins to play and the crowd goes wild. Everyone was up and dancing to the music and having fun, suddenly I feel a hand grip my butt and I turn and see a tall muscular guy grinding up on me and I push him away shaking my finger at him. I brush it off with a smile and continue dancing, but the guy grabs my arm and spins me back around wrapping his arms around me and pulling me against his body.

"Are you crazy, get your hands off me," I shout as I try to wiggle my way out of his arms, but his grip was too tight.

"Don't be like that, I just want to dance with you, pretty lady." He said and leans in and tries to kiss me on the cheek, but I quickly move my head back. "Oh, so you're playing hard to get I see."

He puts his hand on the back of my head and tries to pull my face forward to kiss me again.

WHAM!

I see a fist come flying past my face from the corner of my eye and connecting with the guy's jaw. He stumbles back into the crowd before falling to the floor, I feel someone grab my arm and begin to pull me out of the crowd. Everything was happening so fast, it was like one of those scenes in a movie. Once we reached the VIP area I realized that the security guard was the one that had pulled me from the crowd. Jonathan and one of the security guys were holding Dejuan back as the bouncer was checking on the guy that was laid out on the floor.

"What the hell happen?" Shanice called out to me, running over and putting arms around me.

"Some asshole decided to grope all over me on the dance floor and wouldn't let me go," I replied.

A couple of minutes later they all walked back over to the VIP area along with the bouncer and the security in tow.

"Are you alright beautiful?" Dejuan asks taking a seat in the chair beside me.

I wanted to scream and yell at him for not being right by my side and for not letting the security team handle that guy. Instead I got on to his lap and buried my face into his chest.

"I think we should go," Jonathan said, and the security team nodded back at him.

He phoned the driver telling him to pull around to the side of the building, and the bouncer showed us to the side door so that we didn't have to try and push back through the crowd to get out front.

Dejuan carried me in his arms out to the SUV and helped me inside. Once everyone was in their seats we pulled away from the building and I watched as it faded into the distances. I was happy to get away from there but also sad that the night had ended on such a sour note. Everyone sat quietly on the ride back to the Villa, but Dejuan would glance over at me every once and a while then turn his focus back towards the window.

No one really said much for the rest of the night I guess they figured I wanted some time alone after what had happened at the club. We went to our room and they went to there's saying a quick goodnight before closing the doors. This wasn't exactly how I planned on spending our last night, but I was glad to have Dejuan there protecting me.

I stretched out on the bed and Dejuan walked over and sat on the end watching me closely.

"Are you sure you're alright Renea?" he asks with concern in his voice.

And I could help but melt. I love the way my name sounds when he says it, I sit up and move closer to him. I could also tell that something was bothering him because he had called me by my name instead of saying beautiful. I place my hand on his face and kiss his lips before pulling back to look into his eyes when he doesn't respond. I search his eyes for a minute and all I could see is hurt and anger.

"Dejuan, baby, I'm ok. I promise." I say reassuring him before leaning in to kiss him again and this time he returned the kiss.

He pulls my dress over my head and throws it onto the floor and lies me back on the bed. I watch as he strips off his clothes and slowly eases onto the bed spreading my legs and kissing the inside of my thighs before lightly brushing his tongue against my clit.

"Dejuan…" I moan softly.

Chapter Thirty-Two

Dejuan

"I think I need a do over vacation," I say to myself.

We touch down in LA at about 6 AM and say our goodbyes to Shanice and Jonathan then head home. The last night in Jamaica was crazy and the dude at the club was about to get his cap pulled back until the bouncer stepped in and saved his ass. I'm not down for another man putting his hands on my woman.

Once we get home we crawled into bed burying ourselves under the covers and sleeping most of the day away. I woke up to use the bathroom and when I returned I saw the light on my phone flashing. I had 5 missed calls and 3 messages from Jerome. I kiss Renea on the cheek then head in the livingroom dialing Jerome back. He answers after the second ring.

"Aye man, I need you to ride out to Long Beach."

"What's going on?" I ask.

I knew something wasn't right when he hesitated because that meant whatever was going on was serious and it couldn't be discussed over the phone. I tell him to get the rest of the fellas and meet me at the house in an hour and end the call without saying another word. I lock my phone and walk briskly back to our bedroom and go into the walk-in closet and get dressed really quick.

"Beautiful, I have to run out for a minute. I'll be back in a couple of hours." I whisper to her.

"Where are you going? Do you need me to come with you?" She asks, her voice sluggish.

"No, go back to sleep and don't worry. I'll be back soon."

I kiss her forehead then head out of the house. I climb into the Mercedes and shot out of the garage and speed down the driveway. I hear sirens as I get close to the gate and just as it opens, and I began to pull out two police cars swoop in front of me and block me in. The two officers get out of their vehicle with their guns drawn yelling for me to get out of the car.

"Slowly open the door, stick your hands out, and step out of the car." One of the officers said over the speaker.

The neighbors that live directly across from us come to their door and begin to watch. I step out of the car with my hands in the air, walk around to the front, and drop to my knees first then I lay flat on the ground with my hands behind my back. I knew not to say a word and to do everything they said, so that I didn't end up being one of the next black faces flashing across the screen on the nightly news.

"Don't move," the officer says, coming over and shoving his knee hard into my back and slapping on the handcuffs.

I continued to remain silent not saying a word. The officer pulls me off the ground and shoves me against the car. Renea had stepped out onto the porch and was watching all the commotion until she noticed that it was me leaning against the police car and she came running towards the entrance screaming.

"What the hell is going on?" She said, upset and yelling at the officers.

"Ma'am, I'm going to need you to back up and go back into the house." The officer said holding out his hands to stop her.

She was hesitant at first insisting that the official answer her questions, but the officer repeatedly asks her to go back in the house. She turned to me with a questioning look on her face, but all I could do is nod my head at her. I couldn't explain or say anything to her with the police officer standing there and I didn't want to say anything that they could use against me.

"Call Shanice beautiful, she'll know what to do," I say to her before the officer puts me in the back of the car and slams the door.

I watch her as we pull away from the house until the image of her body was just a blur.

They place me in an interrogation room and remove the cuffs before walking out and closing the door behind them leaving me alone in the cold room. I rub my wrist soothing the pain were the cuffs were so tight and had cut into my skin. I didn't know what was going on or why they'd arrested me, but I was sure it had something to with Olivia Stevens. That bitch has brought nothing but negative energy and chaos to me and my family since she showed back up and that was Maylan's fault.

The door opens and in walks two detectives. The woman detective was thin and tall with long sandy brown hair that was swept back into a ponytail, and she wore a crème blouse and a pair of black pants. The guy he was short and husky wearing a blue suit with a buzz cut and something about him seemed familiar, but I couldn't really put my finger on it.

The lady detective placed a folder on the table and took her seat while the guy stood by the door leaning against the wall.

"Mr. Washington, do you know why you are here?" She asks, placing a recorder on the table before settling into her chair which told me we were going to be here for a while.

"I can't say that I do," I respond in a flat tone.

She leans forward placing her hands on the table cupping them together letting a smile play on her lips as she stared at me. I lean back in my chair stretching out my legs and waiting for her to continue, I could see the game that she was playing, and I wasn't going to fall for it.

"Well, let's jump right into it then," she said opening the folder in front of her and pressing the button on the small recorder. "Mr. Washington, we brought you here today because we have reason to

216

believe that you were involved in the disappearance of Maylan Winchester and Darron Reed."

"Who?"

"Do you not know these two gentlemen, Mr. Washington?" She asks, her eyebrows pulled together.

"I know a Maylan Winchester we went to middle and high school together," I reply.

"And when is the last time you saw Mr. Winchester?"

"I haven't seen him since graduation which was years ago."

I continue to play it cool and not to talk too much, but rather letting her ask me questions picking and choosing the ones I was willing to answer. The more questions she asked, the more I got what I needed from the detectives, they thought that they were smart, but they weren't as good as me.

You see their questions told me what all they knew and what all they didn't know. And eventually, after reading between the lines I would figure out just who the snitch was that they were referring to.

"Look either arrest me or I'm walking out of here. I don't know what kind of games the LAPD is playing, dragging me down here on some bogus charges, but all I know is you better hope that I don't sue you all for the incompetence's of this department." I say in a stern voice then push my seat back from the table and stand to my feet.

And just as I stood up the door swung open and in walked Shanice. She looked at me and then at the two detectives that clearly knew who she was from the look on their faces.

"I'm Shanice Asceno and I will be representing Mr. Washington." She said walking over and placing her bag on the table. "This interview is over and from here on out there will be no questioning my client without the presence of his attorney."

"He's all yours," the detective says nodding towards me with a smirk on her face. "Mr. Washington, you are free to go, for now." The detective says in a cautionary tone.

I nod to her and then Shanice as I exit out of the interrogation room. Renea was sitting in the waiting area as we walked out and once she saw me she ran over and wrapped her arms around me. We hurried out and got in our cars and headed back to the house.

The car ride was quiet and neither of us said a word the whole ride home. I pull onto the street and the house is surrounded with cameras that began to flash as soon as I reach the gate.

"Dejuan, what were you arrested for earlier today?" Ask one of the reporters.

Euro and the rest of security were close by the gate. And once the gates opened the team stepped out surrounding the car and keeping the paparazzi back making sure no one entered. I pulled into the garage just to be safe and when the garage door closed Renea turned to me.

"You better tell me what's going on right now." She said removing her seat belt and turning to face me. "And don't give that shit about protecting me either, I want the truth, Dejuan," her voice was calm but forceful.

I let out a long sigh putting my head back on to the seat. If I tell her everything then she'll probably call the wedding off and run for the hills screaming. I've told her bits and pieces about my past and she accepted those things, but I haven't told her all of the horrible and gruesome details of the things we've done.

"All of this affects my life too you know?" She says softly breaking the silence.

"I—" I begin. "I really don't know where to begin," I replied rubbing my hands across the top of my forehead.

"Start with why the cops coming to our home to arrest you."

I take another deep breath and blow it out before I begin.

"When I met Jerome, Montez, and Lavon we formed a street team. We were D-boys selling only weed in the beginning and then eventually we moved up to guns, car, and X." I stop to look over at her to see if she was following and she waved her hand for me to continue. "Once we'd gotten to high school that's when I meet Olivia we hung real tight all through high school and started dating our junior year."

She shuffled in her seat turning to face forward and I could see from the expression on her face that she was upset with what she'd heard. So, I stopped and waited for her to take in what I'd said.

"Go on," she said softly her gaze now focused outside of the car.

"Olivia's father wanted me to work for him, but I'd told him that I wasn't interested. I liked running the show and I like having things go my way without having to answer to anyone. We meet Maylan our sophomore year and I immediately felt eerie about bringing him onto our team because word on the streets was that he was a snitch. And we later found out that what we'd heard was correct."

She held up her hand for me to stop, so I did, and she opens the door and gets out of the car. That's when I notice Shanice standing in the doorway with her lips pressed into a hard line as she motioned for me to come inside. So, I step out of the car and follow them inside.

Shanice stops beside the island in the kitchen and sits her bag on the stool then takes a seat on the one beside it, before turning in my direction and placing her hands in her lap.

"So, tell me what happened, and I need to know everything or else I can't help you." She says in a sincere voice.

"I know what happened to Maylan and Darron, but I wasn't the one to do it."

"It?" She said, then let out a heavy sigh. "Dejuan are these two men still alive?"

After a moment of hesitation, I answer, "No," then look over to Renea studying her face and body language.

"Did you kill them?" She asks.

"No," I reply, in a stern voice and she puts up her hands.

"Ok. Look Dejuan I'm not here to judge you, but I do have to ask these questions so that I know what I'm getting myself into." She says in a soft but concerned voice.

I start from the beginning and go over what I'd started telling Renea in the car and then going deeper into my past. Eventually, everything that I was saying really got to Renea and she got up and left the room. I wanted to run after her and comfort her letting her know that everything was going to be alright, and assure her that I wasn't that dumb, careless, and heartless young boy anymore. But I remained seated and finished telling Shanice the story.

Once I was finished she let out a deep sigh and leaned back in her seat.

"So, what now?" I ask.

Chapter Thirty-Three

Renea

Who is this man?

After hearing the life that Dejuan once lived, and all of the bad things that he's done to people. I wasn't sure who the man sitting in my kitchen was.

A Killer?

A Dope boy?

How could he have done all those terrible things to people and still live with himself? I really wanted to know, I wanted answers, but at the same time, I really didn't want to know any of it. I mean how can I ever look at him the same and how do I know that part of him is gone, does it just go away like that, or is there a switch that he can turn on or off.

The things he'd told me before weren't all that bad those were things that I could except and move past because I love him. But now knowing that he is capable of murder how do I know that he wouldn't one day have that type of thing done to me.

Just as I wipe a falling tear from my face Shanice knocked at the bedroom door.

"Come in," I managed to choke out before sobbing into my pillow.

"Oh, honey." She says, climbing on the bed beside me and wrapping her arms around me. "It's going to be alright Renea don't cry." She said as she stroked my hair.

"How? He killed those two men."

"And he did what he had to do to those men that were going to hurt the two of you." She said softly.

"What?" I say, turning to face her.

"They were going to try and hurt you and his family."

"Omgosh, why?" I ask, confused.

"I think I better let him tell you that." She says getting up from the bed. "I love you Renea and try to be understanding once you hear what he has to say, call me if you need anything." She blows me a kiss and leaves out the door.

Understanding?

Is she insane, I mean she has to be, right? I would give him a chance to explain because I need to know what is going on so that I can be cautious, but why should I have to be understanding.

He walks into the room and my eyes shoot over to him, his long frame was leaned up against the door. He stood watching me carefully for a moment before making his way over to our bed sitting on the edge. I'd never seen him like this unsure and hesitant I'm use to him being confident and demanding.

"Are you ready for me to finish?" He asks, keeping his eyes on mine.

I sit up in the bed so that I could face him and give him my full attention. I wasn't ready, not at the least but I knew we needed to get this out in the open so that we could clear the air, so there would be absolutely no secrets between us. I waved my hand letting him know it was ok for him to start.

"Ok," he said. "I've been completely clean for a few years no involvement in the streets. Until Tez called me about a mix up with a shipment and he didn't know what to do and he needed me to handle it for him, so I did and that's when I found out that Maylan was back in the picture and that he was messing around with Olivia."

"Wait, but didn't he kill her father?" I ask, a little confused by what I'd just heard.

"Yeah, he did, but she didn't know that. It turns out that Olivia and Jaylyn are sisters, and no one ever knew, but Olivia set up this whole thing back when we were in college because she thought that me and the fellas were the ones that killed her father."

"But that's not true," I say cutting in before he could finish.

My curiosity was peeking, and I understood that this was all happening because of Maylan, and all the lies that he was telling Olivia and Jaylyn about Dejuan and the other guys and it made me angry. So much so that I wanted to protect him, I could feel the hate that was growing inside of me and I was not going to just sit back and allow them to hurt him again.

I wrap my arms around him and press my lips to his and for a second, he froze, confused by what was happening but then he put his arms around me and returned the kiss.

"You don't have to say anymore. I understand, and you did what you had to do."

"Beautiful, I don't want you to ever be afraid of me, I would never hurt you," he says pushing my hair back out of my face.

I no longer needed an explanation. I believed him, but I overreacted as usual. I know that I can trust him, and I know that he's not the same person he was before. I just need to work on not over thinking things. But to be fair I've never dealt with this kind of thing in my life before, and I've never had someone like him in my life so it's going to take some getting used to.

It's been a media circus outside of our house for the last week. I figured after a couple of days that things would let up and another celeb would do something crazy and the media frenzy would go and stalk their doorstep.

I could tell that this was all getting to Dejuan, his mother had called crying a few days ago after finding out about the arrest. We invited her to come and stay with us so that she didn't have to deal with the press knocking on her door asking questions or to interview her. But she declined and opted to go visit some family out of town until it all blew over.

He'd also gotten a call a few days ago from his agent telling him that he'd been dropped from two major endorsements that he's signed with. They claimed it was just too much negative attention coming his way and they didn't need that kind of attention falling back on them. And even though he understood where they were coming from and said he was alright I could clearly see that he was hurting.

"Baby, please come and sit down you've been pacing the floor all morning," I say, pulling him over to the couch and taking a seat.

He stretches out laying his head on my lap and closes his eyes. I massage his scalp with my fingertips hoping that would help him relax a little so that he could calm down. He took a deep breath and then exhaled opening his eyes and looking up at me.

"Thank you beautiful," he said, reaching up and placing his hand on my face.

"We'll get through this, ok."

He offers me a small smile and then shuts his eyes while I continue rubbing his head.

I'm supposed to perform at the Awards in a few weeks and I pray that all of this has blown over before then. I've already canceled three shows and a radio appearance because of all this. I knew that if I'd gone that they were going to bring up the arrest and ask if I could fill them in. And honestly, I didn't want to go through all of that dodging their questions or have to get up and walk out because of their questions.

"Hey, you two, where are you?" Shanice calls out from the foyer.

"We're in here," I call out to her just as she turns the corner.

Dejuan sits up straight on the couch and turns to her. "So, what did they say?"

"Good morning to you too Dejuan." She says in a sarcastic tone. "So, I was able to get your friend out on bond but you're going to have to find him another lawyer." She continues taking a seat in the chair across from us.

"Ok, that's not a problem I have one on retainer." He replies.

"Good, now, as far as I know, they are not charging you with anything because they have no evidence to back their theory so your good for now." She pauses.

"But," I say knowing that there was one coming.

"But… I found out who turned over the video and who's giving the information."

"Jaylyn," Dejuan said, and I could hear the coldness in his voice.

"Yes," Shanice says before pausing and staring at Dejuan.

He gets up and stomps off towards our bedroom and slams the door behind him causing the two of us to jump a little. I wasn't sure what video they were talking about, but I knew that if Jaylyn had anything to do with it then it couldn't be good for us.

Chapter Thirty-Four

Dejuan

I needed to talk to the fellas together, but I wasn't going to take the risk of calling them on the phone. So, I sent word through the hellhounds for Montez and them to meet me this evening and it had to be somewhere secluded because the cops were still heavy on our asses.

We decided to meet out at one the spot that the hellhounds used as their trap house. I had them clear out the spot until we were finished because I don't know who the hell we can trust at this point, and the last thing we needed was someone dropping a dime on our location.

"Yo bruh what's good," Montez said, slapping my hand and then pulling me in to bump shoulders.

"How you feeling man?" I ask, a little concerned because he didn't look like himself.

"I'm maintaining fam. Tell your peoples I appreciate her getting me that bail man, it's no joke inside there." He said, shaking his head as he dropped his gaze to the ground.

This was the first time that Montez had ever been in lock up. He's caught a few minor cases when we were teens but that just landed him in juvie but that was nothing like the real thing. So, I understood exactly where he was coming from and I was going to make sure that he never had to go back, none of us were going to go to that place. We will find Jaylyn and shut her ass up and make sure that video disappears for good.

"Aye man what we gonna do about that bitch, Yo?" Jerome asks.

"We're going to find her ass and have the hellhounds shut her up," I reply.

It wasn't going to be easy to get close to her now that she was being protected by the whatever contact they have in the police department. Which means they probably have someone watching her place and that's if she's even staying there. They probably have her placed somewhere that they know she'll be safe and her sister probably has security following her as well.

"You know my cousin works for the LAPD and she can probably find out where they have her hiding out," Lavon says breaking my concentration.

"No doubt. Yeah check that out for me then and let me know what's up when you get the word. We all need to get new phones after 48 hours, I want you to get rid of that shit and grab a new one. So, make sure you purchase at least four burners. We're going to do that until all this shit blows over." I said, walking over to grab the ones I'd purchased on my way over.

"Bet," they each replied.

I tossed a burner to one of the hellhounds telling him to keep it close just in case we need one of them to handle a situation. He nodded in my direction and then place the phone in his pocket. We finished up the rest of our conversation and I went over the plan once more before we headed out and went our separate ways.

Back at the house, I walked in to find Renea and her parents sitting poolside laughing and talking. I'd kind of kept my distance from her parents after she told them what was going on and about all the things I'd did in my past. I didn't know if they were still going to be as accepting as they were before but if their anything like their daughter then I just might have a chance.

"Dejuan," Mrs. Dubley called out getting up from her seat. "Hello, sweetheart we were just asking where you were." She said with the biggest smile on her face as she rushed over giving me a big hug.

I was a little surprised, but she released me and wrapped her arm around mine and lead me over to the table. I pulled her chair out for her and she took her seat then I turned and shook Mr. Dubley's hand before walking over and kissing Renea then I sat in the chair beside her.

"How are you doing son?" Mr. Dubley asks as everyone turn their attention towards me waiting patiently for my answer.

"Uh—," I paused for a second and cleared my throat. "I'm doing ok."

"Good! I just want you to know that we are behind you a hundred percent anything you need you just let us know." He said, with a broad smile.

"Thank you, sir," I replied looking over to Renea and she winks as her part into a small smile.

The paparazzi was no longer lingering around our house and the buzz on social media had kind of died down. After my PR team released an official statement to the press about the bogus allegations that the cops were trying to pin on me they slowly backed off.

Life was beginning to get back to normal, somewhat. And things were still good with Renea and me, we've been planning the wedding or more like she's been planning the wedding. Every now and again she'll ask my option on a couple of things, but it's pretty much been about what's going to make her happy.

As for my career, the teams have been discussing trading me, but the coach is trying his best to make sure that doesn't happen. I lost a lot of endorsement deals also but I'm sure I'll earn some of them back after all this is over. My fans are staying loyal and my agent has my back one trillion percent so he's not going anywhere.

But as much as I hate to admit it, Olivia and Jaylyn both in the end said that they were going to ruin my life and my career and so far, they're doing a damn decent job.

***

The sound of her ass slapping down into my lap made my dick swell up even more as she rode my dick bouncing up and down. She tilted back so that I had a full view of her perfectly round breast bouncing in my face. I took one into my mouth nibbling on her nipple then sucking it into my mouth.

"Omg, Dejuan, I'm coming baby." She moaned

"I feel you beautiful."

She let out a loud cry as she claimed her orgasm, her pussy gripped my dick tightening around me, and her body trembling as she reached her climax. I tried to hold back but when she reached behind and begin to play with my balls it sent me over the edge. I let out a groan and pushed deep inside of her as my dick spasm and all of my seeds shout deep inside her.

 I leaned back against the seat and she rested on my chest our bodies both drenched in sweat.

I could see that sex with Renea was never going to get boring, she's always reading and willing to get dicked down no matter where we are. She slides off my lap and stumbled to the back of the jet to grab a couple of washcloths for us to wipe off with. We were on our way back to LA from New York, where Renea had performed the night before. We both wanted to stay in New York a little longer, but she needed to get back and prepare for her Awards performance.

"Here you go," she says handing me a washcloth.

She slipped her clothes back on while I cleaned myself up then sat in the seat across from me taking out her phone.

"What are you doing?" I ask, pulling on my jeans on and sitting back in my seat.

"Sending a message to my team. I want to let them know we'll be landing soon." She replies as she taps away on her phone.

"So that's it. You're just going to fuck me then run off." I say with a chuckle.

She looks up from her phone for a moment raising her eyebrow then turns her attention back to her phone and finishes typing out her message. I pull my shirt over my head and grab the burner phone from my bag to check my messages and there was one from Lavon that read.

Lavon: Hit me up once you touch down. I got that info for you!

I shot him back a quick reply and then slide the phone back into my carry-on bag. It'd been three weeks since Lavon talked to his cousin and finally, she'd gotten back to him and the timing was great. I was starting to get impatient with the both of them, the longer that Jaylyn was out there the more harm she could do to all of us.

"Good news?" She asks, breaking my concentration.

"Huh," I said turning my attention to her. "I'm sorry beautiful my mind was somewhere else. What did you say?"

"I ask if that was good news. The message you were reading," she nodded her head towards my carryon bag.

"Oh, yeah. Lavon thinks that he may know where Jaylyn is staying."

She shoots me a disapproving look then sits her phone in her lap and falls back into her seat. "Dejuan, I don't want you to—"

I reach over grabbing her hands and cutting her off, "Stop. I already know what you're going to say, and you don't have to worry beautiful, I got this."

I could see in her eyes that she was scared for me, but she didn't need to be I can handle myself and the fellas and I knew what we were doing. It wasn't our first go-round with an enemy, but it would definitely be my last. No going back, no more stepping in and handling things when shit got rough, or when something goes wrong. From here on out if Tez couldn't handle the situation then that just means that Lavon or Jerome will have to step up and take care of things.

Once we landed I kissed Renea and grab my things and we go our separate ways. While she headed off to rehearse for the Grammy's, I headed to Long Beach and over to the trap house to meet up with the fellas. I sent the three of them a message letting them know that I'd arrived, and I was on my way to the spot. I tucked my phone away in my pocket and gave maverick the address to where we were headed, and he pulled away from the airstrip.

Twenty minutes later Maverick pulls in front of the trap house and looks back at me through the rear-view mirror with a curious look on his face. I offer up a smile and give him a pat on the shoulder.

"Everything's cool Mave. Just stay put and lock the doors, I'll be right back." I say before opening the door and stepping out of the car.

I hear the locks click as I head up the stairs and to the front door. I lift my hand to knock on the door but before I could get my hand knock I hear a loud BOOM inside the house. I jump back from the door and I hear another BOOM, so I head back to the car and motion for Maverick to roll down the window and he does what he's told.

"Give me your gun," I tell him, and he reaches over into the glove compartment and takes out a 9mm and quickly hands it to me.

I run up the driveway and around the side of the house towards the back door. I could hear Tez yelling at someone inside, but I couldn't make out what he was saying. I walk up to the door and see that it's halfway open, so I quickly glance through the crack of the door looking to see if I could see the shooter but there was no one there.

"You're a dumb motherfucker if you thought that you were going to kill me," I hear a voice that sounded familiar and my heart began to pound in my chest.

I push open the door and position my gun in front of me as I slowly walk through the kitchen and down the hallway. I raise my gun a little higher aiming it at the tall figure that stood before me the guy was holding a 357 magnum in his hand. I continued to creep up on him until my gun was pressed against the back of his head.

"Put down the fucking gun," I say pressing the gun into the back of his skull.

He slowly bends down and places the gun on the ground and holds his hands up in the air.

"Fellas are you alright?" I call out to them.

"Yeah man, we cool," Jerome says, coming around the corner first.

I step over to the side with my gun still aimed in front of me and step around to look at the person that was standing in front of me.

"What the fuck," I say gripping my gun tighter. "How the fuck is you alive Maylan?" I said, my voice filled with venom.

He drops his hands to his side and began laughing a loud roar of a laugh that made my blood boil even more.

"Shut the hell up," Tez says walking up on him and hitting him across the face with his 9mm.

He stumbles back then straightens back up and wipes the blood from his mouth.

"Tez, you're a dumb fuck." He said, "You've always thought that you were smarting than me but you're just a simple-minded street hustler." He said spitting the blood on the floor. "Dejuan, I don't know why you trusted this fuck up to take over your business, but I'm glad you did. You made it so easy for me to waltz right in and fuck up the whole operation." He laughed again licking the blood from his mouth.

"What are you talking about?" I ask.

And just as I ask the hellhounds rounded the corner with their weapons drown walking towards Maylan. I kept my gun pointed in his direction as they stood beside him with a big ass smirk on their faces.

"I'd like for you to meet my team of hellhounds." He says holding his arms stretched out to his sides. "They've been letting me know your every move from day one. And oh, the beating that I supposedly took from them back at the port, well let's just say I'm a very good actor and your ex-wife she's a very good makeup artist."

I take a second to let what he said sink in. They'd played Montez from the beginning and he let it happen, he was the one that was calling the shots, and he was the one that allowed Maylan to be a part of his crew. Fuck, I'd known that he was slipping the moment I got the phone call about the shipment.

"So, where is Jaylyn? And Is Darron still alive too?" I ask, curious.

"I'm right here baby, and oh look who I have with me." She says as she walks into the room with Renea and her gun pointed at her head.

"Yeah, now I know this bitch is crazy, Dejuan," Lavon says raising his gun. "I think it's time I blow her fucking wig back. What you think bruh?"

"Move again and I promise I'll put this bitch to sleep." She snaps.

"Bullshit," Jerome said with a chuckle. "The second her body falls your life is over and you know I'm right. So, I call bullshit."

I hear someone begin to clap loudly and then a slender figure steps out from between the hellhounds.

"Olivia," Tez said "Yo, I told you this bitch was playing us bruh.

She walks over and stands beside Jaylyn and Renea stopping at their side before she turns and faces Renea reaching over and stroking her face with the back of her hand. I could see the fear in Renea's eyes as she kept her focus on me. My finger was itching to pull the trigger, but I knew once we blazed then so would they and that wouldn't end well for any of us. Because the truth is there's way more of them and allot more guns on their side then there is on ours.

"So is there anything you want to say to your beautiful fiancée before I put a bullet in her head," Olivia asks.

I couldn't help but begin laughing, lowering my gun to my side, and holding up my hand for the fellas to do the same. We'd played this little game long enough and I was ready for it to be over, I was exhausted from the flight and I had more important shit to do. The look on Maylan's face let me know that he wasn't up on game, so I tucked my gun away at my waist and crossed my hands in front of me.

"You see Maylan your problem is that you think you know everything, and you always think you're one step ahead of everybody else when you're really not." I begin and glance over at Olivia. "You see I already knew about the hellhounds and I was well aware of the staged beating that you and Darron took at the warehouse. The fact of the matter is the only clueless one in this room right now, is you? We've been setting you up for a while letting you see what it is that we wanted you to see and telling you everything we wanted you to know."

He turns to Olivia with a look of anger and betrayal in his eyes then turns and charges towards her, but she takes a couple of steps back and aims her gun at him.

"You bitch, you are just as useless and pathetic as your father." He said venom in every word.

"And you are weak," she responded her tone cold. "The only one of us that is useless or pathetic is you. My father trusted you, I trusted you, and you killed him then made love to me each and every night knowing that you'd taken him from me."

"You're sick," Jaylyn added, stepping beside her sister.

From the corner of my eye, I see a shadow and movement near the window and a smile creeps up on my face. After a couple of seconds, a loud sound echoes through the house and the door behind us flies off the hinges and several men in all black came rushing inside the house.

"Everyone down on the ground," they yell out. "Mr. Washington are you ok?" I hear Jaxon call out to me and I turn searching for him in the crowd of men that had just entered.

"I'm over here," I reply.

"Ma'am put your hands up and back away from Ms. Dubley." The officer told Jaylyn and she did what she was told.

Tears ran down Jaylyn's face as she placed the gun on the ground beside her and dropped to her knees and stretched out flat on her stomach.

Renea ran to wrapping her arms around my neck and squeezing me tight. I handed my gun off to Jerome who was standing to my right and put my arms around her holding her close.

I'd called Jaxon and told him what was going down and he called on a few of his former buddies from the FBI and they'd sent a squat team over to assist them. They handcuffed Olivia and the rest of his crew and escort them out to the van that was waiting for them.

"I hope you enjoy the very long prison stint that you're going to get," I shout, smiling at Maylan and Darron as they place them inside the swat truck.

Chapter Thirty-Five

Renea

The day had finally arrived, and I am excited to be at the Awards. Sitting in my dressing room I watched as people came in and out and I could hear all the voices and the movement surrounding me, but my mind was else were. I closed my eyes and fell into my own space, breathing in and out slowly, trying to calm my mind.

"You are always so damn gorgeous," I hear a Dejuan's voice behind me.

I open my eyes and look into the mirror and I see Dejuan standing behind me and I turn and smile at him. I jump out of my seat and he pulls me into his arms, kissing me on the top of my head so that he doesn't ruin my makeup.

"Baby, I'm so glad that you're here."

"Miss Dubley, we need you to head to the stage." A tall gray-haired man yells into the room.

"I'll see you after the performance beautiful, I just wanted to see you before you went out." He says smiling at me, and I blow him a kiss before he turns to walk away.

"Girl… Whoa, he is so damn fine child." My stylist says as she fans herself with her hand.

"Mm-hmm… he is delicious isn't he." I say lifting my hand and she high fives me as we both laugh.

"You're on in five minutes Ms. Dubley." The stage director calls out to me.

I straighten up in my seat so that she can finish putting the finishing touches on my hair. Then I jump from my seat and run over to wardrobe slipping into my dress then head out towards the stage. My dancers follow behind me to the stage and then fall in place. The music begins, "you're up," he tells me, so I step into place.

I slowly begin to rise to the top of the stage as the lights come up and the crowd goes.

"Hey…." I say as I catwalk down to the center of the stage, joining in on the choreography with the rest of my dancers.

Once my performance ends the crowd explodes. The dancers and I run off stage and head back to the dressing rooms.

"That was so epic," Kiani shouts, handing me a bottle of water and a towel. We walk by a few fellow artists and they give me a few compliments on my performance and I stop to give a quick embrace and to chat with several people.

Once I was back in my dressing room I rushed inside to freshen up and change back into my dress. Dejuan walks into the room along with his mother and gamma in tow.

"Beautiful, you killed that shit." He said walking towards me.

"Watch your mouth boy," Said his Gamma as she hits him on the arm with her purse, then pushes past him and comes over to hug me. "You were stunning up there on that stage sweetheart." she leans in and kisses me on the cheek.

"Awe, thank you Gamma," I reply, smiling at her.

"Yes, baby, you did an outstanding job out there." His mother says coming over and giving me a big hug.

I'd known from the first time I met them that we were going to click, especially his Gamma. She reminds me of my grandmother and it's nice to have that old soul around to talk to and to learn from. My mother and father joined us in the dressing room shortly after, my father presented me with an amazing arrangement of flowers and the waterworks began. After about 30 minutes my team told everyone they had to go back to their seats so that I could finish getting ready and head out to my seat so that I could accept my award.

It took about 20 minutes to touch up my make-up and hair, but I made it back out to my seat just in time to catch Rihanna's performance. I walked away with two award wins for the night, Song of the year, and Album of the year. I couldn't have been more excited, I truly felt blessed. After the show, we said our goodbyes to our parents and headed off to the after party where we meet up with Jonathan. He was partying solo tonight because Shanice wasn't feeling well so she stayed in for the night, but we made sure to keep an eye on him so that he didn't get himself into any trouble.

We drank, we danced, we mingled, and took plenty of photos and by the end of the night, I was completely exhausted and ready to go home and get out of these heels. Dejuan called Maverick and had him bring the car around as we headed out and once he arrived we fell tirelessly inside the car and I kicked off my heels before scooting in closer to Dejuan resting my head on his shoulder.

"I love you, beautiful." He says kissing my forehead.

"I love you too," I reply smiling and wrapping my arm around his.

***

"Who's ready for Elan?" Kerry asks as she steps off the elevator and into the living room holding up a bottle of wine,

I laugh as she stumbles into the room. "Kerry, why are you here so early?" I say sitting my phone on the table.

"Early, who's early? I'm right on time." She replies plopping down onto the sofa, slightly falling over onto me.

"Oh my, I see someone's had one too many mimosas this morning," I say, holding my hand up to my nose.

"Maybe 1 or 2."

"You do know you're like six hours early, right? I don't go for my taping until 2 pm."

"And what time is it now?" she asks

"8:05 am" I reply.

"Oh," She says and tries to get up from the sofa but is unsuccessful, falling right back down on to the sofa.

"Perhaps we should let Maria get you a cup of coffee. You need to sober up." I said, "I'll be right back, stay put."

"mm, yes, coffee. That sounds delightful."

"Looks like someone had a long night or perhaps a very early morning," I whisper to myself as I walk into the kitchen.

Maria wasn't there, so I turned on the Keurig and started a cup of coffee. I carry the tray that had her cup coffee along with all the things some people like in their coffee, just in case she doesn't like it black. Although, I'm sure she's going to need it at its strongest so that she can sober up quickly.

"And here you go," I say sitting the tray on the coffee table in front of her and she sits up straight on the sofa.

"Could you get me something for this headache please." She asks.

"Sure," I say before turning on my heels and heading towards the bathroom.

I dig around in the medicine cabinet searching for some pain relievers, I grab the bottle and shake it. Glad that there was a few in the bottle, I shut the door and head back to the living room and hand her the bottle.

"Anything else?" I ask, and she shakes her head no and takes a sip of the bottle of water and pops two pills in her mouth.

After the tapping of the show, my team and I head to the spot where I'm going to be shooting a couple of shots for my new music video for one of my tracks from my upcoming album. I decided that I was going to have Dejuan be my love interest in the video and I'm sure that it's going to make for good press.

"Hey, Renea. Tomorrow you have another show appearance at noon. What time should I have the team there for hair and makeup?" Kiani asks as she balances her phone on her shoulder and her laptop in her hand.

"Let's make it two hours before the tapping please," I reply smiling over at her.

I'm so happy and grateful that I have such a wonderful team and staff that kicks ass for me on a daily basis. I don't know what I would do If it weren't for them. I actually need to set up a party or something really special to show them that I appreciate all of their hard work.

Shanice, Kiani, and I head back to my place so that we could meet up with the wedding planner and go over a few details. I'd asked Shanice and Kiani to be my bridesmaids and they were excited to be a part of the big day. And so far, I'd made sure to include them in on all of the planning and I'm glad I did because planning a wedding was a lot more stressful then I thought it would be. But we were getting it done and my wedding planner was awesome, she was always there to answer any questions I had and to make even my most ridiculous request happens.

"So… now that all of that is out the way I have something to tell you all." Shanice says, looking back and forth from Kiani and me.

"Ok, spill it," I say waving my hand at her.

"I'm pregnant," She says and Kiani and I gasp and for a minute the room was silent.

"OMGOSH," I scream and jump up and down in my seat reaching over and grabbing her and hugging her.

Her eyes filled with tears and she returned the embrace and Kiani got up and joined in. I was so happy for her, every one of her dreams was finally becoming a reality. She has her dream job, she finally found the man of her dreams, and she was going to be a mom. That was the one thing that she wanted most of all and knowing Jonathan I'm pretty sure a proposal wasn't far behind.

We'd both found the man of our dreams and even though mine came with a little baggage, and almost got me killed. I still wouldn't change a thing he's my soulmate and we were meant to be so that only meant I was willing to weather any storm that came our way.

And speaking of soulmates I think that Kiani might have found hers as well. A few weeks ago, when Dejuan's brother stopped in for a visit we all went out for drinks and the two of them hit it off. The way that Jamie looked at Kiani when she walked in, he was mesmerized or caught in a trance because he couldn't take his eyes off her.

He offered to drive her home as we were leaving the restaurant and she accepted but she hasn't said anything about how that night ended yet, and I wasn't going to press because I knew she would tell me when she was ready to. But hopefully, it went well because she deserves to be happy just like the rest of us, probably more so after all she'd gone through with her son's father.

After a good twenty minutes of sobbing, we fixed ourselves up and tried to get through the rest of the day without shedding another tear at the mere mention of babies.

***

I'd searched high and low for the perfect wedding dress. And after a month I finally told myself the only way that I was going to have the perfect dress was if I designed it myself and that's what I did. I called on two of my favorite designers and they worked together, tirelessly, to make me the perfect dress and reception gown for my wedding.

When I finally received the call that my dress was ready I gathered my girls, Dejuan's mother, and gamma, and we hopped on the jet and headed to New York for my first fitting.

"I'm so excited," Mrs. Taylor said, with a wide grin.

"Child, I just can't get used to planes they make my nerves bad," Gamma said, and I reached over and placed my hand on hers and offered a warm smile.

"Is this your first time flying Mrs. Washington?" Shanice asks.

"No, I flew once or twice in my younger years, but my stomach couldn't handle it then either." She replied with a small laugh.

The flight was smooth, and Gamma was thanking God once we landed. We all hopped in the SUV and headed to the shop to meet up with the designer and my stomach was doing flips the whole way. On our ride over to the shop Mrs. Taylor and Gamma spilled that they'd never been to New York and that was simply not going to do, they had to experience the big apple at least once in their life. So, I promised to bring them back for a girl's trip.

"Welcome ladies," Ralph says as we entered the shop. "I'm so excited and I can't wait to get you into your dress."

After giving each of us a warm embrace he takes my hand and leads me back to the dressing room while his assistant shows the rest of the ladies to the sitting area. I take a seat on the chaise as he disappeared to the back to grab the dress, he returned a few minutes later and propped the dress on the stand unzipping the bag and pulling it off before stepping aside.

Tears stung my eyes as I stared at the magnificent dress that was in front of me. I was speechless, it was exactly the way that I'd imagined it all the way down to the last stitch, it was perfect. It was a mermaid cut, off the shoulder, with white lace, and a long run in the back. Diamonds lined the waist all the way around and ran down the middle of the train of the dress.

"Well don't just sit there all teary-eyed let's get it on you." He says taking my hand and helping me up from my seat.

I wiped the tears away and followed him to the dressing room and watched him place the dress on the hook and walk out closing the curtain behind him. I removed my clothes and slipped into the dress or I tried to, but I needed help, so I ended up calling on his assistant to help me zip up the back of the dress and to help me with my headpiece. After I took a couple of deep breathes we headed out to the sitting area to show the ladies and, so I could take a glimpse in the mirror for the first time.

His assistant opens the curtain and I walk out into the sitting area and they all gasp with a look of aw on their faces and tears filled my mother's eyes.

"Renea you look gorgeous," Shanice says, getting choked up.

I walk over to the wall covered in mirrors and take a look. I raise my hands to my mouth and stare at my reflection, seeing the dress on the hanger did not do it justice and words cannot describe the joy and happiness that I felt inside. This was it, this was the dress, my dress and it fit perfectly hugging my curves just the way that it should.

"Oh, sweetheart, once my son sees you in that dress there won't be a reception." Mrs. Taylor said waving her hand as if she'd just touched something hot and mouthing the words ouch.

We all laughed, and my mother got up and walked over to me drying my eyes with a tissue.

"You're going to be a beautiful bride, my dear." She said kissing me on the cheek.

"Thanks, mom," I replied.

I changed out of my wedding dress and into the gown for my reception and the reaction to that one was just as equally exciting. Shanice and Kiani tried on their bridesmaid dresses and they were a perfect fit which according to Ralph that rarely ever happened. But as for Shanice, she may need to come back in a few months and get hers readjusted now that she has a little one on the way.

Everything was officially complete every single detail now all we had to do was wait for the day to arrive.

Chapter Thirty-Six

Dejuan

I made plans to hang out with Jonathan and the fellas while the ladies are spending the day in New York.

We needed to let loose, so we decided to head out to Las Vegas for the evening and have some fun because we have a lot to celebrate. When Jonathan first arrived, he sat me down and told me that Shanice was pregnant and that he'd planned on proposing to her. He asked if it was alright for him to do it at the wedding and I was all for it, but I told him we should sit Renea down and ask her because the decision was really up to her.

Once the fellas made it to the house I called for the car to take us to the airport. Jonathan wasn't thrilled that I'd invited the fellas to join us in Vegas and it was no secret that he didn't like them being around, but I was hoping that once he got to know them all that would change.

"I'm a be honest with you bruh I'm kind of nerves about getting on this jet man," Lavon said, as we pulled up to the strip.

Jonathan and I looked at each other and laughed. Lavon and Tez had never been on a plane before and come to think of it I don't think they've really ever been outside of California. Jerome, on the other hand, traveled a lot with his family when he was younger his mom was a very adventures woman. So, during the summers she would take them on road trips.

I take my seat and the fellas do the same as the flight attendant puts our bags away.

"Good morning gentlemen. My name is Ashley, and this is Joan, we will be taking care of you during your flight. Sit back and relax and once we're in the air we will serve breakfast."

"Thank you, ladies," I reply and the both of them head to the front of the jet.

"Aye, yo Joan is fine." Jerome said, "I just might have her help me out with a little something, something after breakfast," he continues watching her ass as she walks away.

I shake my head at him and grab my phone, so I can send Renea a message before we take off.

We arrive at the hotel and checked in. The fellas shared a suite and Jonathan and I shared a suite, since I knew exactly how these fools liked to party and even more so how they got down. I wasn't trying to get caught up in a picture with a half-naked female running around the suite late night.

It was still early when we arrived, so I decided to hit the hotels fitness center and get a quick workout.

"I guess great minds think alike," Jerome said walking into the fitness room.

"You know it bruh," I reply speeding up the pace on the treadmill.

He stretches and then steps on the treadmill beside me and begins to run at a slow but steady pace. We spend about forty-five minutes on the treadmill and then switch it up and head over to the weights.

"Aye bruh, thanks for bringing us along," he said.

"Anytime," I reply, "So let me guess those fools are already downing everything stocked in the mini bar."

He chuckles. "Yeah man, they started popping mini bottles as soon as we entered the room."

I shake my head as I grab the 50 lb. weights. "So, how's everything going with your mom?"

"She's doing a lot better thanks to the chemo treatments." He said, and I could hear the pain in his voice that he tried so hard to hide.

"You know I got you right? Anything you all I need I'm here all you have to do is say the word." I say in a sincere tone.

"I know bruh and I appreciate it. But we gonna be alright and plus you've done so much already."

His tone was low and from his body language I could tell that it wasn't really something that he wanted to get into, so I didn't push him instead I changed the subject to something a little more upbeat.

I headed through the lobby and over to the elevators to go back up to my room. I step inside and press the button, as the doors began to close I caught a glimpse a woman waving towards the elevator at me and my eyes got wide, and my heart pounded once I noticed who she was.

"Jill," I said closing my eyes and letting out a deep sigh.

I step off the elevator and quickly walk back to the suite opening the door and shutting it behind me. Could this be a coincident or was she following me again? I push the thought to the back of my mind and head to my room, shower, and then get dress. I step over to the mirror and I must say I'm looking real sexy tonight. The only thing missing is that fine ass woman of mine on my arm. The fellas came over to our suite and we chill out and do a few shots while we waited for Jonathan to finish getting ready.

I'd had at least two before they'd made it over, so I was feeling good. I promised Renea that I wouldn't go all in tonight, which means I'm going to try and take it easy on the alcohol and not let the fellas talk me into chugging down more than I need. I don't really drink so I'm kind of a lightweight when it comes to getting intoxicated but the rest of them they take that shit to the head like a champ.

"Alright gentlemen are you ready?" Jonathan asks stepping from his room and into the living room area.

"Hell yeah..." Lavon shouts

"Let's do this shit then bruh," Tez replies.

We enter the casino and the fellas go wild they bump fist with us and then head their own separate ways. Jonathan and I head straight to the blackjack table which is one of our favorite games besides craps.

The night was going great and we were walking away with nothing but wins. We caught up with the fellas after leaving the blackjack table. Tez and Lavon had already lost half of their money and Lavon was so drunk he didn't know whether he was coming or going.

"Bruh, I'm not tryna lose all my fucking money in here yo," Tez shouts.

"Hold up, hold up. Don't even worry about it because we're about to get you everything you lost back and then triple that. Just follow us to the motherfucking craps table, my man." I say waving for them to come with me.

We walk up to the table and there was a short chubby guy with a cowboy hat on rolling the dice. He'd already crapped out once and by the third time, we all shouted for him to give up the dice.

"New shooter," the stickman calls out. "Place your bets."

I pick up the dice and shake them in my hand blowing on them as one would on a cold day to warm up. I tell the fellas to bet on 8 because that's the number that was going to make us all rich tonight. And at first, they were hesitant looking at me like I was drunk off my ass and talking crazy.

"You're telling me you're going to hit an eight on every roll?" Jerome asks.

"You damn right," I said, "I'm telling you, you better bet on me."

After letting a couple of seconds pass he shrugs his shoulders and places his bet on the table and the rest of the people that remained did the same. I shook the dice one last time then tossed them onto the table watching as they bounced off the back of the table and rolled to a landing.

"Eight," the stickman calls out and everyone around the table cheers.

He grabs the dice and pushes them back to me, I pick them up, blow on them once again, and with the flick of my wrist I send them flying down the table once again. Once they land the stick man calls out an eight and everyone looks at me stunned for a second and grabs their bets and pushes them towards the eight.

Half an hour later Jonathan and I trade places while I run to the bathroom. I finish up and unlock the stall to go out when the door swings open and Jill pushes me back into the stall and against the wall pinning her body against mine.

"What the fuck are you doing?" I say in a sharp tone. "How the fuck did you—"

"Shh…" she says placing her finger on my lips then slowly lowering herself in front me and undoing my pants.

I try to pull her back up but all the alcohol that I'd consumed was making it a little harder than it should be.

She pulls my dick out and licks the tip of it with her tongue circling the head before sucking it slowly. I felt my knees get weak from the warmth of her mouth and I wanted to tell her to stop, beg her not to do this, but the words just wouldn't come out.

She places both hands on my dick and begins moving them up and down as she sucked me in, taking me all the way into her mouth until she milked my shit. I let a loud groan as I explode in her mouth as she continued to deep throat my dick until it was limp. This bitch didn't even let a drop spill, she drank, licked, and sucked up every bit of my seeds.

"Yo," I say resting against the wall.

"I told you, baby, I can get you right," She smiles up at me, "I bet she can't do that, now can she?"

"Yo, please back the fuck up off me," I say trying not to get to angry because I don't know what this girls angle is, and I don't need her crying that I forced her or trying to blackmail me because I lost my shit and choked her ass out.

"Hey, it's ok. I'm just trying to get you ready for round two baby." She says stroking my manhood.

"You need to leave right now," I say pushing her away.

"Aw, baby, don't be like that." She says in a soft and seductive tone. "I just want you to make love to me. Please, you promised." She leaned in kissing my neck then reaches down and lifts her dress over her waist.

My head was swimming, and I hadn't gained full control of my body, so I remained against the wall instead of taking a chance and falling to the floor. I push her hand away and she smiles at me and presses her lips to mine but stops when she realizes that I wasn't returning the kiss.

"Ok, daddy. I see I got you a little weak, so I'll settle for just tasting you on my lips, for now."

She licks her lips then unlocks the stall and disappears out of the restroom leaving me dazed and confused. Her fucking mouth felt so fucking good on my dick, but I knew that it was wrong, and I knew that I'd fucked up. So why didn't I slap that bitch and threw her ass out this fucking stall?

I can't tell Renea that this bitch had my dick in her mouth, or that she randomly popped up at my hotel again begging me to fuck her. Although she did attack me I mean it wasn't like I wanted it, I mean, I did at one point want to fuck the shit out of her but that was when

I'd thought I lost Renea. Man, all them damn drinks and everything got me weak and not a hundred percent.

"FUCK," I growl and push myself off the wall and straighten my clothes then go to wash my hands.

As I walk out the restroom and back into the casino I see Jonathan and the fellas waiting for me with two security guards in tow.

"What the fuck happened to you bro? I thought you'd bailed on us and went back to the room." He said studying my face. "You alright man?" He asks.

"I need to talk to you, now!" I say pulling him towards the cashier's station.

We exchange out our chips for cash and have the security guards escort us back to our suites. The fellas brought a few females that they'd meet at the craps table back to their suite for the night and the two of us retreated to our suite alone.

"What's up?" Jonathan asks once we were back in the room.

I let out a deep breath before I spoke. "That bitch Jill just cornered me in the man's restroom and sucked me off."

"WHAT?" He said his eyebrows pushed together. "Damn man, please tell me that you didn't invite her here tonight?"

"No—what the fuck, Jon," I shout pacing the floor. "I have a beautiful woman and I'm getting married. Why the fuck would I do that Jonathan?"

"Alright man, calm down, I'm just asking a question."

"Well, it's a stupid fucking question," I say falling onto the extremely large couch.

What the fuck was I going to do? Once I tell Renea what happened tonight I'm quite sure she's going to call off the wedding. I let out a small laugh and Jonathan shoots me a look, but I ignore him and shut my eyes continuing to think to myself. How could I be this fucking unlucky with love? I already have two females trying to fuck up my life and now here comes this woman that wants to fuck up my relationship.

"So, what are you going to do?" He asks.

"I don't know man...I can't have Renea finding out about this," I reply.

"Finding out? No, man, you need to tell her and asap." He said, "Bro don't let someone else bring that shit to her it'll only make things worse trust me. She'll be mad at first, but she'll come around if she really loves and trusts you."

I rub my hands over my face and get up from the couch. "I'm a call it a night bro I'll see you in the morning," I said reaching over and bumping his fist before walking towards my room.

I take a long hot shower trying to wash the smell of her perfume off me and making sure that I clean my dick a couple of times as well. Why was this woman so obsessed with me when I hadn't even touched her? Of course, if I'd gone all the way and fucked her then I might understand why she was so clingy. I mean my dick tends to mesmerize the ladies and leave them fucked up in the head, but this chick is going crazy just from seeing the imprint.

My phone buzzed, and I picked it up from the bedside table glancing at part of the message on the screen before opening the full message.

Renea: I hope you all had fun tonight baby can't wait to see you in the morning.

At the end of the message, there was a couple of emojis and a picture underneath of her blowing me a kiss. My heart sank from my chest as I stared at the picture damn I don't want to lose her, not again. I need to figure out a way to get this female out of my life and fast and explain to Renea about what happened tonight.

***

I walk in the house and I hear laughter. I continue into the living room and see all the ladies gathered, sipping wine and enjoying themselves. They looked like they were having a good time and in the back of my mind I was thinking to myself "Damn, this is going to be ugly".

"Hey baby," she says once she noticed me.

"Hey Beautiful," I say as I walk over and kiss her cheek. "Hello ladies," I say turning and greeting the rest of the woman in the room.

"Hey…" they all say in unison.

"Um Beautiful, can I talk to you for a second?" I whisper in her ear.

"Sure, is everything alright?" She asks softly.

 I nod my head and help her up from the floor where she was seated, and we go back into the master bedroom and shut the door.

"Is something wrong?" she asks, "or did you just want to get me alone for a quickie," she says playfully as she gazes into my eyes smiling seductively, but I move her hands and step back from her a little.

"Listen, I need to tell you something. And you're not going to like what I have to say but I need you to listen and hear me out before you react. I promised you that I would never lie to you again and that's why I'm telling you about it myself."

 Her smile fades and she crosses her arms over her chest. "I'm listening," She replies her face now emotionless.

 "Last night in Vegas—," I began but my voice cracks, so I clear my throat and begin again. "Last night Jill was at the hotel that we were staying at and something happened." I paused waiting for her to react, but she didn't.

She stood glued to the floor her eyes cold as she gazed at me waiting for me to continue with what I was saying. So, walked over to the bed and took a sit on the edge as her eyes followed me.

"Renea, I promise you that I never wanted anything to happen with that woman and I need you to believe me Beautiful."

"Just tell me what happened Dejuan. Did you fuck her, is that it? Or did she break into the room and stumble on to your dick?"

"Renea," I said softly walking over towards her, but she throws her hands up and steps back from me.

"Don't touch me," she says disgust in her voice. "You let this happen." She said before trying to walk past me, but I grab her arm and pull her back over to me.

"I didn't fuck her Renea."

"Let me go," she says in a stern voice and I release her arm.

"Please just fucking listen to me—please—hear me out before you just walk away from me." I plead with her.

She stops mid-step and turns back to me her eyes a little softer now and her body less tense.

"Fine," she says walking over to the chair in the corner of the room.

"Beautiful I don't want any woman other than you. You're it for me and you've got to know that by now, I would do anything for you even give up my entire life if you ask me to. I didn't sleep with her, she followed me to the men's restroom in the casino and cornered me and I'll admit I'd been drinking more then I should have so I was weak. She pushed me into a stall and she went down on me."

"And that's it," she says in a voice that confused me. "She just sucked your dick and nothing else?"

"Nothing. I promise you that's it." I reply.

She laughs, gets up from her seat, and walks over to me pressing her lips to mine. Kissing me passionately before pulling back and looking me in the eyes.

"Thank you for telling me the truth. I love you, Dejuan," she said placing her hand on my cheek before turning and walking out of the room.

I stood there in the middle of the room confused feeling like I'd missed something. She wasn't mad or upset, she hadn't thrown me out, or called off the wedding like I was afraid she would. After a couple of minutes, I hear laughter and conversations spark up again filling the house, I walk out of the room and down the hall and look into the living room.

She'd taken her place back on the floor with the rest of the ladies and had her glass of wine in her hand, talking and laughing again like nothing had happened. She was right back in a chill mood same as she was when I entered the house before, and I wasn't sure if I should be scared or maybe she just knew that I was really telling her the truth and was letting it go. Either way, I was going to keep it low key for the next couple of days.

Chapter Thirty-Seven

Renea

When Dejuan told me about what happened between him and Jill in Vegas I will admit that I was upset at first, but I was also happy that he'd come straight home and told me the truth about it.

And although I'm grateful, I don't plan on letting it go that easily. I had my team find out a little information about Jill, like where she lived, and where she worked. Then my girls and I did a drop in. And I can say the look on her face when my girls and I walked into the store was satisfaction enough, but I wanted to make sure that she fully understood the type of chaos I could bring to her life if I wanted to.

"Omg, Renea Dubley," the young sales girl said. "Welcome, what can I get for you today?"

"Oh, I'm just looking around for a little something for my fiancé," I say, turning and winking at her making sure I said the word fiancé nice and slow.

"Well let me know if I can assist you with anything."

"Will do. Thanks!"

We shop around the store for about twenty minutes then headed up to the register to purchase our items. We lingered a bit, so we were able to have Jill be available to check us out, so that we could chat with her. Once we reached the counter we greeted her and began to talk. She listened intently as we spoke and when Shanice mentioned that she was a lawyer her eyes got wide. I could see the panic on her face at the mention of a lawsuit being filed for stalking and sexual assault against Dejuan.

"I'm sure you wouldn't want your boss to find out about the things you do with client information. Now would you?"

"No," she said quickly holding up her hand. "Look, I'm sorry and tell Dejuan that I'm sorry as well. Now can you all please leave, I need this job, and you don't have to worry about seeing me ever again. Please just go." She begged.

We smile at her and tell her to have a nice life then grab our items and leave out the store. When I arrive home I check for his car, but it wasn't there, Dejuan was still out, so I went into our room and laid all the items that I'd bought for him on our bed so that he would see them when he got home. I grabbed two glasses, a bottle of wine, and went into the living room and snuggled onto the sofa with my throw, cutting on some slow R&B and letting it set the mood.

Thirty minutes later he came in the house calling my name and I called out to him letting him know that I was in the living room.

"What's going on Beautiful?" He asks, walking into the room and looking around.

"Hey baby," I say staring at him and biting my bottom lip. "Why don't you go and get cleaned up then come back and join me.

He studies me for a moment then heads back to our room to change. He walks back into the room a couple of seconds later staring at me with a raised eyebrow and I just sit watching him sipping my wine.

"Renea?" He said in the way of a question. "Beautiful, what did you do?" he ask with his lips pressed into a hard line.

"I simply did what you couldn't."

"And that is?" he asks getting impatient.

I smile at him with a devilish grin and press the glass to my lips and take another sip of wine. He laughs and sits the things in his hands on the edge of the sofa and walks over to me, taking the glass of wine from my hands, and pulling me up off the sofa and into his arms. He strokes my hair while looking into my eyes before kissing me hard.

"You know you're crazy right?" he says in between kisses.

"Mm-hmm… I'm crazy for you."

I lean in and kiss him, just as the doorbell rings and we let out a sigh and he smacks me on the ass before leaving the room to answer the door. I hear his brother's voice and another that I'm not familiar with as they come walking back into the living room. Dejuan walks in first and the expression on his face doesn't match his voice, so I knew that there was something wrong.

"Hey Beautiful, looks like we've got company," he said in a way that confused me.

"Hey sis," Jamie says coming over to give me a hug.

"Hey love," I replied standing up and embracing him. "Who's this?" I ask as I release him.

"This is my friend Sean—," Jamie begins but Dejuan cuts him off.

"Sean Winchester?" He said looking from Jamie to me and then over to the young boy Sean. "You're Maylan Winchester's brother, right?" He asks and looks back over at me and I finally understand why he had that look on his face before.

"Yeah, how do you know that?" Jamie asks staring hard at his brother.

"I know his big brother, we went to school together when we were teens," Dejuan replied.

"Oh, word. I heard about you, you use to hustle hard in the streets back in the day." Sean speaks up and says with a smile on his face.

"Yeah, something like that."

The room got quiet for a moment and just as I opened my mouth to speak the doorbell rang again, and I decided that I'd go and get the door this time. I twisted the handle and opened the door only to find Jaxon standing at the door with his gun at his side, and his finger over his lips telling me to keep quiet. I was confused and didn't know what was going on, so I did as I was told. He steps in the door and pushes me behind him and I slowly follow him as we walk towards the living room.

We turn the corner and step into the living room and Jaxon aims his gun straight ahead. I could tell in his expression that something was wrong, so I lean to my left a little to take a look and see why he'd raised his gun.

"Omgosh Dejuan," I cry out feeling my chest tighten and my heart begin to pound hard against my chest.

To be continued....

Acknowledgments

First, I want to give a huge thank you to my husband. Your love for me and the support that you've shown for my dreams, as well as all of my crazy goals that I've set for myself, is beyond amazing and I love you so much. I also want to say thank you to all of my friends and family that helped in making my dreams a reality and a super special shout out to Mark, for proofreading and always giving me the best and honest feedback. And finally, I want to give a major shout out to my mom. Thank you for always believing in me and pushing me to chase my dreams no matter how big or how small. You are my biggest cheerleader and one of the strongest women I know, I love you!

I thank you the readers for purchasing my book and giving me a chance to share my crazy and overactive imagination with you. I hope that you enjoyed the book and I can't wait to bring you more.

About the Author

Author, Wife, and mother of five awesome kiddos! My top three favorite things are books, chocolate, and good music. I've always been passionate about storytelling and impressed by the influence it has on people and the decisions they make in life. As an author I want my readers to get lost in the stories, connect with the characters, and use them as an escape or even a small break from their everyday lives. I've always loved writing poetry, I love writing short stories, and now I can add writing novels to my list of loves.

Website:

www.naetblossauthor.com

Facebook:

AuthorNaeTBloss

Twitter:

@NaeTBloss

Nae T. Bloss

Next in This Series

A FORBIDDEN DREAM

A DREAM ENDING

COMING SOON

DR. HANDSOME

THE UNDERLINED GAME